NEVER ON
SUNDAYS

a novel

JASON M. STEFFENS

"I thank God through Jesus Christ our Lord."—Romans 7:25

"Whatsoever ye do, do all to the glory of God."—1 Corinthians 10:31.

For my wife, Briana, who chooses to love me.

For my children, my arrows.

1.

Will walked out to his garage, pushed the button to open the garage door, and placed his laptop computer in the back seat of his car. He looked at the handle that would open the driver's side front door. He turned his head and walked outside.

It was a Thursday morning in March. The grass was wet with dew. But for the chirping of birds, it was quiet. Most of the people who lived on his street were awake, but there was yet little sign of movement. Will could see a trace of his breath, though it was not so cold he needed more than his suit for what he had intended to do, which was drive the ten minutes to his downtown office. Intentions are sometimes disguises for inertia, he thought. Would he have intended to drive to his office and sit at his desk churning out pleadings, motions, briefs, and endless emails if that was not what he had always done for the past twelve years? If there had been no inertia, what would he have intended to do today?

The position he held defined him. No one could claim he was well-rounded. He read books and everyone thought he had a nice family. Centrally, though, he was a lawyer.

He was good at what he did and compensated well, but there was little chance he would ever be materially rich or a legal star. Not that he sought those things. He didn't, though he liked the things money could buy as much as most people did. He was a lawyer because he went to law school, and he went to law school because he did not know what else to do with his history degree, and he had a history degree because ... well, the Battle of Agincourt, George Washington, and the sinking of the Titanic were more interesting to him than the reflection of light, the periodic table, or from which ventricle the aorta originates.

He had a degree in anything mostly because he fell in love with Ashley as a junior in high school and followed her to college. She was the high-achieving, A-student. Two years after Ashley obtained her graduate degree, she quit the full-time out-of-home workforce to be a full-time mom, working her old job just enough to maintain her professional license. Will provided the main income, pretending like what he did was the important, stressful stuff. He knew better.

Thus, the fame, such as it was, came by accident, it seemed, and lasted briefly. Two cases, one leading to the other even though they were unrelated, changed everything. He was a mid-level partner at a Cedar Rapids law firm, unknown outside of the eastern Iowa civil litigation world in which he practiced. His cases had never warranted a mention in *The Gazette*, the Cedar Rapids-based newspaper. Three days ago his name appeared in the national news and the next morning's *USA Today*.

Because of his client's decision, that was now over. More importantly, the cases—or rather the people he met in them—caused him to awaken out of the existence into which he had fallen and led his family. The question now was whether his awakening would result in a new course. It is so easy to have our eyes opened, but then close them again, pretend it never happened, and go back to doing what has always been done.

It would be wrong to say he could *not* keep doing what he had always done. That path was still open to him. It was the easiest one. No one would question him if he stayed on it. But what had happened over the past nine days, and especially last night, showed Will there was a different way.

If there was going to be a change, he felt he had to resolve to make the change *now* if he would ever make it.

What almost stopped him was the unpredictability that would result. He thought he knew the end of his current path. He had no idea where a new path would take him. That might have been fine if he were alone. He could face unknowns if he was not responsible for providing for a wife and three children. He did not know how his family would take uncertainty when all they had ever known was certainty.

Certainty is a comfort. And a hindrance.

Will resolved that his family would have to embrace uncertainty. The alternative was insufficient. His mind was determined. He had to make his body move.

Standing in the crisp air, he inhaled and exhaled a few more times, staring at his breath. Without further hesitation, but with a pounding heart, he turned, walked back to the door between his kitchen and his garage, and rotated the door knob.

Inside, Ashley stood at the kitchen sink rinsing a frying pan. The three children—Allie (10 years old), Andy (7), and Adam (5)—sat around the kitchen table eating a breakfast of eggs and toast. When Will walked in, Ashley did not look up. It was not unusual for her husband to have forgotten his keys, wallet, or cell phone. She was likely hoping to finish cleaning the kitchen before driving Allie and Andy to school. Allie, on the other hand, immediately looked up and exclaimed, "What did you forget!?"

Will smiled and responded, "Actually, nothing. There is something I would like to talk to you all about."

Ashley's head now turned. His children stared at him. Will was thankful his family was still interested enough in him to stop what they were doing if he had something important to say.

He sat down and began. "I'm sorry." Ashley and their three children continued to stare at him with increasingly apprehensive looks. Will went on, worrying that their apprehension was only going to increase. "I feel that I have failed you as a husband and a dad. No, I don't just feel it. I *know* I have. I have provided for your physical needs. I have worked hard and made good money to give you food, shelter, and clothing, plus most of our wants. But I have not provided for you in any other way. I have given you a good house without giving you a good home. I have not paid attention to you. I have not listened when you talked to me. I do not know how I got to this point. I mean, I can look back and see the path. But I cannot say that I chose it when we started out. It just sort of happened, though only because I allowed it. I think I know the direction we need to head, though I cannot tell you exactly what it looks like or where we end up. I just know I no longer want to be absent when I am here. I want a better marriage."

He looked at his kids. "I want to be a better father. I didn't take you sledding this winter. I want to take you sledding and do lots of other things with you."

He looked back at Ashley. "To do this—to be what God wants me to be—I need to leave the law firm. Maybe I need to start my own practice, one that looks a lot different than the one I have now, or maybe I need to find a completely different career. I want to stop loving the money and the things we can buy with money. I want to love you. I always have, but too often only with words. I feel like I have forgotten, or perhaps never knew, what it is to be a good husband and a good father. I have identified my life with my job and allowed you to do the same. I am no longer going to do that."

Ashley's eyes were fixed on Will. "Is all this because of what has happened the past few days?" she asked.

"Yes," Will answered. "And because of what happened last night."

"What happened last night?"

Will told them. They all listened without interruption. He then asked his family, "Will you trust me? Will you allow me to make this change? Will you go down this new path?"

Will stared at his wife as he asked these last questions. His children continued in silence, staring with some bewilderment at their dad. Other than knowing he was a "lawyer," they had no idea what their dad did for a living. They only knew it was "important," he was gone a lot, and when he was home he usually needed to work in his home office. They now saw their dad's eyes fixed on their mother. They turned to look at her, undoubtedly wondering what she would think of these strange things he was saying. As they did so, a tear rolled down from Ashley's left eye and she smiled. She got up from her chair, walked over to Will, leaned down, and kissed him. Another tear dropped from her right eye onto Will's cheek. She then hugged him and said in a soft voice, "Yes. We don't need your job. We need you. We love you and we will support you. But are you sure? I didn't think you would ever do this. I thought our not having you was just how things would always be."

"Yes," replied Will. "I am sure. And if I do not make this decision now I do not think I ever will. So I am making it now."

"Will this mean you can play with us more?" asked Andy. "Will you fix your bike and go bike riding with me?"

Will laughed. "It means many things, one of which is I will be spending more time with you, including going on bike rides."

Ashley looked like a weight had been lifted off her. Will smiled at her and continued, "It will take me a little while to extract myself. I need to go to the office now, but this is real." He then looked at his children. "I will be back home tonight, and we will most definitely play."

Will kissed and hugged his wife and his three children. He then drove to what would soon be his former office, to what would soon be his former life.

2.

Ten days earlier, Monday evening

Will walked out of his office at six o'clock. He had meant to leave a half-hour earlier to get home in time for the start of supper. At 5:15 p.m., one of his law firm partners had walked into his office. Fifteen minutes later, Will was not sure why. The conversation began with "So, do the Cubs have enough pitching to win anything this year?" and devolved into why the workroom staff had trouble keeping enough French Roast coffee pods stocked in the break room, leaving only various light roasts and flavored versions. In the end, resolution to those two issues remained elusive and the partner departed.

Before Will could figure out what he had been doing beforehand, an email arrived:

> From: Alan Bonner
> To: William Jacobson
> Subject: new claim
>
> Will, I need your help on this new claim that came in this afternoon. Johnson Engineers has

been sued by the owner of the new medical building. There are a number of other defendants and the claim appears to be for defective construction and design. I acknowledged receipt of the claim to the insurance company. Please contact Bill Smith at Johnson Engineers and let him know that we have been retained by his insurance company to defend his company, gather his initial knowledge, and begin work on an answer to the petition and initial discovery requests. Can we remove this to federal court?

Will replied to the email and said he would work on it. He then called Bill Smith, but was put into his voicemail. Will left a message. After spending fifteen more minutes replying to three more emails that came into his inbox, Will realized he would not get done what he had meant to get done before he left the office, which was finish preparing for tomorrow's deposition in the most interesting case he had. He gathered the documents he needed for that deposition and headed home.

When Will walked in his house ten minutes later, his family was at the dinner table eating. Will's plate of food sat on the table in front of his empty chair. "I'm sorry for being late. Some things came up shortly before I was going to leave and I couldn't get away."

Ashley looked at the folder of documents her husband set down as he took off his suit jacket. "You will probably need to warm up your plate in the microwave," she said.

He did so. The rest of the meal conversation consisted of the kids chattering faster than anyone could keep up, not that Will tried. If you had asked him what his children just said, he would not have been able to answer. Will finished his meal in ten minutes, including reheating time, and got up from his chair.

"What do you have planned tonight?" questioned Ashley. Will heard in her tone a hope that her husband would forget the papers he brought home. "It would be a good night to go to the library together," she continued. "The kids need some new books. Maybe we could get some ice cream afterwards."

The three kids screamed in unison, "Ice cream!"

Will looked at Ashley and his kids. He wished he had it in him to say yes. "I can't tonight. I have a deposition tomorrow I need to finish preparing for."

Will left the kitchen before the disappointment in his family's faces enveloped him. After changing out of his suit, he entered the family room that contained his home office desk, a sectional, and an entertainment center. He set his papers on his desk. He had thought hard all day. Worrying about his clients' problems with the knowledge there was an opposing side thinking about how to ruin his solutions took a lot out of him mentally. He had trouble bearing the thought of looking at those papers so soon after getting home, no matter the importance of tomorrow's deposition. He picked up the TV remote, hit the power button, and switched the channel to the early evening sports news show on the sports cable channel.

An anchor appeared on the screen. "Moving away from the push to the NBA playoffs," he said, "we have some breaking news from the spring training camp of the Indianapolis Hawks. Our senior baseball reporter Preston Edwards is on site in Phoenix and we go to him live now. Preston, we hear there is some unexpected and potentially un-

settling news out of the camp of the team many are pre-
dicting will win the National League pennant this year.
What can you tell us?"

The screen switched to a split-screen, with the anchor
on the left and baseball's most recognizable reporter on the
right. Preston Edwards began, "That's right, Bob. Right
now the details are murky, but one source has confirmed for
us that second-year star Roy Adams was absent from the
team's facilities yesterday, apparently on his own and without permission. Today, he was scheduled to play in the
Hawks' spring training game against Chicago, but he was
held out of the lineup and sent to the Hawks' minor league
camp facility for participation in practice drills. We do not
yet know why Adams failed to show up yesterday. We also
do not know if removing him from today's lineup before the
game was part of a team punishment for his absence. We
have not been able to interview Adams. Personnel in the
team's front office are conducting an investigation and the
team is not revealing further information at this point.
None of his teammates are talking yet either. The story is
developing and we anticipate having more soon."

"This seems unusual given what we know about Roy Adams and his character," the anchor offered. It was a statement posing as a question to give the appearance the anchor had a function in this report.

The reporter continued, "That's right. After being called
up on the first of May last year, Adams appeared in 135
straight games for Indianapolis. Everyone knew Adams
would be good. He turned out to be great. A model of consistency, grit, and determination, Adams also boasted MVP-
caliber numbers, finishing first in the National League in
on-base percentage, fifth in slugging percentage, and steal-

ing 40 bases in 42 attempts, along with earning a Gold Glove for his defensive work in centerfield. He was by all accounts a model citizen and teammate. His Hall-of-Fame bound manager, Earl Vinson, even described him as the most teachable player he has had in twenty-five years as a big league manager, not that Adams needed much teaching."

"What will this mean for the team going forward?" the anchor asked.

Edwards answered, "It is too soon to say, but before Adams arrived last year the Hawks were 10-15. They appeared destined to again finish with a losing record, something they had done each year since joining the league as an expansion team four years ago. With Adams, Indianapolis went 82-55 the rest of the way, finishing just two games behind eventual division winner St. Louis, giving the young franchise its first winning season, and providing one of the most exciting division races in baseball. Attendance jumped ten percent in the second half of the season and the Hawks sold out their last thirty home games. This year, the Hawks are the consensus favorites to win the National League pennant. If there is a rift between Adams and the team, that will negatively impact both the team's on-field success and revenue."

"Thank you Preston," the anchor said and turned back to the off-screen audience. "We will certainly continue to update you on this developing story."

As the report concluded, Ashley walked in the room. "I thought you needed to work," she offered in a slightly accusing tone.

"I do and I am going to," Will replied. "I just wanted to see the sports news for a minute before picking it up again." Then, in a poor attempt to shift the focus away from having been caught not doing what he said he was going to do and to show he was capable of paying attention to his wife, he asked, "Did you hear about this story? Can you believe someone who gets paid so much to play baseball would just not show up for practice without a good explanation and then expect to play in the game the next day?"

Ashley's look conveyed the feeling that there were few things in life for which she cared less. "We are going to the library and then to my parents'. They said to make sure you knew you could come. I told them you needed to work. We will be back in a couple of hours." Ashley left the room and called for the kids to get their jackets. Getting them out the door and visiting the library would be a lot easier if Will helped. Will sensed his failure and tried to put it out of his mind. He turned the TV off and sat at his desk.

There are few depositions that make or break a case. Tomorrow's had a chance. In most, witnesses simply confirm information an attorney already knows by other investigation, written discovery, and court filings. A deposition is a device to gauge what kind of witness the person will make at trial and to ensure there are no surprises at trial. Surprises often came anyway.

Tomorrow was different for a number of reasons. For one, the witness was the pastor of the Baptist church he had sued on behalf of his client, the Midwestern Baptist Association. He had never sued a church or deposed a pastor before. Whatever the decline in religious activity in America, the American populace still afforded pastors and other religious leaders more than a modicum of respect. A jury would be predisposed to believe his testimony and perhaps agree with many of his beliefs, even if unwilling to act and think in accordance with them. That was especially true if he did not come off as a TV evangelist, though Will had difficulty picturing anything else. In any event, it seemed more important than normal for Will's words to not appear rude in the deposition transcript in case some of it was read during the trial.

Another reason tomorrow's deposition would be unusual was that neither the Baptist church nor the pastor as a witness were represented by an attorney. The pastor, Nate Sanders, would be there alone. Will understood why some people chose to represent themselves. Paying a lawyer through the discovery process and a trial is expensive. However, the process is so layered with rules, protocol, and insider tics that it is difficult for a self-represented litigant to get to the trial without something having gone irreparably wrong. Even if they get to the trial, their chance of conducting it with even a hint of apparent competence is almost zero. Self-represented litigants often try to act like a TV lawyer, which just looks foolish in real life. The thing that sometimes saves self-represented litigants is judges effectively taking off their robes to serve as their advocates through not-so-subtle guidance and even less subtle favoritism.

Will was only nominally religious. He was a member of a large Protestant church, though membership did not require participation or attention. As a child he attended most Sunday morning services. He stopped going to church in college and told himself he was too busy during law school. Once they started having kids, he and Ashley felt they needed to take them. They made no attempt to reason out why. An hour a week on Sunday morning, though, was not too much of an inconvenience. Plus, they had met some nice people there.

Over the past year, their attendance had faded. They only made it about once a month now. For Will, Sunday morning was about the only time he did not work and he much preferred sleeping in and watching the National Football League pre-game shows or a wildlife documentary. The kids, of course, welcomed the chance to sleep in and then get up and watch cartoons. Multiple televisions, in separate parts of the house, made such sedentary escape possible.

When the Jacobson family did attend church, they were not very involved. They came at the last minute, sat in the furthest pew from the front still available, and then quickly left after the service, speaking to as few people as possible lest they have to make conversation or—worse—be asked to help out in some area of the church's ministries.

With documents he was reviewing for the deposition on his desk in front of him, Will reflected on the state of his religious participation, though not too deeply. His thoughts, as far as they went, led him to think he would be anxious while around a pastor tomorrow.

3.

Roy Adams entered the locker room of the Indianapolis Hawks' spring training facility at nine o'clock in the morning. A number of other players were already there getting ready for the day's routine and receiving treatment from the athletic training staff. As they became aware of their now-controversial teammate's entrance, they subdued their voices. Roy noticed this without acknowledging it. He walked straight to his locker.

His locker was next to Malik Jones's. Malik was just 25-years-old, three years older than Roy, but was already entering his fourth full year in the big leagues. Malik had been a highly touted prospect when he arrived. The Hawks drafted him in the first round of the MLB amateur draft during his junior season at LSU. He spent five months of the next year at the Hawks' double-A affiliate. The Hawks then called him up to be their starting center fielder during the final month of the team's inaugural big league season. Malik spent the next two seasons in that spot. He played well, if not up to the expectations the scouts—and consequently the media and the fans—had for him. Roy and everyone else in the game knew that expectations, regardless of whether they are tied to reality, are so often the standard by which others judge a player's success and failure. That was probably true outside of baseball as well.

Roy's arrival caused people to forget about Malik as they transferred the expectations they had for him to Roy. The team moved Malik to left field and he had another solid but unspectacular year. Despite the shift of adoration and hope, Malik quickly overcame his jealousy and the two had developed a friendship. Winning helped.

On this morning, Malik arrived at his locker shortly after Roy had arrived at his. "Welcome back," Malik said to Roy.

Roy grinned involuntarily. "Thanks."

"I know you talked about it, but I didn't think you would actually do it."

"Yeah, well, this is real," Roy responded.

"However real you think it is, be careful," Malik cautioned.

"What do you mean?"

"I mean you can go from hero to goat, loved to hated, very quickly in this business."

Roy nodded, but then replied, "It's just a game."

"Not to a lot of people and not with the amount of money involved."

There was silence for a few moments before Malik spoke again. "I am not just talking about the fans and the media turning against you. You have already lost some of the people in this room. It will be hard to regain their trust and friendship."

Roy nodded. He wondered what kind of friendship he ever had with them.

"What does Jenny think of this?" Malik asked.

"We haven't talked about it much. I told her my plan on Friday. She wondered what would happen, what the team might do, and I didn't know at that point. We haven't been able to talk much since then. She gets into town tonight."

Malik nodded and asked, "Is the team going to let you play today?"

"I'm not sure. I have not seen Earl yet."

Roy finished dressing and told Malik he would see him out on the field. Roy headed there without speaking with any of his other teammates, bypassing the office of his manager, Earl Vinson.

He entered the light of a clear, seventy degree morning. Everything appeared peaceful—and perfect. The mirage was shattered by a voice calling out, "Roy! Roy! Can you talk a sec?"

He turned and saw Preston Edwards. There was much in Roy that wanted to brush off the reporter, give him a scowl, do anything but act friendly. He fought off those thoughts and walked toward him. "Hi Preston," Roy said in a friendly voice. Roy was struck by how his decision to act friendly placed a positive countenance on the reporter's face.

"Are you in the lineup today?" Edwards opened.

"I'm not sure yet. I actually expected you would know more about that than me," Roy replied.

Edwards grinned. Roy could tell the reporter knew something, but did not intend to reveal what it was. Instead, Edwards moved to his next question. "What comes next Sunday?"

Roy chose obfuscation. "I'm not even sure what comes tomorrow. I'll continue to work through this with my team."

Some reporters, like lawyers, keep asking questions of their subjects in the hope some unexpected, revelatory answer will blurt out. Sometimes it works. According to statements he had made in media panels over the years, Edwards was different. He had come to believe asking too many questions—or asking the same question in five ostensibly different ways—mostly just wasted time and unnecessarily caused strain in the discourse. He had by now trained himself in such a way that gotcha reporting was uninteresting to him.

Edwards shifted from questions to discussion. "Whatever you do from here, what you did was a bold move. It has the potential to impact a lot of people, though the few who know about it wonder how far you are really willing to take it."

"People wonder that because they either do not believe in much or are unwilling to fully act on what they believe," Roy replied.

"That's a bit presumptuous of you, don't you think? It's hard to know what is going on inside someone else's mind."

Edwards' response caused Roy to regret his comment. It was so easy for him to ascribe motives and thoughts to others. He realized he knew almost nothing about who Edwards really was. He had typecast him based on Edwards' reports on TV. In actuality, he knew nothing about Edwards' life, his beliefs, or the depth of his thoughts. Roy's sense of moral superiority evaporated. Roy was working hard to be a better man. He realized, again, how far he had to go to be the man he ought to be.

Roy decided to shift the conversation. He was curious about Edwards' report the previous night. "Last night, why didn't you report the reason I was absent on Sunday? You knew, right? Why didn't you say?" Roy asked.

"Sometimes I know things I do not report because the information is not sufficiently substantiated," Edwards answered. "Some things are just better left unsaid. And sometimes a source gives me information on the condition I not report it yet."

Roy thought about this. "The front office doesn't want the public to know yet."

"That's fair to say," Edwards responded. "But that won't last forever. Listen, when you are willing to talk about this, will you consider doing so with me?"

Roy began to think about how he could control the story so the team did not. "I'll think about it." The two exchanged cell numbers. Roy turned and headed out to the field to began his stretches, wishing he did not find himself plotting ways to undermine the organization so it first did not undermine him.

4.

Will entered one of his firm's large conference rooms with his client representative, George Bannon, Vice President of Legal Affairs for the Midwestern Baptist Association. Despite his title, Bannon was not a lawyer. He was just in charge of overseeing the outside counsel the Association retained.

Inside the room, Will saw the deponent—Pastor Nate Sanders—standing with his face looking out the glass window toward the street twelve floors below. The court reporter sat at the head of the conference room table, working to finish setting up her equipment. The pastor turned when he heard the entrants and walked toward them.

"Hi," Will said as he reached out his hand and shook the witness's. "I'm Will Jacobson, the attorney for the Association."

"Nice to meet you, Mr. Jacobson," Pastor Sanders replied.

"Please call me Will."

The pastor nodded and then shook hands with George Bannon. "Hi George. Nice to sce you again. It's been quite awhile. A few years at least."

Bannon smiled awkwardly. "Yes, it has. Well, you know, with the lawsuit and everything, we felt it best to not communicate except through the lawyers."

Will had never seen Bannon so uncomfortable before.

Who was the *we* and what *lawyers* was he talking about? There was only one lawyer—him—who had been involved in this case. Two things occurred to Will: First, Bannon had expected the church to hire an attorney when he ordered the Association's lawsuit. Its going without counsel was a surprise. Second, Bannon was as uncomfortable around Pastor Nate Sanders as Will had expected himself to be. As it turned out, Will felt fine. He wondered what caused Bannon's uneasiness.

The participants took their seats and the court reporter had the pastor swear to tell the truth. After Will explained to Pastor Sanders how depositions worked and asked some preliminary questions, the substance of the deposition began.

Q (Mr. Jacobson). Without telling me the substance of any communications with attorneys, have you individually or the church collectively retained an attorney to assist you in defending the lawsuit that brings us here today?

A (Mr. Sanders). No, I do not have a lawyer. The church also does not have a lawyer.

Q. Why not?

A. We have not seen the need to undertake that expense. If the Lord wants us to remain on the property, He will work it out. If he does not, He will open some other door for us.

Q. Does the Lord not sometimes work through lawyers?

A. I do not have any experience with that.

Q. We will get through this deposition faster if you answer the questions I ask. I did not ask about your experiences with lawyers. My question was whether God sometimes accomplishes his purposes through lawyers, as he sometimes does with pastors?

Will wondered at his own surliness. His question had nothing to do with the lawsuit. He had simply been offended at what he thought he heard in the pastor's answer—that lawyers were useless to God. Thankfully, the pastor did not respond in kind.

A. I had not thought about that, but I suppose the answer is yes.

Q. Please provide me a history of your work in the ministry.

A. I graduated from North Phoenix Baptist College twelve years ago in May. For eleven years after that, I worked as a youth pastor in southern Indiana, the first five of those without a salary, taking odd jobs here and there to cover expenses. Over time, I decided I had gained enough experience and learned enough from the head pastor that I could be useful as a head pastor myself. I candidated at a couple of churches and ended up in Cedar Rapids about a year ago.

Q. What is involved in candidating for a church?

A. I visit the church, preach for them, meet with the people, and interview with the leadership of the church.

Q. How many churches did you do that for?

A. Three. One in Michigan, one in Missouri, and the one here.

Q. Did they all offer you a job?

A. We say 'called to be the pastor,' but yes.

Q. I take it Pine Road Baptist Church here in Cedar Rapids happened to be the best opportunity—what made it so?

A. Actually, it was worst of the three.

Q. The worst?

A. Well, from a human perspective anyway. I had several pastors I respect tell me to not take it.

Q. What made Pine Road Baptist Church the worst church to take from "a human perspective?"

A. It offered me the lowest salary, it was averaging less than fifty people on Sunday mornings, it had stopped having Sunday evening services altogether, and—as you know—the church did not have title to the property where it meets or the next-door parsonage. The other two churches, on the other hand, offered me more money, were averaging more than one hundred on Sunday mornings, and owned their own buildings, parsonages, and land. In short, the other two positions were almost ideal for a new pastor to step in and keep things going as they were, except for the continual improvements every person and church needs to make. Here, there was and remains a chance the church would lose its property, including the house in which my family and I live. The loss of a church building could lower the attendance further, reducing the church's ability to support a pastor and his family after paying all its other bills.

Q. So what made you turn down the Michigan and Missouri churches and decide to come here?

A. The answer to that is complicated in the sense that it is hard to put in words.

Q. Do your best. Was it something you just felt?

A. I would not reduce it to a feeling, though feelings were involved. It was something more permanent. But it is hard to put it into anything other than the language of feelings.

I preached a few messages at each church. I usually do not recycle messages. By that, I mean I do not usually preach a message I have preached on a prior occasion. The reason for that is the principle that the teacher studying for the lesson almost always learns more from studying than the teacher's students learn from listening. In the process of preparing messages, I am greatly blessed and I lose out on some of that if I preach again what I have already preached.

However, there are certainly times when circumstances require, or at least make it preferable, to repeat a message. The time I spent canidating at these three churches was one of those times. It was a lot of work to get my family to each place and I was trying to fulfill my final responsibilities as assistant pastor at the church in Indiana, including training a new assistant pastor. So, I ended up preaching one particular message in all three places. It turned out doing so was helpful in the decision on which call to accept.

Q. How so?

A. The message was centered around the theme of the potter and the clay. The Bible uses that analogy a few times—in Isaiah chapter 64, Jeremiah chapter 18, and Romans chapter 9. We are molded by God. We should yield to that molding. He knows what's best for us and we must realize this life is not about us. We will not have true joy if we are not who God has designed us to be. Our rebelling from God's purposes for our lives, hardening of the clay if you will, leads to either being carried about from one temporary emotional high to another, often leaving a path of destruction in our wake, or living an almost absent-minded life, not thinking about what we are doing and not really caring.

I ended up receiving different reactions to that message from each of the churches. The church in Michigan appeared to receive it enthusiastically. After the service, it seemed as if each person there came up and congratulated me on what they termed "a wonderful message." But many of those people also said something like, "I have been allowing God to mold me for years and he has blessed that. I have been trying to get so and so to see they need to be molded as well." It appeared they didn't need me, or any other pastor. They just needed, in their own eyes, someone to tell them what a great job they were doing.

The church in Missouri also received the message enthusiastically, except instead of telling me how great they were, they just shook my hand and smiled, then went about talking with others about the concerts they had tickets for, the vile movies they watched the night before, and what they were going to watch that night. I gave that message on a Sunday morning in that church and—though the church had Sunday evening services—hardly any of those people came back. So, where the church in Michigan, in their own eyes, did not need me or anyone, the church in Missouri appeared to not want me. I was frankly surprised when they still asked me to be their pastor.

Q. So, does that mean the people of Pine Road Baptist Church both needed and wanted you?

A. Not exactly. I received almost no reaction at all from them to that message. Most of them quietly shook my hand and walked out the door. Eighty percent of the congregation had left the parking lot within a couple of minutes of the end of the service. In their own eyes, at least, I'm not sure they needed *or* wanted me. However, I was certain God could use me to help them.

5.

Will thought it was strange the pastor would make a decision based on his perceptions of the reactions to one sermon, but he caught himself before accusing him of that. It is easy to look foolish when you assume things before having all the information, and one rarely has all the information, even a lawyer in a deposition (or perhaps especially one). There had to be more to the decision.

Q. Were there other things about your visit to Pine Road Baptist Church that day that caused you to accept the position there?

A. Yes. The church had a couple of families who did stick around for awhile after the service that morning. They were the leaders of the church. They wanted to make sure the church followed a Biblical direction. They had been keeping the church going while it was without a full-time pastor.

Earlier, I mentioned that Pine Road had stopped having Sunday night services. Sunday night services, or a second service after a potluck, are common in Baptist churches. When I came that day, I actually did not know the church had stopped them. I did not learn that until my family and I were talking with these other families after the Sunday morning service. I must've mentioned something about being back that night or what I would be preaching on that night or asking what time the service started. The other families started looking around at each other when I said that, so I stopped talking. There was a momentary silence, then one of the girls—she would've been twelve at the time—tugged on her father's sleeve and whispered, though loud enough we could all hear, "What is he talking about?" He looked at me and said, "We actually do not have a Sunday night service. It has been some time since we had one. The attendance got so low we just stopped having them." He said this slowly, but it still took a moment to register in my mind.

Sometimes things become so routine to us, either in a good or bad way, that we fail to recognize others live differently. Sunday night church was like that for me. There had not been a week in the prior seventeen years I had not been in church on a Sunday night. I realized I had not encouraged the congregation to be back at night. I had likely been too focused on making sure everything went well during the morning service. Still, I knew I would somehow make sure my family and I would be in church that night somewhere, though I did not know the area and what might be open.

I looked at the man and said, "If you will unlock the doors to the church at six o'clock, I would like to hold a service, even if my family is the only one here singing and listening to the preaching."

It was remarkable. The man did not hesitate. He nodded and said, "I will be here to open the door and we will be here for the service." The other family then said they would as well. Then one of the ladies said she would call the members right after lunch and let them know about the service. And she did. My request to hold a Sunday night service had given them a choice: Christian service and worship of God, or what they always did on Sunday nights, which might not have been bad, but was certainly less good. I knew God would reward their faithfulness and I wanted to be around to see that, if they would have me on a permanent basis.

Q. Did anyone else come to that Sunday night service?

A. Yes, though it was not a big crowd. There were six people in those two families, plus my family, so another six, making twelve. The one lady's work to call all the members resulted in two more people coming, two ladies, though their husbands decided to stay home.

It is unfortunately common to see families where the husband and father fails to spiritually lead his family, thinking the work he does to provide food and a roof is sufficient service. Anyway, that made fourteen of us.

Then there was one guy who walked in during the middle of the hymn singing and sat down in the back pew. He had not been there in the morning. I learned later that none of the members had seen him before. He was in his early twenties, I would guess, and had a baseball cap on that appeared to cover short hair. He had a couple of days facial hair growth, stood about five-foot-eleven, a real fit guy. His clothes were dirty, like he wore them to work construction or in a factory and had not washed them, though he did not smell bad.

After the song, I welcomed him. The rest of the people there turned around and said "hi" as well. He did not say anything. He just nodded his head in acknowledgement. We then went on. I have since wished I asked him his name when he walked in. He did not say it and I still do not know it. He slipped out during the closing prayer and we have not seen him since.

~~~~~

Will saw the court reporter's fingers slip. She turned her face away from the witness and bent down. She fumbled through her purse and rose back up with a tissue in her hands, cover-ing her face. She blew in the tissue, paused, and blew again. She placed the tissue in her lap, swiveled back around in her chair to face her machine and the witness, and said nothing. Will had hired this court reporter many times before. It was unusual for her to interrupt a deposition like this, though Will was always careful to take regular breaks even if he and the witness did not need one. He asked her if she was fine to proceed. She silently nodded her assent.

~~~~~

Q. Anything else you can tell me about your decision?

A. Yes. I have four children. While we were at the church in Michigan, the people of that church were nice to them, but it was in an over-the-top way. They showed no actual interest in them. They would ask them questions, but not wait for the answers before going into their own experi-ences about whatever subject it was they were asking my kids about. Then they walked off smiling at what a great job they had done engaging the children.

In Missouri, the people tended to look at my children suspiciously, waiting to catch them in the act of doing something wrong. Rather than talk to them, they just stared at them. Like most parents, my wife and I work hard to raise our children to do right, but our children are like other children. They misbehave sometimes. After one of the services, one of my children—my oldest and my only daughter, Samantha—started running in the foyer area while playing with another child. Out of the corner of my eye, I saw one of the members stop her and tell her there was no running inside the church. That might be fine advice, but I was close by, the other child was not scolded, and the scolding stopped the forming of a friendship between my daughter and the girl she was playing with. After that, my daughter came to my side and did not leave me. Something like that happened a few other times. It was as if the people thought my children should be perfect, and thus perfect examples to their children, while they themselves were excused from being good examples to their own children. I, not my children, have been called to be a pastor.

Here at Pine Road, my children received more mixed receptions. In other words, it was normal. Some were kind, some were indifferent. It felt more real to them, and they told me so, though not necessarily in those words.

All of those perceptions of and reactions to my kids at the churches in Michigan and Missouri were correctable, but it is accurate to say they were factors in the decision to come to Iowa.

There was also the issue of who I would be succeeding at each church. At the church in Michigan, the last pastor had only been there for a year. Prior to that, the church had five pastors over the past eight years. I could never get a clear explanation for why there had been so many pastors and why none had stayed for very long. I only know that most of them had left voluntarily for other positions elsewhere. It is possible the church had no idea why its pastors would not stay for long. All of us lack self-awareness to some degree. Maybe the church did something to run them off, even if unintentionally. Maybe they didn't support the pastor financially or by being good followers. All of that is just speculation, but the high turnover rate indicated a problem.

At the church in Missouri, the prior pastor had been there for ten years. The reason they were looking for a new pastor was because he had suddenly passed away as a result of a brain aneurysm. The church clearly loved him, which is a good thing. A church should love its pastor and the pastor should love his church. However, from the statements they made to me, the reason they loved him so much was because he made them feel good about themselves. Those statements, combined with their behavior and conversation, led me to believe the pastor had avoided one of his most important responsibilities: naming sin specifically and calling people to repentance.

Q. Why is that something the pastor should do? Doesn't the Bible say "judge not?"

A. Yes. It also says "judge righteous judgment." Are those two statements contradictory? If they were the only statements in the Bible, yes. But they are not. It is important to look at the context of those statements, both the immediate context and the context of the rest of Scripture. We should also presume the Author intended consistency.

Q. Why should we presume consistency? And wasn't there more than one author of the Bible?

A. One author, multiple transcribers. As for presumption of consistency, you do the same thing when you are interpreting laws passed by the legislature or reading case opinions, correct?

Q. Yes, we do.

A. And those make no claim of divine origin.

Q. That is certainly true. Do you know what those churches did after you turned them down?

A. Both of them found other pastors. The church in Michigan ended up hiring someone who led them in the direction they were naturally inclined to head.

Q. What do you mean?

A. He removed the church's independence by joining them to a conference, added a contemporary service, and lessened some of the standards the church had in place prior to his arrival.

Q. I am going to come back to what you mean by lessening of standards. Before I do, what happened with the church in Missouri?

A. They hired someone I know as an acquaintance, a good pastor. I believe George knows him as well. He did his best to keep that church on a right path and get the people to live in a way pleasing to God. It appears some of the leadership resented that, they got others to follow them, and they called a special meeting last month and voted him out as the pastor. Everything that has happened since I took the call to pastor Pine Road Baptist Church instead of those other two churches has confirmed this is where I am supposed to be.

Q. Even with this lawsuit?

A. The lawsuit has not been pleasant, but it's not over yet. Sometimes men mean things for evil, but God means them for good.

Q. Do you believe this lawsuit is evil?

A. That's not what I said. I said sometimes men mean things for evil. That could be true regardless of whether the thing itself is evil.

Q. Fair enough. But I will ask the question anyway. Do you believe the thing itself, this lawsuit, is evil?

A. I had not formed a judgment about that before you asked that question. I do believe our church's defense to the lawsuit is justified. I also believe there are better uses of all our time and resources.

Q. Do you understand the purpose of this lawsuit?

A. I believe so.

Q. Please put in your own words what the lawsuit is about.

A. The Association is trying to take our property.

Q. Your property?

A. Our church's, including the parsonage.

Q. You realize the title to those properties is in the name of the Midwestern Baptist Association?

A. Yes.

Q. And has been for the past thirty-five years?

A. Yes.

Q. Since the church was founded?

A. Yes.

Q. And that the Association bought the property thirty-five years ago for the specific purpose of establishing a church there that would be part of the Association?

A. I know the Association bought the property and that the church, which was part of the Association and had been established about a year prior, moved into the building erected on the property. It would be speculation to know what the Association leaders purposed thirty-five years ago.

Q. You also understand the Association furnished the money to erect the building?

A. Yes, though the church added onto the building with its own funds twenty years ago.

Q. Are you aware of any instance in which Pine Road Baptist Church has claimed to be the owner of the property? And before you answer that question, please take the time you need to think about it. For each such claim of ownership, I will want you to provide me with as many details as possible, including when the claim was made, who made it, to who it was made, the reaction of the person to who it was made, and whether the Association was aware of the claim if it was made to someone other than a person working for the Association. But don't worry about those details yet. First just please answer my initial question about whether you are aware of any such claims of ownership.

(The witness paused.)

A. I do not recall ever making that specific claim.

Q. Did you ever make it non-specifically?

A. What do you mean?

Q. Well, you said you did not recall making that "specific" claim, which could imply you recall making the claim in some nonspecific manner.

～～～～

The pastor paused. He looked unsure, like he recognized the importance of these questions but did not understand why. Still, Will had little doubt he would tell the truth no matter what.

～～～～

A. I don't recall making that claim in any manner, except to the extent I may have implied it to you in answer to one of your earlier questions during this deposition, or in answering the written petition that started this lawsuit.

Q. What about anyone else on behalf of the church? Do you know of anyone on behalf of the church that has made the claim that the church, as opposed to the Association, owned the property, whether before or after you became the pastor?

A. I do not.

Q. Let's take a short break. Let's start again in ten minutes.

6.

Will went back to his office. There was a voicemail message from Bill Smith of Johnson Engineers, the client in the new case that came in the day before. He would be sending all the documents in his company's project file. *Great*, Will thought, *more documents to review, most of which would play no role in the outcome of the case*. After everyone spent a bunch of money on lawyers and lost opportunities, there would be a settlement designed to avoid the risk of an unpredictable jury.

He wondered again why he was sitting where he was, though he had long resigned himself to his circumstances. This was and would remain his career and this was and would remain the system in which that career existed. The middle man taking a cut of the shuffling of money. It was hard to beat back the cynicism. Will had some partners who were good at it. Actually, they did not appear cynical at all. Rather, they appeared to—and probably did—believe the law and their role in it was noble. Sometimes, when he was around them, their positive attitudes infected Will. Mostly he just wondered how in the world anyone could match up the picture of Atticus Finch with what he did. Of course, no one ever saw the day-to-day business of Atticus Finch. Maybe he was a money shuffler as well. Harper Lee didn't tell us about that. A money shuffler given one chance to make a lasting difference.

Will forced himself back to the drudgery, which right now meant the email from Bill Smith. Will needed more than all of the paper documents in the Johnson Engineers project file. He wrote and sent a short email reply letting Smith know he received his voicemail, that in addition to the paper records in the file he would also need all electronic documents and email and instant communication messages, and that he was in a deposition today and so would try to reach him by phone tomorrow.

When the compose window disappeared from his computer screen, Will noticed twenty unread messages had piled up already that morning. He would have to deal with them later.

Will grabbed more coffee and walked back to the conference room. George Bannon stood outside the door. "Are you ready to go back in?" Will asked. "Do you have any questions before we do?"

Will had not paid attention to Bannon during the deposition to this point. There was no need to acknowledge him during it; he was there to observe. Now that Will had taken time to look at him and converse with him again, Bannon looked even more fidgety and uncomfortable than he had at the outset of the morning. He looked like he wanted to say something. Instead of opening his mouth, though, he nodded in a way to indicate he had nothing to discuss and was ready to go back in.

Will walked in with Bannon trailing him. The court reporter was standing in the room alone. "What happened to our witness?" Will asked her.

Bannon interjected first. "Maybe he got tired of this and left."

"I don't think we've worn him out yet," Will replied.

"He came back from the bathroom a little while ago," the court reporter answered, "and saw I was the only one in here. He mentioned something about having a policy of not being in a closed room alone with a woman not his wife, mother, grandmother, or daughter, and that he would wait in the reception area. Then he just left the room. I have been doing this for twenty-five years and that is the first time that has ever happened to me."

"Did he say when he would be back?" Will asked.

"I assumed he would come back after you did."

A receptionist cracked the door and stuck in her head. "Mr. Sanders is in the reception area. He asked me to let you all know he will come in when you are ready for him again."

"Thank you Jane," Will said. "Please tell him he can come back in."

The receptionist left and a few moments later Nate Sanders walked in and took his seat without comment. Will, Bannon, and the court reporter looked at each other. The court reporter smiled, Will shrugged, and Bannon smirked as they each took their seats.

As Nate Sanders had sat in the reception area, he wondered whether he should have recommended that Pine Road Baptist Church hire an attorney. He felt entirely out of his element in that conference room.

Certain thoughts comforted him. He had no doubt he would eventually be able to use this experience in sermon illustrations. Also, whatever distress he felt now, it was nothing compared to the persecution believers had faced in the past and faced in the present in other parts of the world, or the things he had helped people with as a pastor. One of the easiest ways to remove feelings of oppression is to stop thinking about one's own condition and start thinking about how to meet the needs of others.

Nevertheless, it would have been nice to have someone else sitting in there with him. When the receptionist informed him they were ready for him again, he tried to put the isolation he felt out of his mind. He silently asked God to give him wisdom in his thinking and answers, as well as increased faith to trust Him for everything. Though the others did not know it, it was this prayer that accounted for Nate's silent entry into the room and the taking of his seat with a slightly bowed head.

"Are you ready to proceed?" the lawyer asked.

Nate looked up. "Yes," he answered.

Will nodded at the court reporter and continued.

Q. We have come back from a break a little longer than anticipated, lasting approximately fifteen minutes. During that time, did you speak to anyone?

A. I spoke with Miss Martinez here very briefly and then with your receptionist and another couple in the reception area.

Q. Did you speak about this case or this deposition?

A. No.

Q. What did you talk about?

A. When I walked back in the room, I saw that Miss Martinez was the only one in here. I mentioned to her that I prefer not to be alone with women that I am not related to and that I would wait in the reception area. In the reception area, with the receptionist and the other couple waiting, we mostly talked about the weather and who we thought might win the NCAA basketball tournament this year. In other words, we were on the verge of solving some of the world's major problems before you called me back in here.

Q. Lawyers have a bad habit of interrupting important things.

A. I'll leave that comment alone.

Q. Prudence is a virtue.

A. I agree.

Q. Okay, let's get back into the questions that matter for this case. When you came to Pine Road Baptist Church a year ago, what were you told about the status of the property?

A. Even before I accepted the position I had been told the Association had title to the property. That was one of the reasons other pastors recommended I not accept the position.

Q. Who informed you about the property ownership issue?

A. The church had an elderly gentleman it was bringing in to preach for it occasionally, a person who had pastored a few churches in the past but because of health issues had stopped full-time work. He told me about the church's affiliation with the Association and about the Association having title to the property, including the parsonage. He wanted to make sure I knew what I was getting into before I accepted the position. Later, one of the members also informed me of the issues.

Q. What was the interim pastor's concern?

A. That the church would lose its building and I would lose my home if I moved into the parsonage.

Q. Sitting there at that time, a year ago, why did you and he think that might happen?

A. Well, there is always uncertainty when someone else has control.

Q. True, but the Association had owned the property for thirty-five years without there being a problem.

A. Yes, but our concern was justified, for we are sitting here today with the Association trying to take the property from us.

Q. Let's talk about how we got to this point. When was the first time you had a conversation with someone at the Association?

A. It was after I became the pastor, but not for some time after I started. Probably four months after I started. When I came, I was busy getting acclimated, visiting the members in order to get to know them, visiting the few visitors we had, starting to get things set up in the way I thought they should be, and working a part-time job outside the church to help our family's income, as the church was not able to pay me much, though the providing of a home is of great benefit.

Q. Who did you have that conversation with? Was it with George Bannon here?

A. No. I believe George did not take a position with the Association until about six months ago. We received a letter from the Association informing us the church was behind in its cooperative support payments to the Association. After receiving that letter, I called the Association's office. I initially spoke with a receptionist or secretary in the office. When I told her the purpose of my call, she transferred me to someone who had a title like 'assistant membership director.' I have not spoken with him since, but I believe his last name was Patterson. Phil, maybe?

Q. Does the name Peter Patterson sound familiar?

A. Yes, that's who it was.

Q. What was the substance of your conversation with Peter Patterson?

A. I informed him we had received the letter and we would not be making any more payments to the Association. He asked me why—was the church in financial difficulty? Now, it was true the church did not have a lot of revenue at that time, and still doesn't, and the cooperative support payments would not have been a high priority for financial reasons alone, but that was not the reason. I told him the real reason: Pine Road Baptist Church was not interested in being part of the Association any longer.

Q. What did he say to that?

A. Not much. I don't think he knew how to react. He seemed not to expect it at least. He finally said "okay" and that he would pass that information on to the membership director and the Association's board of directors. It was not a long conversation. He did not even ask me why.

Q. Did the church members support that decision?

A. They did and they do.

Q. When did you make that decision?

A. I knew when I accepted the position I would lead the church out of the Association. The members—or, at least, the leaders of the church—knew that before I accepted the position.

Q. Why did you want to end the church's long history with the Association?

A. We will always be appreciative of the vision the Association's leaders had, and the work they performed, to start a Baptist church in that part of Cedar Rapids. I do believe, though, that the better practice is for a church to be independent, with Christ as its head, the pastor as an undershepherd, and the Word of God as the guide for faith and practice. Adding an association, conference, or denomination adds a layer of authority not founded on the Word of

God. It risks conflict if, for instance, the authority outside the church takes a position the church is convinced is contrary to the Bible or God's direction for that church. That type of conflict is common actually. That does not mean churches of like beliefs cannot or should not work together to accomplish certain goals. It does mean it is best they remain independent entities, as that is the Biblical model and the pattern of the early churches.

Q. Doesn't the Bible mention bishops?

A. It is another word for overseer of a church, as is pastor or elder. There is no indication in the Bible that a bishop or pastor had authority over more than one church at once. Your client, I am certain, even agrees with me about that. Churches of like belief helped one another, but they did not cede their independence in the process.

Q. Is it wrong for a church to be part of an association or conference or denomination?

A. The Bible does not expressly say that churches should not join associations or conferences. It does lay out a model for church authority that does not reference multi-church overseers. It references different churches by location, which indicates there was not, as Catholics believe, one universal church. Denominations that consider themselves a singular church with multiple locations, with a hierarchy between Christ and the pastor, are thus further away from the New Testament model than conferences or associations. Conferences and associations, such as the Midwestern Baptist Association, do not technically have such a hierarchy, though in practice it ends up that way. I want our church to follow the pattern of the early churches as laid out in the Bible.

Q. What do you mean by associations or conferences in practice having a hierarchy like denominations?

A. If a church belongs to an association or conference, it is known by that association, as an association church. For instance, Pine Road Baptist Church has been known as a Midwestern Baptist Association church. The Midwestern Baptist Association has a board and officers. They are responsible for directing and coordinating the activities of the Association. They also make statements on doctrinal, cultural, and political issues. Many people consider the position of the Association to automatically be the position of each church in the Association. They view associations and conferences as no different than denominations, where the position of the organizational hierarchy is the position of each church within the denomination. Most of the time that is no problem because the larger organization and the local church are aligned in their positions. When there is conflict, though, the local church is left with keeping quiet about its own position or disputing the organization's position. That latter choice risks creating confusion and disorder.

Q. Doesn't each church being its own entity also risk confusion and disorder?

A. Globally, yes, but not within the particular local church and not with respect to others' view of a particular local church's position.

Q. Any other ways that conferences and associations act like denominations?

A. Well, you also have associations of associations. For instance, there is an organization called the Baptist World Alliance. It has been around for about one hundred years. Its members are Baptist associations, conferences, denominations, whatever you want to call them. The last I checked, it had more than two hundred of them around the world. The Baptist World Alliance's goal is unity, and not necessarily just among Baptists. Unity is fine and great, but not if it comes at the expense of truth. Collectively working together can result in some good works, but to keep everyone happy and in the organization, you have to countenance error. To choose unity at all costs is to choose to believe in nothing at all. Ultimately, you do not even believe in unity because you cannot tolerate those who refuse to unite. The Midwestern Baptist Association has not joined the Baptist World Alliance and I have not heard any indication it will, but I would not be surprised if it eventually joins it or something similar.

Q. Let's back up. Are there other reasons you did not want Pine Road Baptist Church to be part of the Midwestern Baptist Association anymore, other than wanting to follow what you believe to be the Biblical model?

A. The Association and our church are heading in different paths. Even if we felt the Association model was the best one, we disagree with some of its current positions.

Q. In what ways?

A. For several years now, the Association has been helping start churches that do not even have "Baptist" in their names. While the term "Baptist" as we use it is not a denomination, it *is* a distinction. It identifies a certain set of beliefs. The Association is saying some people consider the term "Baptist" offensive.

Q. Isn't it in some instances? For example, "Westboro Baptist Church," the military funeral protesting church?

A. That group's use of the term "Baptist" may be offensive—as well as its use of 'Westboro' and 'church' for that matter—but the term itself is not offensive merely by that group's misuse. The term Baptist has a long heritage, with distinctive meaning, that one group's misuse is incapable of interrupting.

Anyway, I have yet to meet a person who actually considered the word "Baptist" offensive. To me, it appears the Association's move away from that distinctive marking has less to do with wanting to avoid offending people than it has to do with a loss of doctrinal conviction. The Association no longer believes some of the things Baptists have historically believed. People have called themselves Baptist because that term signifies a set of beliefs. If the Association no longer believes some of those things, it is no surprise it is dropping the "Baptist" name in its newer church plants.

What is really curious, though, is with its newest churches, the Association is even forgetting the word "church." They are called things like 'The Bridge' and 'Pathways', names with no meaning when applied to a church.

It is a wonder the Midwestern Baptist Association has not dropped the "Baptist" from its own name, though I am sure that is coming. Lately its leaders have referred to it as the "MBA," which is a bit comical given that acronym is already taken by something more famous.

Q. Any other ways in which your church and the Association are, as you say, heading in different paths?

A. The naming convention the Association has adopted is emblematic of a de-emphasis of some of the standards to which Association churches have historically held. The issues include Bible translations, music, acceptable forms of entertainment, and how we dress. In each of these areas, we are holding our ground because we believe the historical stands are based on Bible principles. The Association is, on the other hand, in our eyes, becoming more worldly.

Where we continue to use one translation, the King James Version, the Association no longer holds to that and its churches use varied translations, some of which disagree with each other.

Where we sing traditional hymns, or newer hymns with a traditional sound and message, the Association is encouraging its churches to adopt rock sounds to attract younger people.

Anyone is welcome into our services, and we are glad for visitors, but when they come they will find the leaders of our church and many of its members dressed well, men looking like men, with suit jackets and ties, ladies looking like ladies, with dresses or long skirts. The Association is encouraging the leaders of its churches to dress down to help people feel more comfortable.

We are by no means stuffy. We like to enjoy ourselves in church. We shout "Amen!" We sing loud. But we are also respectful, formal, and reverent.

Q. Do you mean to say the Association's churches are not those things?

A. I can't speak as to all of them.

Q. What can you speak to?

A. Let me put it this way. We believe there are standards Christians should adhere to. Really, every single person and organization has standards. Everyone draws a line some-where. You find some clothing and music acceptable and some not, for your home and for your law firm.

It is a matter of how you base your decision on where to draw the line. Our church has standards based on the Bible. The Association used to hold those standards as well. We believe the Association has moved its standards less because of a desire to adhere to the Bible than because of convenience.

I am sure the Association's leaders believe some of these standards are merely preferences and not convictions based on Bible principles. I could take you through each standard we hold and show you the Bible passages on which they are based. In any event, it is sufficient that Pine Road Baptist Church and the Midwestern Baptist Association no longer see eye-to-eye on where to draw the line. To keep our standards, we cannot associate with the Association any longer, just as to keep your standards you would not accept partners into your law firm that did not hold to the abilities and ethics to which your firm holds.

Q. Do you plan to have Pine Road Baptist Church join some other conference or association?

A. No.

Q. Are there no other acceptable associations or conventions?

A. There may be some whose beliefs, practices, and standards align with ours. However, for the reasons I mentioned, we intend to remain independent. This conviction is not unique to us. There are thousands of independent Baptist churches in this country. Additionally, many non-Baptist churches, commonly called nondenominational or New Evangelical churches, operate independent from any denomination, conference, or association.

7.

Nate noticed George Bannon's snorts and sighs had increased in volume and frequency over the past fifteen minutes as he had answered the lawyer's questions about the church withdrawing from the Association. Nate had always admired George. The snorts were beneath him. Perhaps the conflict between the church and the Association was making his outward disposition less cordial. Conflicts can do that.

Nate did his best to ignore Bannon so he would not lose his focus. It appeared Will Jacobson was doing the same.

~~~~~

Q. In your church's answer to the petition, it denied that the Association was entitled to possession of the property. Tell me everything on which you base that denial.

A. I'm not sure I understand your question.

Q. I'm not trying to trick you. I promise. That does not help me at all. I need to know what you are going to tell a judge or jury about why the Association should not have possession of the property for which it holds the title.

A. Well, the church has been in possession of the property for thirty-five years. It has paid for all of the maintenance and utilities. Twenty years ago, it put on an addition at its own expense. More recently, it installed new carpet and a new roof. It also added a chair lift in the back stairs to make it more handicap accessible. There are many other little things it has done. The only reason the property has value outside of the land is because of how the church has maintained and improved the property.

Q. Did the Association ever help with those costs?

A. Not that I am aware of.

Q. Did the church ever ask for the Association's help with those costs?

A. Not that I am aware of.

Q. And the Association has always allowed the church to possess the property rent-free, correct?

A. I believe that is true.

Q. Thank you. That is all the questions I have. Unless you have anything to add, the court reporter will now stop transcribing.

A. I don't think there is anything to add.

~~~~~

Will looked at the court reporter and nodded to indicate she could stop. She turned from her gadget setup and began to unplug it all and put it away.

Will stood. George Bannon and Nate Sanders followed his lead in rising from their chairs.

"Thank you for your time today," Will said to the pastor. "It was a pleasure meeting you. I am sorry it has to be under these circumstances."

"Yes, me too," Nate replied.

"Do you need help finding your way?"

"No, I'm fine. Thank you."

Will walked to the conference room door and opened it. He turned back around and saw Pastor Sanders look at Bannon. "George, it was good to see you again," Nate said to him. "As Mr. Jacobson just said, I am sorry it is under these circumstances."

"Yes, I am as well," Bannon responded, somewhat unnaturally it seemed to Will.

"Please tell your parents I said 'hello.'"

"Yes, okay. And you say 'hi' to your family from me."

Nate nodded, turned toward the door, and walked out to the reception area.

Will and Bannon soon after exited the conference room. Will motioned his client representative down a hallway into a smaller conference room where they could talk. Will closed the door and began, "Well, I thought that went well. Sanders will make a good witness. By that I mean the jury will probably like him. How much a jury likes the witnesses plays a large role in determining how a jury will decide. That said, the information he has, the things he will be able to testify about on the witness stand, should not affect the outcome. The law and relevant facts are on our side. However sympathetic he and the church may be in the eyes of the jury, we confirmed by this deposition they do not have any surprises that would put the facts or the law in their favor. The property belongs to the Association. It can kick the church out if it wants."

Will saw that Bannon was not listening. He was seated and staring coldly out the window. As Will stopped speaking, Bannon looked up at him and said, "Why didn't you press him more?" Bannon's tone was even more accusatory than his words.

"What do you mean?" Will asked.

"I mean, why didn't you make him feel more uncomfortable? Nate needs to feel the pressure of this lawsuit. He needs to give in before a trial, and to do that he needs to be made to feel uncomfortable. He needs to get to the point where he has to hire a lawyer so we can start putting financial pressure on his church. I feel like we wasted an opportunity. Everything that happened in there was too pleasant. You were too kind. You hardly even challenged his baseless criticisms of our Association or countered him with facts of all the good our Association does."

Will's mind went into a mixture of defensiveness and appeasement, caught between defending himself against what he saw as a ridiculous attack on his methods and the desire to ensure the money kept coming in from the one who paid him. He recovered from his initial dumbfoundedness and said, "You know him better than I do, but based on my observations of him today I do not believe we could pummel him into submission. In any event, that is not important. The facts and the law are on our side. We should win this. That said, I will give some thought to how we can put more pressure on them to agree to our terms."

Whenever Will was presented with a difficult demand or question from a client, he found it best to put them off with a *let me give it some thought* reply. That usually pacified them for the time being. Whether it worked with Bannon he wasn't sure, for Bannon merely resumed staring out the window.

After what seemed like ten minutes, but was more like thirty seconds, Bannon broke the silence. "Nate kept criticizing the Association. Our positions, our doctrine. You did not try to counter his points at all. You could have brought up all the good things our Association does, helping start churches, supporting missionaries, food banks, daycares with scholarships for the poor, all of that stuff."

No, no, no, Will thought. That is not the point of a deposition. Why do clients, even so-called sophisticated ones like George Bannon, not understand that? The goal of a deposition is not to score points. The goal is to gather information to avoid surprises at trial and to evaluate whether the case needs to be settled. It's not a debate.

Out loud, Will responded, "A lot of what he said helps explain the church's motives and outlook, but isn't relevant to the issues that impact the outcome of the case. The discovery process, including depositions, is our opportunity to gather facts. To the extent we need to do any disputing or arguing, we can do that at trial and in pre-trial motions. However, we won't want to do that over every issue or we will annoy the judge or jury."

Will knew that answer would not pacify Bannon.

It didn't.

There was more silence.

To break it this time, Will asked, "Anything else you'd like to discuss about the deposition or any other aspect of the case?"

George Bannon stood and shook his head while saying, "No."

Will provided a brief explanation of the next steps in the lawsuit and then walked Bannon to the reception area. It was less than a cheery goodbye.

A few moments later, Will was back in his office at his desk. He had never before had a client rebuke him for his handling of a deposition. Who Bannon wanted him to be was not who he was. There were "bulldog" lawyers, but Will did not have that disposition. Will preferred to get along with everyone. Most clients were fine with that, though here and there during his twelve-year career there had been clients who wished he was cordial to them and the judge but certainly not to the other side. Even those few had come around to accept his methods, as he generally got good results. There were definite advantages to having a reputation that did not cause the opposing side to put up significant barriers to cooperation. Thus, Will's personality fit what he also believed to be the best way to practice law. Most of his clients had appreciated that. He knew some wouldn't, but Bannon's outburst surprised him.

For much of the rest of the afternoon, Will played back in his mind the deposition and his previous communications with Bannon. His worry about it killed his work efficiency. Will was certain Bannon had not previously said he wanted Will to put extra pressure on the church or its pastor. Bannon hadn't even said anything during the morning break. If he thought Will was not conducting the deposition properly, why didn't he say it then? Instead, Bannon had acted like everything was fine.

Will admitted to himself that he was not good at recognizing nonverbal cues. His wife could attest to that. It seemed to him there was some benefit to that particular ineptitude. Recognizing that someone was trying to convey a message through head movements, facial expressions, and/ or body language was different than deciphering that message. More often than not he would misread the message if he recognized it in the first place. Or, he might start "recognizing" messages not really there. At least, it appeared to Will that when people thought *he* was saying something nonverbally, it was more likely he was thinking about something unrelated and mundane, like how good a slice of pizza and a Coke would taste right then or whether to buy a new computer mouse because the current one just didn't feel right. Once, his wife raised the possibility of going on a weekend trip with a couple of her friends. As she talked about it, Will allowed his mind to wander to the time when he was a boy and had a chance to win $500 if he made a three-point shot during halftime of a semi-professional basketball game. He had missed. As he was thinking about how he wished he would've shot it from a different angle his wife saw something in his expression that told her that her husband did not want her to go. He had to spend the next week convincing her that whatever his body language conveyed he really did not mind if she went and thought it would be a fun thing for her to do.

Will brought himself comfort by noting that—whatever his deficiencies in recognizing communication symbols—*guys* did not "talk" like that. Women were the ones speaking things not said and hearing things not spoken. A man said his mind out loud and if George Bannon failed to do that at the appropriate time it was his own fault. Still, the anxiety Will felt for disappointing his client remained.

One of Will's law partners walked in. "Are you going to the First Bank reception?" he asked.

Will slumped. He had forgotten about that reception. "Eh, uh, I don't know," he replied.

"You should. Big client and all, and could be bigger. They will have a lot of people there and it would be good if we had a good showing."

Will looked at the time on his computer. It was already 4:30 p.m. His tasks list looked the same now as it had when he finished the deposition of Nate Sanders. "What time does it start?"

"In a half-hour."

"Okay. Let me see if I can get a few things done here." The partner left to recruit others. As soon as he left Will realized there wasn't much chance he would actually accomplish anything in the remaining time before the reception. First, he had to call his wife to let her know. She picked up the phone and said, "Hi, you're going to be late, aren't you?"

"Yes. I had forgotten First Bank had invited our firm to a reception tonight. It starts at five. I should be home between six-thirty and seven. Don't worry about supper for me. I am sure there will be hors d'oeuvres at the reception."

"It's already cooking."

"I'm sorry."

"Okay. We'll see you later."

The phone clicked on the other end. It wasn't an angry click, but a resigned one. At least, that was the best Will could hope for. He had now disappointed one of his clients and his family today. If his other clients knew how little progress he had made on their cases today, they would be disappointed in him as well. He now had to go to a reception he did not care about. Earlier today, he had missed the monthly board of directors meeting for the community nonprofit organization on which he served.

Will could sometimes feel fine about himself if he was at least successful in one area of his life, if at least one person liked him. There was none of that today.

Before leaving for the reception, Will turned his attention back to Bannon. Will was not so blind to his occasional inability to impress others that he was unwilling to admit Bannon simply may have been upset at Will, regretting the decision to hire him. It appeared there was something more. Will *had* noticed Bannon's lack of composure on first seeing Nate Sanders that morning. He wondered if their paths had crossed even before Pastor Sanders became the pastor of a church belonging to an association for which Bannon now worked.

Thanks to today's deposition, Will knew a good deal about Pastor Sanders' background. He knew much less about Bannon's. Their conversations had not involved much that was not business related.

Will began searching for information about Bannon's background on the internet. Bannon's social media accounts were private, but the Midwestern Baptist Association's web site did have a staff page with a one-paragraph biography of him. It did not take long for Will to read that Bannon had graduated from North Phoenix Baptist College, the same college from which Pastor Sanders graduated. Bannon had graduated one year before Sanders. He had been valedictorian of his class, which did not surprise Will.

How big was the college? The college's web site said it graduated two hundred the past year. A dozen years ago that might have been less. Bannon and Sanders must have known each other there, and perhaps well if today was any indication.

He would have to find out about this, for more than just curiosity reasons. A client's motivations often impacted settlement negotiations and litigation tactics. Will's analytical mindset sometimes caused him to forget that. Bannon's outburst at him would help him remember that for awhile.

Will was not able to quickly find other connections between the two. He put his computer to sleep, put on his suit jacket, and began walking the block to the First Bank reception.

8.

Nate had taken the elevator to the first floor of the building, which housed a bank, and exited out onto the downtown sidewalk. Rather than turn left toward the parking lot in which his car sat, he turned right.

He pulled out his cell phone, turned it on, and called his wife, Tara.

"How did it go?" she immediately asked.

"I'm not really sure, but I don't think very well."

"I'm sure you did great!"

His wife's confidence in him made Sanders smile. "Well, I'm not so sure about that. I answered his questions truthfully and as best I could. I just don't think the answers are helpful for the case."

"Do you think they will let us keep the property?"

"Right now, it doesn't look like it."

"Our house, too?"

"If they take the church property, they will take the parsonage as well."

"I know. You've told me that before. And we knew that when we came. It's just I was praying this morning God would show them something during the deposition that would convince them to drop the lawsuit and allow the church to keep the property."

"Keep praying. Though things seem bleak right now, we don't see the big picture like God does." Nate wished he could hide these things from Tara. He didn't want her to worry.

"I will," she responded. "Are you outside?"

"Yes, instead of going to my car, I decided to walk around downtown for a bit. I thought it might help me relax after the tension of the deposition. Plus, since we have been here, we haven't really spent much time downtown. I wanted to try to get a better feel for the area. I suppose you can hear the wind."

Nate had reached the Second Avenue bridge over the Cedar River. It was a windy day, something he could feel more over the river outside the defense of the downtown buildings. He turned south so he could walk back east along Third Avenue.

There was a pause in the conversation and then Tara asked, "Was George there?"

"Yes," Nate answered.

"What did he say?"

"Not much. We shook hands at the beginning. I mentioned we had not seen each other in awhile. He replied with something about not being able to talk because of the lawsuit."

"Hmm. Anything else?"

"He didn't talk during the deposition. I don't think he was allowed to. When it was over we asked each other to say 'hi' to our respective families. So, uh, he says 'hi.'"

"He's not married yet, is he?"

"Not that I am aware of. I just asked him to say 'hello' to his parents from me. He could use a wife, though." Nate laughed.

"Yes. It is a good thing *you* have one."

Nate laughed again. "It most definitely is a good thing. Without you, I would probably be eating a single-serve frozen pizza for supper tonight."

"And walking around wearing dirty, wrinkled clothes."

"Hey, I know how to do laundry!"

"But being able to do something and actually doing it are two different things, right? I know someone who preached about that just last week."

Nate smiled again. She was really good at making him smile. "True, true. Anyway, you know I just married you because of your cooking, right?"

"I only knew how to make grilled cheese when we got married."

"My point exactly!"

Tara laughed and then replied, "Right, and I just married you for your money."

They each laughed.

When they caught their breath, Tara asked, "So that was it from George?"

"Yes, unfortunately. I didn't get a chance to ask him how he came to be employed by the Association."

"Did it seem like he understood our position, that he was sympathetic to our church at all?"

"I did not see a lot of his reactions. He was looking away a lot and most of the time I was so focused on answering the lawyer's questions that I did not look at him. I did hear him sigh a lot, though. He seemed uncomfortable, but not because he felt sorry for us. It was more like he was angry. But I probably should not even say that. It's just speculation. Only God knows what's in his heart."

"Was the lawyer nice to you?"

"Actually, he was. He wasn't what I pictured he would be.

He was about my age. He was respectful and didn't act like he knew everything. He had a lot of questions about the differences between the positions of the Association and our church. I don't think he quite understands, but he did seem genuinely interested."

"How do those issues impact who gets the property?"

"I'm not really sure. They might not. But the lawyer—his name is Will Jacobson—was curious about them for part of the deposition."

"Okay. What time do you think you will be home?"

"I am going to walk around here for awhile longer and find a place to pray. Then I am going to go to the church to do some things. So, I'll be home in time for supper."

"Okay, see you then!"

"What is for supper, by the way?"

"Grilled cheese."

Another smile.

~~~~~

As he finished speaking with his wife, Nate had turned down First Street on the east side of the Cedar River, walked past the tallest building in the city—the Alliant Energy tower—and crossed Third Avenue. As he walked back east along the south side of Third Avenue, he came and stood in front of the Paramount Theatre entrance. The building's restoration to its former glory had recently been completed. It had sustained significant damage in the June 2008 flood. Nate saw a poster of upcoming Cedar Rapids Symphony events. That would make a nice date with Tara. He resolved to bring her here to a symphony concert soon.

Nate walked a few blocks further until he came to a trail that crossed his path, heading north and south. He made another mental note to see where this trail headed. He would first need to clean the chain on his bike and put some air in its tires. He hoped he would follow through on that intent. As Tara just reminded him, it is easier to think about doing something worthwhile than to actually do it.

Past the trail, on his left, stood the Cedar Rapids Museum of Art. Nate had never visited the place. In fact, he couldn't remember ever walking through an art museum. He crossed the street and walked in the entrance.

He soon found himself in a room containing paintings by Grant Wood. He had heard the name and recognized some of the paintings, but did not realize Grant Wood's ties to Iowa until reading a short biographical sketch of him in the room.

Nate sat on a bench. After glancing around for awhile, he fixed his eyes for some time on one painting. It contained rolling hills of farmland, with a series of plush, green trees. To the right sat a farmhouse. The house was important. It meant the fields would look the way they looked, for someone lived there. That person planted and tended the field and would harvest its crops. But the house itself needed to be built on a sure foundation and then maintained with all diligence.

So much depended on right choices. And then work. But all of it remained a miracle, the handiwork of God, such that the man who made the house and worked the fields, along with the man who drew the scene, owed everything to the One who made them, strengthened, forgave, and comforted them, and made a way to redeem them, if only they would accept that free gift.

The painting, and the thoughts that came to him as he studied it, helped Nate put today in perspective. The church building was important. But there would be another building, as long as Nate and the church members remained willing laborers.

After a half-hour in the museum, Nate walked back outside. Green Square Park was across the street. It seemed like a nice place to pray. He walked across the street and sat on a bench. He began praying. His mind recalled many things for which to thank God. He also asked for wisdom to pastor the church. And he asked for good to result from the Association's lawsuit.

Before long, a train horn in the vicinity interrupted his prayer. A track abutted the park. He looked up and saw the train coming from the south. One of the endearing—or annoying, depending on your perspective—features of Cedar Rapids: a train passes along a north-south route through downtown a few times a day, blocking the east-west traffic.

Nate recalled one of the church members mentioning that a famous actor was once staying in the downtown hotel after performing in a musical at the Paramount and complained when he heard the train's horn in the middle of the night. It seemed a petty complaint, to be awakened once by nothing more than a train horn. Pastors are awakened by more distressing things—usually phone calls from people who are going through tragedies—on what seemed like a regular basis. But then Nate considered that even that thought was petty. After all, it was a privilege to be of such use and help to others.

It is so easy to get caught up in our own problems, that are hardly problems at all, really.

Nate took out his phone and began putting some of these thoughts into a note-taking app he used for sermons.

A blessing and a curse. That was the choice God set before the Israelites in Moses's final sermon before he passed away and the Hebrew nation crossed the Jordan into the promised land. Obey God and His commandments and be blessed. Follow after other gods and be cursed. Choices dictated the result.

Yet it was also true that God gave us blessings despite ourselves. How often did we miss those because we saw them as a curse? If the train tracks had not been built where they were, would Cedar Rapids have prospered as it had? What other consequences would there have been? And these are just train tracks.

We sometimes stand so close to things we cannot see them for what they really are.

As Nate continued typing into his phone, it rang.

"Hello," he answered.

"Oh, hi, uh, hello," the voice on the other end stumbled. "Is this Nate Sanders? I mean, Pastor Sanders?"

"Yes, it is."

"Oh, okay, this is Kay Martinez, the court reporter from the deposition this morning."

"Yes, sure."

"I found the number for your church. Someone there answered and said you weren't there, but gave me your cell phone number. I hope it is okay I called."

"Yes, that is fine," Nate said. Her voice sounded anxious. "Is there something I can help you with?"

"I'm not sure. It's about my son."

"What about him?" Nate asked.

"I haven't seen him in three years. He's twenty-two-years-old now. He walked out when he was 19, almost without a word. I was wondering if you could help me find him."

That was a first. Nate had never been asked to find a missing person before. His first instinct was to bluntly reject her request. Thankfully, he would later realize, he paused and found a way to respond more gently.

"I'll do what I can. Is there something in particular you had in mind?"

"During the deposition this morning, you talked about having a visitor during that first Sunday night service you held. Do you remember that?"

"Yes, I remember. I still wish I knew his name and had been able to speak with him." Nate now also remembered that Ms. Martinez had seemed agitated during that portion of the deposition.

"Was he Hispanic?" she asked.

"Huh?"

"You never mentioned his skin color. Was he Hispanic looking?"

"Yes, he was." That did not exactly narrow things down, Nate thought. Nevertheless, Kay Martinez was excited.

"Then it's possible," she continued. "The way you described him otherwise, it could have been him. I thought he might eventually try to find a church. I wish he would have kept coming back to yours. Then I could at least find him."

"Is he missing? Have you notified the police?"

"When he first left, we—his father and I—notified the police. They looked for him and found him fairly quickly. He wasn't trying to hide, except from maybe us and his former life. There was nothing for the police to do. He was an adult in their eyes. He writes me now and then to let me know he is okay. But there is never a return address. I don't know where he lives or what his phone number is or how he is doing. It's been three years, but I think I already mentioned that."

"What's his name?"

"Donald." Nate would not have guessed that name. "Well," Ms. Martinez continued, "his friends call him Donnie or DJ. Or they did call him that. I guess I don't know what his friends call him now, or if he has friends."

"If your son was the young man who came to the church that Sunday night a year ago, why do you think he would have come to church?"

"He grew up in church, a Baptist church. I took him every Sunday. Well, mostly anyway. Sometimes we got too busy. Actually, we were too busy a lot when he was in high school. That's my fault. But I think he loves God. I think if he doesn't have church in his life he will feel empty. That's why he came, he didn't want to feel empty."

She was talking as if it was a certainty that the visitor had been her son. She was also confident in his motivations despite the fact she had not talked with him in three years. But maybe she was right. It was impossible to determine right now.

Nate replied, "Okay. I am pretty sure I would recognize the visitor if I saw him again, though he was wearing a ball-cap, so it might be hard. But if I do, I could call you."

"That would be great. That's really all I meant by asking you to help me find him. He might show up at your church again. I just want to be able to talk to him and see how he is doing."

"Okay. I have your number here in my cell phone now that you called it. What about your husband? What is his name and would I reach him at the same number?"

"I'm sorry. You misunderstood. We were never married, Donald's father and I. It was a high school thing that went too far. Neither of us have ever been married, in fact. But his name is Eddie Valenza. Donald has his last name. Donald Valenza. Eddie and I do keep in touch. Always have. I will text you his cell number after we hang up. If you see Donald, it would be good if you let one of us know as soon as possible."

"I will." Then Nate realized he needed to qualify his promise. "Wait. If I am able to talk to him, I will mention that you would like to speak with him. If he tells me to not tell you where he is, I won't be able to. But I will, with as much urging as I can muster, impress on him that he should reach out to you."

"I understand," she replied. "Thank you."

"Sure. No problem."

"I'll let you go now. Thank you for listening to me and offering me some hope today."

"Before you let me go, can I ask whether you are attending church anywhere now?"

"I'm still a member of the same church I took Donald to growing up, but I haven't been there in quite awhile."

"Well, I don't want to take you out of a good church, but if you need one, we would love to have you visit us at Pine Road Baptist Church. You are welcome anytime."

She replied with nothing more than an "okay." Her mind was on her son and not on church. They ended the call.

A few moments later the text came from Ms. Martinez with Donald's father's phone number.

The day certainly had been interesting, Nate thought, though not one he was eager to repeat. He started back to his car and wondered what else would happen. As it turned out, the rest of the day was normal. He returned to the church, continued preparing for the midweek service (teaching through the book of Isaiah), fixed a broken door handle to one of the Sunday School rooms, went home, had supper (it really was grilled cheese on this night), and came back to church to oversee follow-up visits to people who had attended the church.

9.

Tuesday evening

Roy arrived home at the apartment he had recently leased in Phoenix. He intended to use it during spring training and during the off-season. His wife, Jenny, had helped pick it out, but she had not yet spent a night in it. It was a little nicer than what he would have picked out for himself, but since they married two summers ago Roy had allowed her to make most of the home-related decisions.

Given his draft position, Roy received a nice signing bonus, but his income playing minor league ball was small. They lived in one-bedroom apartments in the cities in which Roy was assigned. They ate ham sandwiches on white bread and lots of pasta. They were happy. In fact, Jenny's happiness was one of the few things Roy wanted in life and he worked hard to make sure of it.

Roy's time in the minors ended up unusually short: a half-season following the draft and the first month of the next season. That was less grooming than even Malik had received. The Hawks had sustained injuries to three outfielders in a matter of weeks. They had no choice but to call up Roy. Then he played so well they could not send him back down.

When the Hawks added Roy to its major league roster, the immediate jump to the big league's minimum salary caused an exponential increase in the expense of Jenny's tastes, not that Roy minded. If she was happy, he was happy.

So here Roy found himself in the nicest place either of them had ever lived. Neither had grown up in families with much discretionary income. Jenny was already scouting places for them to live in Indianapolis during the season.

Jenny's flight from Iowa had arrived an hour ago, as the Hawks' spring training game was concluding. She told Roy not to worry about trying to pick her up; she would have coffee with a friend and be at their apartment soon.

On his way home, Roy had picked up a meal for them at a French-Asian fusion restaurant Jenny had heard about and wanted to try. He set their dining room table with a candle in the middle. He could not wait to see his wife after being in Phoenix for three weeks without her.

While he was waiting for her to finish up her coffee chat with her friend and arrive at their new apartment, Roy turned on the national sports news. It was immediately about him.

"We now go to Preston Edwards in Phoenix with an update on the Roy Adams situation from yesterday," the anchor said.

The reporter Roy had talked to that morning appeared on the screen and began talking: "Roy Adams was back in the lineup for the Hawks' spring-training game today, going one-for-three at the plate and making a nice defensive play in centerfield before being lifted for a replacement in the sixth inning. While Adams is not yet talking about the situation that caused him to be away from the team on Sunday and pulled out of yesterday's lineup, we did obtain additional information from a source associated with the team. According to the source, Adams was not with the team on Sunday as a result of his own voluntary decision. He was not injured and apparently there was no sickness or tragedy in his family. He also was not in trouble with the law.

"Outside of that information, the source was not able or willing to confirm the actual reason for Adams' absence, except the source did provide this interesting tidbit: It appears that Adams informed the team on Friday that he would be absent on Sunday. The team did not excuse his absence, which Adams knew, and he failed to appear anyway. For now, whatever caused his absence, Adams' appearance in the lineup today indicates that he and the team have made up. The team does not expect further absences. That doesn't mean this story is going away. There is still the mystery of why Adams missed Sunday and the long-term effect his failure to show up will have on his relationship with his teammates and overall team chemistry. So far, none of them are speaking on the record about the situation."

Roy's immediate thought turned to his teammates. He did not want them to think he did not care about them or the team's success. The opposite was true. It was just that sometimes other things had to take priority. It was interesting that Edwards had said his teammates were not speaking "on the record." The implication was that they were speaking off the record. But which ones and what were they saying? Whatever the case, he shouldn't be surprised. He once had the mindset many of his teammates had. If he still had that mindset and one of his teammates did what he had done Sunday, it was likely he would be furious and talking to reporters about the situation as well. The one thing that was likely inhibiting them was their desire to avoid the team's censure for talking poorly about one of its stars and its most marketable player.

Edwards had eliminated some possible explanations for Roy's absence on Sunday, but he did not report the actual reason. He had to know. If he knew, Roy felt confident about why the team wasn't confirming it. It had to be because the team believed the reason, if known, would reduce the amount of money it could make off Roy.

Roy did not have time to think about the report further, as just then Jenny opened the door to the apartment. Roy saw Jenny put her bags down as she walked in and closed the door. Then she looked up and smiled at him. The return smile that came to his face was wide and automatic. She ran to him and wrapped her arms around his neck. He put his arms around her waist and lifted her off the ground. When he set her back down they kissed.

"It is so good to finally have you here," said Roy.

"Oh, I am so glad to be here!" Jenny replied and kissed him again.

"I got supper set up for us."

"This looks great!"

"I thought you would like it."

"I love it."

They sat down to eat. Their conversation was fast as Jenny talked of their friends back in Iowa and Roy of spring training. Midway through the meal, though, Roy noticed Jenny was uneasy. Her constant smiles at their reunion had subsided. "What's the matter?" he asked. "It seems like something is bothering you."

"Nothing!" she replied in protest, putting on another smile. "Everything is great!"

A few minutes of silence passed. Jenny looked up at Roy and then down at her plate again. While fiddling with her remaining food and continuing to look down, she asked,

"So, what did the team say about you missing Sunday? Were they upset?"

"I knew there was something bothering you," Roy replied.

"Not bothering me," Jenny said defensively. "I'm just curious."

"Okay. Well, don't let it worry you." Roy wished he could make his voice exude more confidence than it was presently mustering. "Did you see any of the news reports?"

"No, I just heard a few things while listening to the radio, about them not letting you play yesterday. The reporters didn't know the reason."

"Yeah, I was supposed to play. When I got to the park in the morning, one of our coaches immediately grabbed me and told me to go to Earl's office. Earl's conversation with me was short. He told me he and the front office had decided to take me out of the lineup for that day and I was to report to the minor league facility to work out. Earl did put me in the lineup today and no one from management has said anything else to me about it."

"Why do you think they haven't said anything else?"

"I think they hope it will pass."

"Will it?"

The question struck Roy. *Did she want it to pass?* "That depends on the team," Roy answered. "I hope they will eventually understand, or at least tolerate it."

"Do you think they will?" Jenny asked.

A year ago, if asked such a question about what the future held, Roy would have answered—as most people do— with something like, "They'll come around. Everything will be fine." But he was like everyone else who offered such assuring words: He had no idea. He now knew it was better to speak truthfully. "I don't know," he said.

Jenny looked up at Roy and proceeded, "You know, when you told me on Friday you were going to tell the team you would not be with them on Sunday so you could attend church, I wasn't sure you would really do it."

"I don't regret it. Everything that happened on Sunday confirmed to me it was the right decision."

"What about what happened on Monday?"

"It wasn't as bad as I expected."

"What about next Sunday? Will you be taking me to church or will you be going to the ballpark?"

"When you put it like that, it makes the decision simple, doesn't it? Though perhaps not easy. As I said when we talked on Friday, if I am going to start doing this, I need to keep doing this. I want to be a Christian, a husband, and eventually a father, all before a ballplayer. I am convinced we will have the best marriage possible if I make sure we have the right priorities."

"What are your teammates saying?"

"So far, not much. Malik told me some of them are not happy, but I do not know which ones yet. Did Cammy say anything while you two had coffee at the airport?"

"Yes, though she was mostly trying to get information out of me, asking a lot of questions. You know how you can often tell what a person thinks about something by the way they ask questions? I could tell she thinks you are crazy."

"Well, there's crazy in a good way. Like, 'that's *crazy*.' And then there's crazy crazy."

Jenny smiled. "I'm sure she meant the latter one."

"She won't be the only one."

There was a momentary silence.

Roy said, "Preston Edwards, the reporter, wants to interview me about this."

"Don't do it."

"I don't plan on it right now, except I was wondering if it would be the best thing to do in order to control the story. Why don't you think I should?"

"There are so many risks. I mean, what if it goes bad? Or, what if you think it goes good, but the reporter edits it in a way that makes you look bad?"

"You're probably right."

Another silence passed. "You see that this is best, right, no matter what happens?" Roy asked.

Jenny hesitated before answering. "I do. I just get worried about what will happen."

"Don't worry," Roy responded. Then his desire to comfort his wife overpowered his new conviction to say only what he knew to be true. "Everything will be fine."

10.

Wednesday morning

Roy awoke to the smell of eggs and bacon in a frying pan. He got out of bed, walked through the short hallway separating the bedroom and kitchen, and found Jenny cooking breakfast. He loved the way she looked in her pajamas and disheveled hair.

When she saw him, she gave him a big smile. "Good morning," she said.

Roy smiled back. "Good morning to *you*." He walked up and kissed her on the cheek. She even smelled good. It was a wonder to him how she could smell so good having just woke up and over the smell of breakfast. "It looks like it was a good thing I picked up some groceries."

"No doubt. I did not think you would have anything here for us. I was surprised to find this stuff for breakfast. There's even orange juice in there."

"You have done a good job domesticating me."

"I hope that's not a bad thing."

"No, not at all. Like most men, I would be in a lot of trouble without a good wife."

Roy grabbed the orange juice from the refrigerator and

two glasses. Jenny dished the bacon and eggs—along with some toast—onto two plates and they sat down at the dining room table adjoining the kitchen.

They prayed for their breakfast and for the day. When they looked up and grabbed their forks, Roy asked, "Did you sleep well?"

Jenny replied enthusiastically, "Yes! I love this place! I feel so at home here. I love being with you here."

"I am glad you like this place. I like it, though I like it a lot more with you in it."

Jenny smiled. "I am sorry if I seemed worried about everything when I got here yesterday," she said. "I don't know what it was. You are probably right. Everything will work out."

Had he really said that? Roy thought to himself. He probably had. That was a mistake. He certainly did not know if things would work out. It depended on what one meant by "work out."

Jenny continued, "I didn't go to church on Sunday and then the conversation with Cammy at the airport. That was probably a bad combination. It didn't put me in the right mindset."

Roy did not know Jenny had not gone to church on Sunday back home in Iowa. He decided not to press it.

"Are you coming to the game this afternoon?" he asked her.

"I don't think so. It looks like the weather is not going to be that good. At least not that good for Arizona in March. I thought I would go to a few home stores to find things to decorate this place."

"What!? You don't like my decorations?" Roy asked her with mock incredulity.

"That college baseball trophy you put up in the corner over there does *not* count as a decoration."

Roy laughed. "But it is so pretty!"

"How about you worry about the baseball and I will worry about decorating our home? Or, homes I should say, since this is just a spring and winter one."

"That is probably a good idea."

Without making her feel bad for skipping church on Sunday, Roy wanted to bring the topic of church back up. "I am so glad you are happier about everything this morning. And going to the midweek service at Independent Bible Baptist Church, the one pastor told us about, tonight should also help. It really does help to be in church to have a right perspective about everything. Plus, since our game today is during the afternoon, I will be done with the team in time for church tonight, so there will not be a conflict with the team."

"Oh, okay, yeah, you are probably right."

"Trust me. You will like it. It is a very simple, sincere church."

"How was it when you went on Sunday?"

"It was really pleasant. The people were very nice. It is not a very big church. And you will get a kick out of this: The pastor has to be about eighty-five years old. No joke. He could be our great grandpa. He has apparently been the pastor there for fifty years now. That is just incredible. But his mind is still really sharp. He talks fairly slowly, but clearly, and his messages were good on Sunday. Very Biblical. It seems like he has a lot of wisdom."

"Did he talk with you?"

"Yes, he greeted me before the morning service and we talked little bit again after the evening service."

"Did he recognize you?"

Roy laughed and replied, "I am pretty sure he didn't. I would be surprised if he has watched a baseball game since the days when Maury Wills played shortstop for the Dodgers."

"Who?"

"Nevermind. I'll just say that it doesn't appear that he keeps up with the game."

"That is too bad. It is a good game."

"Oh, you are coming around to it now, eh? When we first met, you hardly knew the difference between a ball and a strike. I had to explain to you what a shortstop did."

"I am coming around to the game's virtues," Jenny said playfully.

"But not so much to cause you to come to the ballpark this afternoon instead of shopping for home decorations."

"True." She smiled.

After a pause, Jenny asked, "Did anyone in the congregation recognize you?"

"If they did, they did not say anything. A number of them greeted me and welcomed me to the services. A few asked me where I was from. I replied that I was from Iowa, but was in town on 'business.' It is really not a very big congregation. Smaller even than our church in Iowa. But it was certainly a welcoming church."

~~~~~

Roy spent another hour with Jenny before heading to the ballpark. They watched a home improvement show. Jenny gathered ideas and Roy pretended to listen to them. It had been a good morning.

11.

Roy entered the locker room. His entrance caused less of a hush than it had yesterday. The buzz over his skipping out on Sunday and the team effectively suspending him Monday had subsided a small amount, at least temporarily.

He had not been at his locker longer than it took him to put on his uniform when the team's manager strode up to him. Roy saw him coming. He was hard to miss. He played in the big leagues for fifteen years, most of the time as a power hitting first baseman. He then spent a few years in the minor leagues as a hitting coach and then manager before his first big league manager's job twenty years ago. The Indianapolis Hawks had hired him away from his previous job soon after Major League Baseball had granted its ownership group a franchise. As a result, even before the Hawks fielded a big league team, this man had been its face.

He had taken on weight, but remained—at sixty-five years old—a tall, imposing figure. His high standards but caring attitude added to his authority. It perhaps helped that he shared the first name of another legendary manager.

"Hi Earl," Roy said with some apprehension. Roy did not exactly fear Earl Vinson, but he very much wanted to obtain his approval.

"Roy," the manager responded. "John Reinhold wants to see you."

"He's here?" Roy asked. "Now?"

"Not just now, but twenty minutes ago. He is upstairs."

People figured Earl was the most powerful person in the organization, even above those in the front office. He wasn't. That rank belonged to John Reinhold, the majority owner. Reinhold had made his money developing software and then in financing software startups. About the time Major League Baseball was considering new franchise locations, Reinhold got bored with making obscene amounts of money. He decided to pursue a professional sports franchise to occupy his time. The group of people he put together became the surprise winning bid for the Indianapolis Hawks franchise, though it was not so much a surprise to those who knew that baseball's commissioner was the financial backer to Reinhold's first software product.

Reinhold put on a front that made it seem as if he deferred almost everything about the organization to Vinson. A few knew better, though it was unclear whether Vinson did.

Roy walked up the two flights of stairs to the executive offices. On entering, a young woman receptionist greeted him. She immediately recognized him. "Mr. Reinhold is expecting you. You may go right in. He is in the conference room down the hall. He is using that as his office while he is here."

Roy thanked her and turned down the hall, walking past the offices of the front office personnel. Only the president's office was empty. He only had nominal power anyway. Loud voices came from the offices of the general manager, the assistant general managers, and the vice president for business operations, at least creating the appearance of busyness.

When he arrived at the end of the hallway, Roy found the conference room door slightly ajar. He gave a quick knock and opened the door. "Mr. Reinhold?" he asked into the room.

Roy saw the owner sitting at the conference room table. Short stacks of papers were spread out in front of him. The room itself was surprisingly undistinguished. Roy expected it to look more high-class, like it belonged to and was used by the super rich. Instead, the conference room table and chairs, while nice, could have existed in most small business offices in the United States. At the left end of the room as Roy walked in, there was a short bookshelf, on top of which sat a coffee pot and a pitcher of water. Hanging on the wall to the right was a large-framed picture of the Hawks' new stadium in Indianapolis, like what anyone might be able to purchase at a shopping mall kiosk. The room's natural light came from the windows opposite the door. They looked out over a portion of the facility's parking lot. The field was unobservable from here.

Roy remembered a magazine feature he had read once about Reinhold. He only spent money—real money, anyway—on the things that mattered. He wasn't wasteful with his money or his time.

The owner looked up at Roy over his reading glasses. "Come in, Roy," he replied. "And please call me John. I mean that. I have never become accustomed to having people put a 'mister' before my name. Besides, someday you'll be as rich as me if you keep hitting the ball like you do and invest your money wisely. Rich people don't call each other 'mister.'"

Roy did not know how to respond. It occurred to him that perhaps rich people, or at least the uber-rich, did not know how to have normal conversations with the less than uber-rich. "Yes sir," was all that came out of his mouth.

"No, that doesn't work either," the owner corrected him. "You call someone 'sir' if they have been knighted. I am still working on that." Reinhold smiled, leaving Roy to wonder whether he was serious or not. Either way, the awkwardness was just increasing. Roy wished this was not their first encounter so that he understood the owner's idiosyncrasies.

Roy responded, "Where I come from, calling someone 'sir' is a sign of respect. I meant nothing more than that." Roy immediately second-guessed his decision to verbalize that thought. Why was he disputing with the man who paid his salary?

The owner's reply did not put Roy at ease. "Hogwash. You need to unlearn such childish notions of showing respect. You do not show respect by showering flattering words on them. You show other people respect by being the person you need to be in order to be successful. Otherwise, you are just belittling them by pretending they are needful for your own victory."

Roy stood silent, scrambling his mind to find a response that would not cause another rebuke. There was a hint of wisdom in Reinhold's words, but it seemed off, distorted, but Roy did not know how to articulate why.

When the owner saw that the player would not open his mouth, he spoke again, moving to the direct question at hand. "There is no point to platitudes or pleasantries, not that this conversation has yet entered the realm of pleasantness. What do you plan to do on Sunday?"

Roy knew what his response to this question would be before he walked up the stairs. Faced with it directly, he was able to muster a response in kind. "I plan to attend church, both morning and evening services. I will not be with the team on Sunday."

Moments of silence passed between the two. The owner appeared to be studying Roy to ensure his response was certain. It was.

The owner nodded and stood up. "Did your parents attend church often?" he asked.

"No sir." Whatever Reinhold's objections to words of respect, Roy wasn't about to abandon what his father had taught him about respect. It seemed right. He was thankful for that teaching, even though he now wished his father had also taught him about the importance of church. Perhaps he never would have ended up in this predicament.

The owner stared at Roy again. "Hmm. My parents weren't churchgoing either. But somehow church has become important to you. I clearly see that. You have demonstrated it. While I have never been a churchgoing man, I do try to live by what you all consider an important principle: The Golden Rule. Do unto others as you would have them do unto you."

"That is certainly a good rule to live by," Roy responded. *But how do you understand that rule?* Roy wondered.

"I expect people to seek success. It's what I seek. Whatever I decide to do, I want to be successful in that thing. Right now, that means creating a World Series-winning baseball team. Preferably, a team that wins multiple World Series championships. In fact, I want to build a foundation here where eventually the Indianapolis Hawks become the new New York Yankees, the team everyone loves to cheer against because we are so successful."

"I love baseball, sir," Roy responded. "And it is always more fun winning. I would like to be a part of that."

"Then we both want success."

"I do want success, sir. But whether we want the same thing depends on what you mean by 'success.' It is possible we do not mean the same thing."

Reinhold studied Roy further before speaking again. "There are only three things worth pursuing: money, fame, and power. If you can combine them, all the better. If I stand in someone's way, I expect them to try to push me out of the way. I intend to do that to them. *That* is showing someone respect. Recognizing and treating them as a formidable foe. If someone does not likewise treat us that way, they are not showing us respect."

Avoiding the philosophical issues, Roy asked, "Do you feel I am in your way?"

"More like a distraction. But we can still put you aright."

"How so?"

"I mentioned earlier that you will be a rich man someday. Really rich. You are already famous. But if you keep walking down this path you think you are on, the money will never come, the fame will prove to have been fleeting, and you will have no hope for power. People will forget you, Roy."

Roy had to find out. Now was the time. Would the team ever allow what he was trying to do?

"Is there no middle road?" he asked.

"There rarely is," Reinhold answered. He paused and then said, "If we have in mind to do something, the best way to do it is to remove distractions."

That's what he called me, thought Roy. *A distraction.*

Reinhold continued. "If you look around this room, you will notice I have nothing in here but the papers requiring my attention, the ones I need to review and act on. There is not a single electronic device. No phone, no smartphone, no computer, no tablet. In fact, I do not own any such devices and never use them. I decided ten years ago that they distracted me too much and I removed them from my life. They got in the way. I have not used them since."

That was remarkable considering how Reinhold had made his money. "Didn't you start off working in the technology industry?" Roy asked.

"Yes, but when I stopped writing software code and moved into funding startups, using electronic gadgets became a diversion. I now pay people who need to use them as part of their jobs. But for the high-level decisions I make, they are unnecessary."

"What about as a form of entertainment? Or as communication?"

"I choose other forms of entertainment," the owner said vaguely. "And I communicate by speaking, having others deliver messages I give to them to deliver, or by writing actual, physical letters. So, getting back to your original question—no, there rarely is a middle road, if you really want to avoid compromise and accomplish your purpose. But tell me what you think you mean by pursuing a middle road in this situation?"

"Play me every day of the week, but let me have Sundays off."

"That is impossible. If you are honest with yourself, I think you already know that. We play everyday to win. We also play everyday to make money. We cannot create exceptions for anyone, even someone as good as you. If we allow you to take one day off per week, your teammates will feel abandoned. You will lower morale. And whether morale affects on-field performance of the team or not, your absence means a lesser player plays. It will mean losses, and that may mean missing the playoffs, and that will mean less money and fame, not just for you, but for me and everyone else associated with this organization, including your teammates. And what if someone else also asks for Sundays off, and then someone else?

"Whatever your resolve, I do not think you have fully considered the consequences of what you propose to do," Reinhold concluded.

Roy weighed how to respond. "There are more important things than money, fame, and power."

"You are mistaken. I have looked. There is nothing else. You won't find it."

"I already have."

Reinhold looked away and then said softly, "This isn't over."

"That's up to you," Roy responded.

The owner swiveled his head back around to stare at Roy. "It is always up to me. It always has been."

"Then what do you plan to do with me?"

"Today, I plan to play you. And I plan to play you tomorrow, too. After that, we will see. For now, you are part of this team. Act like it. Remember why you first chose this life. Learn to embrace it. We are going to win the World Series this year, or soon, and we are going to become the most dominant franchise in this league. We are going to do it with you and others I bring in to help you. Then, when your playing days are over, after you have the money and the fame, abandon any notion of power if you wish and attend church all day everyday if it is still of interest to you."

Roy nodded, but refrained from speaking further.

The owner finished, "Go play." He sat down, took up his pen, and returned his gaze to his papers.

Roy turned and slowly walked out of the room, back through the hallway, and down to the locker room, where he grabbed his glove and batting gloves and went to the field to begin his morning stretches.

12.

Roy finished taking batting practice and returned to the locker room to eat lunch before that afternoon's game. Shortly after he got his food and sat down, Malik Jones sat down next to him with his own plate.

"Jenny get in fine yesterday?" Malik asked.

"Yes, she did. It's good to have her here."

"Yeah, I am glad Whitney has been here with me. She is good for putting things in proper perspective. Balance is good."

"Not according to the man who pays our salaries."

"Huh? What do you mean?"

"Oh, nothing, nevermind."

"Okay, well, is Jenny coming to the game today?"

"No, I don't think so. It is not quite as sunny as she likes it. She was going to do some shopping for the apartment. Decorations and stuff."

"Yeah, you better leave that up to her."

"Oh, I will."

"Well, I will tell Whitney that Jenny is in town. I am sure Whitney will want to get together with her. They haven't seen each other since we were all at the fan convention in January."

"That would be great."

"Say," Malik continued, "I have been talking to a few of the guys, including Al." Al was the team's bench coach, the coach in charge when Earl Vinson got thrown out of games, which happened to him more than most managers. "We are thinking about starting up a Bible study group for the Christians on the team and anyone else who wanted to come and listen. Something that would meet regularly, starting soon here and continuing through the season. Al was involved in one when he was a coach for the Braves. He said it was really good, that it brought the team closer together. We would like to get as many people in it as possible. Staff included. Would you join us?"

Roy got excited, but he hadn't yet processed whether his excitement was due to joy or apprehension. "What would it be like?" he asked his friend.

"The way Al described the one he was in before, the group will meet once a week, share prayer requests, commit to pray for one another, and study some portion of Scripture. Maybe we will even sing some songs. I don't know all the details yet, but I'm sure we could tweak it until we get it right."

"Who would lead it?"

"Since Al has been part of something like this before, he would, though he and I talked about making you his understudy, so to speak. We think you would be great for the job eventually."

"Does that mean he and I do the teaching or preaching? I don't think I'm qualified for that. Al is a nice enough guy, but I'm not sure he's qualified either."

"It could mean that, but Al mentioned bringing in different speakers, pastors, ministry leaders, whatever, each week or for a series of weeks. It might depend on what city we were in."

"What day of the week would the group meet?"

"We talked about it being a Sunday morning thing. You know, we always have games scheduled on Sundays, so that would avoid having a scheduled meeting on an off-day. The Sunday games are usually early in the afternoon, so we would come in a little earlier in the morning. It's the normal day of worship. We'll even take up collections for the guest speakers."

"You're talking about creating a church?"

"Sure, man, whatever you want to call it. It will be really great!"

"We can't have a church."

"Why not?"

"We don't have a pastor. We don't have a common set of beliefs."

"What are you talking about? Consider Al the pastor. And our set of beliefs will simply be the Bible."

"It's more complicated than that," Roy responded.

"It doesn't have to be," Malik answered. "You, me, Al—we'll make sure the speakers we bring only teach things based on the Bible. And others on the team will see our faithfulness and joy. It will open them to the Gospel. It will allow us to have church and play the game we love. We get it all, without compromise. It might even improve our play on the field, getting reminded each week Who we are all doing it for."

Roy stared down and picked at his food. It sounded like compromise. He was a relatively new Christian, though, and had trouble explaining the Biblical basis for what he believed to be right.

Then another voice called out to them, "Hey Roy! Malik!" Al Tanner, the bench coach, came up to them and put his right foot on a chair, his forearm resting on his knee. "Has

Malik been filling you in on our little plan? Actually we should call it a big plan!"

Roy had never seen Tanner so enthusiastic.

"Yes, sir."

"Wonderful! I see no reason to wait on this. We should start this Sunday morning. We have to head over to play in Tempe that day, but we don't leave here until noon. We could start at half-past-eight, before morning stretches. I have a call into a man I know would be a great first speaker. He runs an organization called Winds of Change Ministries. He speaks all over the place. If he can't come, and he might not given his busy schedule, he has others in his organization that probably could."

"Winds of Change Ministries?" Roy asked.

"That's right!"

That sounded hokey to Roy. He wanted to laugh, but when he looked at Malik, his friend showed no signs of thinking that was anything but the best named Christian organization in the world.

"What church is that ministry affiliated with?" Roy asked.

Tanner replied, "Church? No, it's a para-church organization. Helps all sorts of churches. Really dynamic teaching."

Roy did not want to be rude to these two. They appeared genuine. But he had to say no.

"It sounds like you could create something good here. But Malik said you wanted to meet on Sundays. My pastor recommended to me a church down here. It's the one I went to last Sunday. I'm going there again tonight, taking Jenny now that she is in town. I think I should continue to go there while I am here."

Malik remained silent. Having opened the door, he now appeared to be yielding to Al's efforts to pull Roy in.

Al responded, "I completely understand Roy. It's good you would want to follow the recommendations of the man or woman—which one is your pastor?"

"Man," Roy answered.

"Right," Tanner continued. "Man. As I was saying, it's good you would want to follow the recommendations of the man who helped you become more of a Christian –"

"Actually, a Christian in the first instance," Roy interrupted.

"Huh?" Tanner asked.

"Not more of a Christian, but a Christian. I was not a Christian before I met him and he showed me the Gospel as stated in the Bible."

"What were you?"

"I wasn't anything. Actually, I guess it would be accurate to say that I was lost in my unbelief."

"Right. Well, again, it's good you would want to follow his recommendations. And we just sprung this on you. No need to make a hasty decision. We did this in Atlanta, though, and it was really special. Give it some thought. Let us know later. In the meantime, Malik and I will get the word out."

Roy said "okay" as a way of ending the conversation.

"See you guys on the field," Tanner said as he left them.

Soon other players joined them with their lunches. Neither Roy nor Malik brought the topic back up around them. They finished eating and separated to begin individually preparing for that afternoon's game.

13.

The game that afternoon started at one o'clock local time. It was cloudy, unusually so for Phoenix in mid-March, but the forecasters expected the rain to hold off.

The Hawks were playing in their home park. When the public address announcer called out Roy's name as the starting center fielder and leadoff hitter, the crowd cheered loudly, louder than any subsequently announced player. When Roy ran to his spot in center field, the fans sitting in the outfield grass beyond the fence of the spring training stadium yelled his name and clapped loudly. Whatever had been the effect of the team's suspension of him on Monday, it had not extended to any noticeable loss in his popularity. Adams' jersey remained the most popular one in the stadium's merchandise shop. The lack of news on the reason for the suspension had probably helped blunt fan backlash to this point. Plus, Roy knew, it is easier for fans to forgive someone who is great than it is for them to forgive someone who is mediocre.

Despite the cloudiness, it was still seventy-five degrees and there was nothing more than a slight breeze.

It had been a good morning with Jenny. It was a good afternoon to play baseball, the game he had loved since his dad first started taking him to the games of the minor league affiliate team in Cedar Rapids.

When he was nine-years-old, Roy's dad signed him up for a week-long camp put on by that minor league team. On the final day, they played a game. Roy went two-for-three and—in the final inning, while playing second base—dove for a ground ball up the middle, snagged it, rose, and fired home to the catcher to cut down what would have been the tying run. The minor league team's best player, who would go on to play ten years in the big leagues, looked at him and said, "Wow. Nice play kid." Roy realized then that he was good at baseball.

Within a few years, Roy and his dad realized Roy was better at baseball than most people were at anything else. The summer after his eighth grade year, Roy's parents transferred him into the Catholic school system in Cedar Rapids. The high school team's varsity coach had promised them Roy would have a spot on the varsity team immediately. It also looked to be a better team than the city's public schools over the next few years. The coach was true to his word. Roy became the varsity team's starting center fielder, a spot he held for four years. By the summer after his tenth grade year, the varsity coach had him batting third in the lineup. The school won the 4A state championship that summer and the next.

Most good athletes play multiple sports in high school. Roy had shown some progress in basketball, football, and track in middle school, but he gave them all up before high school in order to focus on baseball. His parents had not pushed that decision on him. It had been Roy's. Baseball was what he loved. Removing the other sports from his life allowed him to spend off-seasons at baseball camps in the south, improving his agility at a local training facility, and taking batting practice.

Following his senior year, the New York Yankees drafted him in the tenth round of the amateur draft. By that time, he had committed to play college baseball at Creighton University in Omaha. He had his pick of schools, but he wanted to stay close to home, partially for his parents, but mostly because he had started dating Jenny, a small town girl from neighboring Jones County. She would be attending Kirkwood Community College in Cedar Rapids that fall.

It also helped that Creighton hired Roy's high school baseball coach as one of its assistants, a move undoubtedly designed to seal Roy's commitment. Creighton had a successful baseball program, but Roy was the school's highest rated recruit in its history.

The Yankees based their decision to draft him in the tenth round on the possibility they would be able to offer him just enough of a signing bonus that he would back out of his commitment to Creighton in favor of moving to professional baseball life immediately. The Yankees offered him more than most tenth round draft picks. Unlike drafted college players, Roy had the option of going to college and, under Major League Baseball's first-year player draft rules, re-entering the draft after his junior year of college. The Yankees would have lost the rights to him and wasted its tenth round pick.

Still, a number of people advised him that the money the Yankees offered was not enough. He could obtain more if he had a great few years as a college player and ended up as a first or second round draft pick. His parents told him a college education would be a good fall-back option, or at least help him develop business skills to manage his even-

tual professional baseball wages and marketing opportunities. The Creighton coaches, now including his high school
coach, emphasized that the college game would help him
advance as a player, especially his power stroke. His friends'
advice focused on the fun college would offer.

In the end, he chose college. He kept his commitment
to Creighton. He made the Creighton athletics department
look smart in its hiring of Roy's high school coach. He obtained good grades, making his parents proud, though they
were under no illusion that anything other than baseball
was his future. In his three-year career, he set numerous
Creighton hitting, baserunning, and fielding records. When
he announced he was leaving following his junior season,
during which he led Creighton to a College World Series
appearance, everyone knew it was time. The Hawks drafted
him in the third round, offered him substantially more than
the Yankees had three years earlier, and professional baseball became his life. His dream since he was eight-years-old
became reality.

Roy's decision to turn down the Yankees and spend
three years in college had turned out great. He played as
hard as ever, but had avoided serious injuries that might
have lowered his draft value. He got the contract and the
signing bonus everyone thought he could get. While he
ended up in an organization with much less tradition than
the Yankees (in fact, it had no tradition), it was run by smart
people making smart baseball decisions. The Hawks would
be contenders soon enough.

Only Roy and Jenny knew this, but choosing Creighton
and three years of college ball over accepting the Yankees'
offer hardly had anything to do with the advice he received.
It was not about pleasing his parents and his high school

coach, experiencing college life, developing as a player, or making a bid for a better draft slot and more money.

Instead, it was because for that first summer the Yankees were certain to send him to their minor league affiliate on Staten Island. Staten Island was more than one thousand miles from Cedar Rapids. That was four times further away than Omaha was from Cedar Rapids. It meant he would never see Jenny. Jenny was the reason he chose college. The drive to Omaha for her or back to Cedar Rapids for him would take no more than four hours, a straight shot on Interstate 80 after the quick drive on Interstate 380 between Cedar Rapids and Iowa City.

Roy did not want to take the chance that the physical separation would result in emotional separation. Jenny was thrilled when Roy chose college over the Yankees. It was a choice of her over his dream of playing professional baseball, a game she still hardly understood.

Yes, everything about that decision had turned out perfect.

As Roy now stood in the field before the first pitch of this spring training game, he looked down at the grass. Everything about it was just right. The color, the length, the thickness. As he worked his way up in the baseball world, the ballfields kept getting better. He had loved playing the game on rocky, all-dirt infields and uneven, poorly kept outfields in Little League. But the field he stood on now was pure. Somehow the fields in Indianapolis and the other major-league stadiums on which he would play when the regular season started would be even better. Whatever professional teams paid their groundskeepers, it was worth it. They were the best in the world as far as Roy could tell.

As Roy prepared defensively before each pitch, he thought about the goodness of his life. He was doing what he wanted to do, what it seemed he was meant to do. How many people get to do the thing they love? Everything he felt told him he was in the right place. This place made him happy, with or without the adulation of the crowd. Honestly, he loved the adulation as well.

After the first two batters of the inning grounded out, the third batter hit a fly ball to right-center field. Roy saw it clearly off the crack of the bat. He sprinted back and to his left. As he neared the spot where the ball would fall, his sprint slowed and turned into a glide. He reached up and the ball fell in his glove mid-stride. His momentum carried him to the outfield warning track. He took the ball out of his glove with his right hand. He looked up and saw and heard the fans yelling "Roy!" He flipped the ball to them. They cheered again. Roy then turned and ran back to the dugout.

In the fifth inning, with the score tied at one and a runner on third base with one out, the opposing team's batter hit a line drive into short right-center field. Roy again read the ball well and immediately started running in and to his left. The ball was slicing away from him, toward right field. The right fielder, however, was nowhere near in a position to try to catch it. Roy never hesitated. He dove head first and stretched his glove hand—his left one—out in front of him. In the middle of his dive, he felt the ball slam into his glove. He squeezed tight and his body struck the ground.

On other occasions, he might have allowed himself to continue sliding through the grass. That was great fun. But there was that runner on third.

Roy sprang up. He saw the runner had tagged and, following the catch, had already started sprinting toward home plate. Roy took the ball from his glove, reared back his right arm and, in a motion both violent and graceful, rapidly brought it forward, releasing the ball at the exactly the right time. The ball flew back to home plate in what seemed as fast and as straight as it had been hit to the outfield. The catcher did not move. He caught the ball at the level of his knee. As he squeezed it into his catcher's mitt, he swung around to his left and swiped the sliding runner with it. The umpire yelled, "Out!"

Roy pumped his fist. Even if this was just spring training, making great plays—plays few in the world could make—was fun. As he jogged into the dugout, the fans stood and cheered and clapped loudly, especially those behind the third base dugout, the home dugout. The loud ovation continued for a full minute after Roy had disappeared inside.

In the bottom of the inning, Roy singled to left. Earl Vinson sent in a pinch-runner for him. His day was over, as it would be for most of the regulars soon. They rarely played a full game during spring training. He received another loud cheer as he left the field for the pinch-runner.

He spent the rest of the game in the dugout, enjoying the camaraderie of his teammates. He had spent much of his life around people who loved baseball as much as he did. It is fun being around people who love the same things.

Roy felt the pull of the game he knew. Between his participation in the banter among his teammates and watching the game unfold, Roy was—not for the first time—deeply struck by how privileged he was. He played a game. Not only that, he was paid a lot of money to play that game. Even if football had passed it in popularity in the United States, helped along by gambling and fantasy games, hundreds of millions of people passed though baseball's turnstiles. Many of those people wished they were in Roy's position.

As he stood with his arms hung over the dugout railing, eating sunflower seeds, all of this—what he did for a living, how much he loved it, how much he was paid for it, and how many people paid to watch him—occurred to Roy as ridiculous. And wonderful.

Roy knew his feelings were swaying him toward a decision.

Malik's idea could work, he began to think. It was possible to have a church service, a Bible study, whatever one wanted to call it, with the players, no matter how many or how few were interested. They could meet, pray together, sing some hymns, read the Scriptures, study them. That is what church is, right? It could be good enough. Lots of people—people who call themselves Christians and say they love God—hardly attend church at all. What Roy would be doing with his teammates would be better than not attending church at all. He could still attend an actual church during the offseason.

Maybe John Reinhold was right. Maybe Roy had not thought through all the consequences of not being with the team on Sundays. Maybe there were consequences that were too great, or at least tipped the scale in favor of reversing course in order to stay with the team full-time.

There was so much good he could do if he focused on baseball full-time. If he remained good at this game, and especially if he continued to get better, his fame would give him a platform to speak out concerning the things he believed were important. The media would continue to put microphones in his face. Not everyone would agree with him, but people would listen to him, and some might change their mind because the words came from him. He could make a real difference. The lasting impact he could have in the lives of others would overcome the triviality of playing a game for a living.

Then there was the money. Lots of players wasted theirs. He, on the other hand, could do so much good with it. Making the amount of money he would make playing baseball would allow him to give more to his church, more to missions and building programs. He would also have plenty to give to other charities. Like the providing of jobs, impactful philanthropy was only possible by people with a lot of money.

It felt good to help people. He could help more with more money.

He would never hurt anyone playing this game. On the contrary, he would bring many people joy. Baseball provided a wholesome diversion, relieving them from life's stresses and reminding them that life contained joy and greatness.

Roy also thought about Jenny. She was undoubtedly anxious about the dilemma Roy had put them in. He knew she would stand by him and support him no matter the choice he made. Neither one had any serious relationships before they met. They had never given their hearts away to anyone else.

Jenny had loved him before she knew there was a chance Roy would earn a lot of money. She loved him before she even knew he was good at baseball. In fact, before she met Roy, she hardly knew anything about baseball. His joking to her earlier that morning about her lack of baseball knowledge was funny because it was true.

Yes, Roy thought, it was possible to be a good Christian playing this game full-time, even on Sundays. Sunday baseball had been a regular part of the major leagues for a hundred years. Roy knew he was not the only one in the game who took his faith seriously. Others, both before him and now, managed to both honor God and play baseball and other professional sports that required extensive time away from church.

As Roy thought about these things, the game ended. He took another look at the field before turning into the hallway leading to the locker room. Some of the clouds had parted and rays of sunlight were shining through the breaks onto the field. The temperature had warmed a few degrees, toward the normal high for Phoenix in mid-March. Roy could not shake the feeling—and did not want to—that this was a good place, the place where he belonged.

14.

Will sat down to eat supper with his family. He had managed to make it home on time tonight. However, it would be a quick meal. Allie, 10, had piano lessons and Andy, 7, had his first Little League baseball practice (inside a gym) tonight.

"Are you going to come with us or take one of them?" Ashley asked Will as they were all eating as fast as they could. All, that is, except Adam, 5, who had yet to understand the concept of hurrying.

Will responded, "No. I had a lot of documents come in this morning that I did not get a chance to review. It's a new case. Important client, all that. Alan asked me to work on this case. I need to start going through those documents tonight. Are you able to drop Allie off for her lesson and then take Andy to the gym before getting Allie again to go back and watch the rest of Andy's practice?"

Ashley sighed, though Will knew she had expected an answer like that. It would have been unusual for him to say he could help with the kids' activities. "Yes," she answered. "Do you want to keep Adam with you here?"

104 · Jason M. Steffens

"I would love to, but I would not really be able to give him any attention. I suppose I could let him watch cartoons while I review those documents."

"Cartoons!" Adam shouted. "Yeah!"

Ashley gave Adam a side glance that told him his outburst was unwelcome.

Will continued, "It would be easier for me to get work done if you were able to take him with you."

"I'll take him with me," Ashley said. Adam sighed. Ashley gave him another side glance, this time out of pity. "Do you mind if we stop and get some ice cream after Andy's practice."

This time all three kids were excited and shouted.

"No, not at all," Will answered. "You should do that."

"I thought it would be something fun to do and a nice reward for practicing well."

"Yes, definitely."

"Do you want us to bring you anything back?"

"No." Actually, Will *did* want ice cream, but he turned it down as penance for making his family do things without him again. He consoled himself that his work allowed his family to go buy ice cream treats without thought of the cost or how it fit into a budget.

Pastor Nate Sanders stood behind the pulpit and led the congregation in the singing of two hymns. The Wednesday night service crowd was still quite small, small enough that he did not use the regular pulpit, which stood on a platform, but instead set up a temporary one in front of one of the two columns of pews. On Wednesday nights, everyone sat on just that one side of the small auditorium. The crowd seemed smaller than it actually was because the elementary aged kids had a program in the basement of the church building and some of the members volunteered their time to lead that.

This gathering—the ones who showed up in the middle of the week—comprised the most faithful. Nate knew they would be the members most interested in the status of the litigation. Many of them had spent a portion of Tuesday morning praying for him during the deposition.

After the singing of the two hymns, Nate gave them an update on how yesterday's deposition had gone, the types of questions he had received, and how he had answered them. As he did so, Nate saw a head with a ball-cap on it rise from the half-stairs in the back that led to the auditorium. Before yesterday, he would not have thought much of it, but now he hoped it would be the court reporter's son.

It wasn't. It was the teenaged son of one of the members, arriving late. The rest of the family slowly followed him in.

Nate thought about deviating from his prepared lesson to one on punctuality. Before he became a pastor, he often wondered how pastors were able to come up with a new sermon or lesson four times a week, one each for Sunday School, Sunday morning, Sunday evening, and Wednesday evening. He had since discovered innumerable issues that a pastor needed to address. Lots of times his congregation needed to hear about a topic a second time. And then a third. And he needed the benefit of studying it again.

Then it was also beneficial to do in-depth verse-by-verse studies of books of the Bible. That always took longer than at first expected, as Nate found he continually learned something new or gained a greater understanding as he studied a passage of Scripture.

His concern now was less whether he would be able to develop a new sermon for the next service than whether he was sufficient to convey the message. He learned so much in study. Would he be able to get the congregation to understand? When it came down to it, he knew he could not adequately convey the message without God's help.

When he began as a youth pastor years ago, he had also worried that some of the members of his audience—usually the youth group, but occasionally the full congregation—would think the message was about them, when all he had been trying to do was teach and preach God's Word without anyone in particular in mind. He later learned to stop worrying about that as well. Now he liked to tell the congregation, "If you think I am preaching this message about you, then let me assure you: I am." In truth, every Bible message Nate preached he intended for everyone.

So despite his temptation to change his message to focus on punctuality, he decided to stick with his prepared lesson. After all, it too could apply to punctuality, if only its hearers would understand its implications for their lives.

~~~~~

The clouds had completed their parting. The skies were full of blue, there was nothing more than a breeze, and it was seventy-five degrees outside as Roy and Jenny pulled into the parking lot of the Independent Bible Baptist Church of Mesa. The lot was gravel. There were about fifteen cars parked in the lot as the time for the start of the service neared. The building was a one-story metal structure. A rectangular sign hung over the double entrance doors stating the name of the church. Below the name, the sign read: "pastored by Johnny Edwards." And then below that: "since 1933."

Roy put the car in park, turned it off, and looked at Jenny. "This is it," he said, smiling.

"It's not much, is it?" Jenny replied, more as a statement than a question.

"Pastor recommended it. I trust his recommendations."

"Has he been here before?"

"I don't think so. I think he knew someone who knew the pastor here, and then he also called here and spoke with him awhile before recommending it to us while we were here. He made a good choice. It might not look like much, but the services were good on Sunday and the people were friendly. It'll certainly do for the remaining short time we have in Phoenix."

"So," Jenny said, smiling back at Roy and pointing at the sign above the doors, "does that mean the church has been here since 1933 or the pastor has been here since 1933?"

Roy chuckled. "He is old. But he is not *that* old. ... At least, I don't think he is that old." Jenny laughed. They picked up their Bibles and walked inside.

They were greeted by Pastor Edwards. As he had been on Sunday when Roy met him, he was tan with thin white hair. He was wearing a suit too big for him. The suit's style gave away its age. It seemed likely the pastor had bought it when he was quite a bit younger and heavier. His back was hunched. "Hello!" he said smiling at them and shaking Roy's hand. "Good to see you again!"

"Thank you. It is good to be here again. This is my wife, Jenny. She got into town yesterday."

"Miss Jenny, nice to meet you!" the pastor replied.

Jenny smiled at him—it would have been hard not to—and said, "You, too."

Pastor Edwards then looked back at Roy and said, "Now, what was your name again? I seem to have misplaced the visitor's card we had you fill out on Sunday. It was Sunday you were here, right?"

"Yes, that's right," Roy responded. "My name's Roy." Roy hesitated before adding, "Roy Adams."

"Ah, yes. I will have to come up with a way of remembering that! In town on business, right?"

Roy smiled. "That's right. We should be here a few more weeks before heading back north to Indianapolis."

"Well, consider this your church home while you are here. There is a potluck next Sunday. We hope you will be able to join us. Come on in. We are about to get started. It shouldn't be too hard to find a place to sit, as our Wednesday crowd usually isn't too large, but the folks who are here will treat you kindly."

Roy and Jenny found a place in one of the back pews and the pastor headed for the short podium.

"He really does not know who you are," Jenny whispered as they sat.

Roy shook his head. "That's good with me."

~~~~~

Will sat at his home office desk. The paper files on the new case had come in and the assistant of Bill Smith, the president of Johnson Engineers, had emailed him the electronic files. Will pulled them up on his computer. He quickly reviewed the lawsuit papers and the contracts for the construction project. It turned out the initial information Alan Bonner had given him about the lawsuit was incomplete, probably because he had received incomplete information as well. The insurance claims representative that hired his firm probably did not have all the information when he gave it to Bonner. As with most things, information passed from one person to another by word of mouth rather than through the primary source proved inaccurate or incomplete. It was the old game of 'telephone,' in which a person whispers a message to someone else and that message is relayed around the room until it ends up back with the original person as something entirely different, played out in real life.

The owner of the new medical building had been the entity to sue Johnson Engineers, but only after it had first been sued by an employee of a contractor performing maintenance on a rooftop air handling unit. The plaintiff's allegation was that he had tripped over a service pipe running from the unit and fallen over the roof edge to a second roof twenty feet below. The roof edge had been unguarded. His petition alleged he did not see the pipe because it had been covered by snow.

After suing the owner of the facility, the owner filed cross-petitions against the designers and constructors, alleging that if anyone was at fault it was them. Johnson Engineers had been the mechanical engineer on the project. In his initial review of the series of contracts that governed the work on the design and construction of the building, it appeared to Will that meant Johnson Engineers had decided on the location of the air handling unit and the pipe on which the plaintiff tripped. It was unclear how much of a role the architect, structural engineer, and mechanical contractor had played in these issues.

There were a lot of questions to work out. Why was the pipe in that spot? Why was there no protective guard at the roof edge? Why did the injured plaintiff not pay more attention, especially with snow on the roof? How badly was the plaintiff injured? Will's review of documents would probably do less to answer them than it would to raise more of them.

It was unlikely the case would go to trial. They hardly ever do. There is too much risk, unpredictability, and cost for both sides to put the outcome of a case in the hands of a jury or a single judge. The collective defendants would pool their money and pay something to the plaintiff to leave them alone. Until then, the defendants' lawyers would do a bunch of work—racking up huge bills—finding ways to blame each other's clients so as to shift the allocation dial of who would pay what.

Collectively, the defendants would portray the injured plaintiff as careless, that he could have prevented his fall if he had been more attentive.

And then there would be the fight over the extent of the plaintiff's injuries. The plaintiff's lawyers would portray his injuries—whatever they were—as so debilitating that meaningful work and life's enjoyment would be impossible. The defendants would portray him a complainer and his efforts at rehabilitation half-hearted.

It was how the game was played. And it would be played until the eve of trial. Fear would prevent them all from settling until shortly before the trial was to start. They wouldn't want some fact to arise after settlement to reveal they offered too much or accepted too little. Likewise, fear would prevent them from actually proceeding to the trial, as the jury just might throw off everyone's carefully calculated estimate of the worth of the case and how the settlement should be allocated.

In this system, truth mattered, but it was incomplete, and all sides would put so much gloss on it than it would be difficult to see how they all existed in the same world.

Still, the case would settle. The near certainty of a settlement did not relieve Will's anxiety about the case, though. A mistake on his part—not analyzing something correctly, missing some evidence, or missing a deadline—could lead his client's insurer paying more than it would otherwise have to pay, or potentially missing an opportunity to get out of the case without paying anything but his fees.

It was just shifting money around, but it was a lot of money and it wasn't his.

After the lawsuit papers and contract documents, Will decided to start reviewing the email correspondence. Emails were often the only contemporaneous, unfiltered thoughts on issues the designers and contractors on a construction project faced. But as with any other document review, getting through the mundane to find the relevant and interesting was sleep-inducing. There was so much endless back and forth over whether this beam could be moved to accommodate that pipe. The Catch-22 of legal work was this: No one should have to pay the rates lawyers charged to have them review so many pages of mostly irrelevant documents, but no one would spend their time doing the close review necessary if they were not paid those rates. The result was that neither the payor nor the payee were happy.

A half-hour in, Will felt himself drifting. Keeping his eyes open, let alone concentrating on what he was doing, became more difficult than running a marathon, something he always wanted to do but wasn't sure why.

Then he came across an email that kept his attention, mostly because it was so short. It simply read: "No one has stopped the ball yet. Point guard has open lane to the hoop."

A basketball analogy, but for what? Will could not tell based on the surrounding pages, which seemed unrelated to this one.

The author was Donnie Valenza. There were several recipients, but Will did not recognize their names except for Bill Smith, the owner and president of Johnson Engineers. The other recipients appeared to be Johnson Engineers employees, given their email addresses.

There was nothing in the subject line of the email. That was one of Will's pet peeves. People were either misusing the subject line or not using it at all. The most common misuse was putting the entire content of the email in the subject line instead of the body. That or not using it at all made it harder to understand the email when reviewing it later.

Will marked Donnie Valenza's email so he would be able to find it later and added to his tasks list the need to ask Bill Smith who that person was and what his email meant.

He then finished his review of the email correspondence and moved on to the field notes and design documents, dozing off before he came close to finishing.

~~~~~

Nate came to the conclusion of his message. "Turn again to Colossians 1:18." He paused as the congregation flipped the pages in their Bibles. "See again it says Jesus 'is the head of the body, the church: who is the beginning, the firstborn from the dead; that in all things he might have the preeminence.' Colossians chapter one is filled with reasons *why* Jesus should have the preeminence. We have redemption and forgiveness through Him and His shed blood. He is the image of the invisible God. The firstborn of every creature. He created all things and by Him all things consist. He reconciled us who were alienated from God, and He did it by *dying* for us.

"And yet we would put anyone or anything else in the place of preeminence?

"To be preeminent is to be before all. Have you put things into your life, or allowed things to remain in your life, that are before Jesus? If so, repent of that now. Give Jesus the preeminence due Him as the One who made you and redeemed you. As it says in Philippians chapter two, 'let this mind be in you, which was also in Christ Jesus,' a mind humble before God, willing to obey Him. Resolve this evening, and each morning, to conduct your lives and your conversation so it is clear to God, yourself, and those around you that Jesus is more important to you than anything else. It is there you will find joy and peace, with God, yourself, and those around you."

Nate closed his Bible, prayed over the congregation, and called them forward for an altar invitation, a chance for them to seek God and His will for their lives.

~~~~~

Roy listened intently as Pastor Edwards continued a study through the book of Second Corinthians, chapter 5, verses 18-21. "To be an ambassador is to carry the message of the one who called you to another," the elderly pastor told the congregation with conviction. "An ambassador cannot substitute his own message for the one he has been called to carry without violating his oath of faithful service. His devotion must be to the message imparted to him by his employer. He otherwise ceases to be on ambassador.

"God called you to be an ambassador. An ambassador for who and for what? The text says you are an 'ambassador for Christ.' You are to bring His message to the lost. The message you bring is one of reconciliation with God. We have all been, or currently are, in need of reconciliation with God. Our having fallen short of the glory of God causes this need. But God, in his grace and mercy, gave us a gift. That gift is Jesus, the perfect son of God, who became sin for us, that God would judge him and not us who deserve the condemnation.

"People need this message, for this life and the one to come. We are the ones to take it to them. As ambassadors of countries are privileged to serve their homeland, how much more are we privileged to serve the One who created us?

"It starts in our homes. We must bring this message to our family and others in our lives. It then proceeds to our communities and ultimately the world.

"Consider now whether there are things in your life that inhibit you from fulfilling this calling. If you are to be faithful to it, to fulfill the position of 'ambassador,' you must purge those things."

Roy and Jenny walked out of the church building following the service and after they shook a few hands. If anyone recognized Roy, they did not say so. It was possible some did, but not with enough confidence to seek confirmation of it in front of him.

"That was a good message," Roy said as they walked to their car and stared out at the horizon of the approaching night sky. "It seemed as if he was speaking directly to me."

"Yeah," Jenny replied passively.

Roy sensed his mind being pulled into different directions. Or maybe it was more than two.

Jenny's face brightened and she said, "It is such a beautiful night. Let's drive somewhere!"

"Where?" Roy asked.

"Anywhere!" Jenny answered. She skipped over to the passenger door and waited until Roy reached it to open the door for her.

"The lady asks and she shall receive," he replied. Jenny got in the car and he closed the door. As he walked around to the other side, he looked back at the simple church building. He then got in the driver's side. They took off to find roads they had not driven before, heading nowhere in particular.

15.

Will called Bill Smith of Johnson Engineers. Even though they had exchanged emails setting this time for a call, an assistant told Will that Mr. Smith was not available. She would have him call Will back.

Will wasted the next hour of his day, not wanting to get too involved in anything because he thought his client would be calling him any minute. The minutes dragged on. Will reviewed his junk mail, deleted emails that did not require a response, and filled out sheets recording his billable time.

Finally, Bill Smith called back. Without an apology for the delay, he opened the conversation in what seemed to Will to be forced nonchalantness. "Say, my people were going through the email correspondence we sent you. They found one that does not appear to belong. We are not sure how it got in there."

Will did not hear anything he said after "my people." *Who says "my people?"*

"I am sorry, could you say that again?"

"Yes, I am not sure if you had a chance to look at it yet, but there is one email message in the emails we sent you that does not belong as part of this file. We are not sure how it got in there."

"I started going through them last night," Will responded, "but can't say I have a good grasp of which ones are important yet. Which email does not belong?"

"The author was Donnie Valenza. It did not have a subject line. The message was something about basketball."

Will remembered the email that had awoken him slightly during his document review the previous night. "I actually had pulled that one out to ask you about it," Will said back to his client.

"Oh, why?"

"Just because it seemed unclear. I was going to ask you what it meant. As you mention, it looked like it had more to do with basketball. Also, I was going to ask what role Donnie Valenza played in your firm's work on the project."

"I will have to check. He may have done a little bit of work on the project as someone in training. He is no longer with our company. It is possible his name would show up on the time records for his project, but on the other hand maybe not. We are not sure what his email means now, but it looks like he was using the company email system to talk about personal recreation business, which is against company policy."

"If you are not sure what his email means, is it possible his message was a metaphor for something about the project, since the email is in the project files?"

"No, no. We are sure it is unrelated."

How was he sure? Will continued to wonder, but decided against pressing that point. He did ask, "You said Donnie Valenza no longer works for you; do you know where he is now?"

"I will have to check. We probably have a last known address, but that would have been from some time ago. He was a young kid when he worked for us. You know how they are. He has probably moved out of the state."

"Yeah, probably. Let me know what you find, though."

"Uh, yeah, sure," Smith replied. "Anyway, you could go ahead and just destroy that email, since it is not part of the file. We would not want to produce it to the other side since it has no relevance."

"Right," Will said. He extracted the email from the electronic files for this case, but he did not delete it. Instead, he put it in another spot on his hard drive.

Smith then moved the conversation to other topics. Will extracted from him what he knew or thought about the case. Smith was certain no regulation or standard either prohibited the location of the pipe on which the plaintiff tripped or required the design of a guardrail near the rooftop air handling unit. He was also certain the plaintiff was at fault for tripping over the pipe and he was not hurt badly. In any event, if anyone on the project team was at fault, it was the architect or the mechanical contractor, all for various reasons not necessarily consistent with one another.

It was the typical client response—All the problems resulted from the fault of someone else and it was ridiculous they were named as a defendant in the case at all. *So*, the implication went, *get us out of this case right now and for no money*.

After fifteen minutes, Smith ended the call, saying he had to go to a meeting. Will was happy to let him go. It saved him from having to explain, again, that Johnson Engineers was going to be in this case for awhile and it was going to have to spend a lot of money in the process. Perhaps it deserved to be in the case, notwithstanding Smith's protestations.

16.

Roy was in the lineup for Thursday's game. The Hawks travelled by bus the short distance to Salt River Fields in Scottsdale to play the Colorado Rockies. Roy played his scheduled five innings, though not well. He struck out twice against a mediocre pitcher. Thankfully, though, no balls were hit to him in center field, for his movements felt weighed down. The conflicting emotions he felt the previous day had not fully subsided, though he thought he knew his decision.

Before the game, Malik and bench coach Al Tanner again questioned him about his interest in the team chapel. He brushed them off again, not giving them a definitive answer, but at the same time not showing any enthusiasm for it. He regretted being equivocal. It was such a human thing to avoid straightforwardness when there is fear it will hurt someone's feelings, even when straightforwardness is the thing they need because it has to come out eventually.

When Roy exited the game, he went into the visitor's locker room of the Rockies' spring training facility. There were a few people in there as the game continued. The athletic trainers and the massage therapist were working on a couple of the players. Roy ignored conversation with them.

Roy showered and was mostly dressed at his locker when, consumed by his thoughts, a voice right behind him startled him. "Hi Roy," it said.

Roy turned to see Preston Edwards, the reporter. There would not be media-player interaction during regular season and playoff games, but such barriers were much lower during the more relaxed atmosphere of spring training. It was thus not surprising a reporter was in the locker room.

"Hi Preston," Roy greeted him. "What do you know today?"

"I know the church you were at last night. My guess is that is the one you were at on Sunday as well."

"What did you do, follow me?" It seemed something below this reporter's caliber, but Roy considered that he did not really know him.

"I have a source," Edwards replied simply.

"John Reinhold," Roy guessed, "or someone that works closely with him or wants to please him."

"There are options other than me following you or the owner of the team being the source."

"I suppose so."

"And you know I cannot reveal sources."

"Right. So, you are going to report this and you want a statement from me?" Roy was not ashamed of the church, but he started worrying that the reporter's own beliefs would lead him to do a report that painted the church in a bad light, bringing unwanted notoriety to its pastor and members.

"I still want that sit-down interview with you when you decide to go public with all this. But, no, I am not going to report what church you are attending instead of playing baseball."

The team was doing something to keep him muzzled, Roy thought.

"Then why are you telling me this?" he asked.

"Isn't it obvious? If you go through with this, most fans and media are going to turn on you. You have probably already considered that. There will also be many that will admire you, fans anyway, if not media. But they, too, may turn against you when they find out the type of church you have chosen."

"What do you mean by that?"

"You know, most people like the Bible, what little they know of it. But few are willing to fully believe and live out what it teaches. Either they reject what they do not like or are convicted by their half-heartedness, with that conviction manifesting resentment. Either way, people inclined to sympathize with you won't understand you because they won't understand your church. It is too conservative, too fringe. And then there is the attention you will bring on it. The media narrative will not be kind."

"The media or you?"

"I will be fair to all sides. I am just telling you how it will be."

"What do you know about the church when you have never been?"

"I have not been to your church here, or where you started going to church in Iowa—I know about that one, too—but I grew up in a church very much like it. I even spent a year in a Baptist Bible college after high school before going on to journalism school at Northwestern."

Roy was taken aback. The first question he could think of in reply and that came out of his mouth was, "Are you saved?"

Edwards continued standing as Roy sat, giving him the appearance of a teacher over his pupil.

"I used to say 'yes' to that question when preachers asked for a show of hands at the end of a sermon, but I never was, not as you understand it."

Roy's heart sunk at whatever or whoever it was that had caused Edwards to turn his back on what he had been taught as a child. Edwards gave no hint of noticing the pity on Roy's face as he continued, "I consider myself a seeker. The journey is more important than the destination, as they say."

"What if what they say is wrong?"

"Then I will at least have enjoyed myself along the way."

"Drifting seems like an unpleasant way to live a life."

"And you think you are not drifting?"

Roy sat there and thought about the question, about where his life was headed. "I know I am not. I know where I am going."

"And where is that?"

"In the path God has laid for me."

"How do you know God is the one laying the path?"

"Because the path is His Word. It is only a question of whether I will obey it or not."

"The Bible is a nice book, but there are a lot of subjects it does not address. Playing baseball on Sundays, for instance."

"The Bible may not say 'thou shalt not play baseball on Sundays,' but it says everything about priorities. If something stands in the way of my service to God, including assembling in a local church with other believers, then I must put that thing aside. What am I teaching others if I put professional baseball before God?"

"So you have made your decision then?"

Roy nodded in assent.

"Well," the reporter continued, "I did not come here to debate the Bible with you, though I do think you should consider other sources of truth and knowledge. As I indicated, I wanted to warn you that if you choose rebellion—for that is what it is, rebellion—against your employer, your teammates, and your fans, it is going to be mentally and financially painful. I cannot imagine you have thought through all the consequences."

Rebellion—an interesting word choice, Roy thought. What had weighed him down since last fall, when a preacher had knocked on his door and he had made the decision to repent of his unbelief and sin and put his faith in Jesus as the Saviour of his soul, was that his life remained in rebellion against God, that he had repaid Jesus's sacrifice for him by ingratitude in the form of living his life as he wanted. Rebellion against God was what he did not want to do. He wanted to live peaceably with all men, but he could not obey men rather than God.

"The consequences are not very much up to me, either way," Roy replied in-artfully.

"To each his own," the reporter concluded.

A cliché he does not really mean, Roy thought but did not say. It was time for this conversation to end. Roy stood up and made a motion away from his locker. "I need to go meet with someone." It was time to make his intentions clearly known.

"Sure, no problem, Roy. I am here when you are ready to talk on the record."

Everything is on the record, Roy again thought in silence.

Edwards walked off and Roy headed upstairs to the executive offices. He reached the receptionist and saw out the window behind her that the game was still going on. "I need to see John Reinhold, please."

"Let me see if he is available," the receptionist replied. "Please have a seat." Roy remained standing. She picked up her phone and whispered into it, casting a side glance at Roy. "Okay, he will see you, Mr. Adams."

Roy offered his thanks and walked back toward the conference room where he and Reinhold had spoken the day before. As he knocked on the closed door, his heart pounded. A voice inside the room beckoned him in. He opened the door. Reinhold was there along with the team's general manager, head scout, and one assistant general manager.

"I am sorry to interrupt you, sir," Roy said to Reinhold.

"No problem, Roy. We can make time for you."

The owner made no motion to dismiss his front office employees. Roy had not discussed this issue with them. He did not know what they thought of it all, though it was easy enough to surmise.

Roy said, "I cannot give professional baseball my life. I must and want to give it to God. I will play for you, but not on Sundays."

The owner sat there in silence. The rest initially deferred to him, but then the general manager could not contain himself. "Malik spoke with you, right?" he said. "About the team chapel?"

"Yes."

"And you have considered the media and fan reaction?"

Roy stood resolved. "Yes."

Roy saw Reinhold look at his employee with a stare that told him to say no more. Reinhold himself made no indication he was going to say anything.

Roy walked out of the office.

As he walked back down the hall, a second assistant general manager stepped out of his office. He had not been in the conference room. He must have seen the anxiety on Roy's face, for he asked, "Did you make a final decision?"

"Yes."

The executive guessed correctly. "You chose church."

"Yes."

"You are throwing your life away, Roy."

The bluntness of the man's pronouncement shook Roy. The man hardly knew Roy, but his reaction would probably be like most. Roy recovered and managed a reply. "No. It is just that someone else has a claim on it."

17.

Friday afternoon

Roy was again in the lineup Friday afternoon. He tried to treat the day as any other, as if nothing had changed and everything would continue as it had. However, the few teammates who spoke to him did so almost by mistake. They quickly backed away once they realized their error. It was if there had been a memo sent to everyone but him that they should avoid contact with him. He had found Malik in the outfield shagging balls during batting practice before the game and informed him that the team chapel idea seemed nice but he would not be able to participate. Malik just nodded and said, "Okay man, it's your call." He then jogged off to shag another fly ball. His manager and coaches did not say a word to him.

All of it had been disconcerting, but the day paled in comparison to what awaited him at home.

When Roy arrived at his apartment and walked inside, he saw Jenny sitting on their couch. Her hair covered her face, but he heard her softly crying. "What's the matter?" he asked.

Jenny looked up at Roy. More tears dropped from her eyes and down her cheeks. She pivoted her head in the opposite direction and back down, picking up an empty 8x11 envelope with its former contents stacked on top. "Someone handed these to me outside the building," she said.

"What do you mean?" Roy asked. "Who was it?"

"I don't know. He did not say his name. I had just returned from the grocery store. I was about to enter the building when he walked up out of nowhere and said, 'You're Mrs. Roy Adams, correct?' I nodded my head and told him 'yes,' but I wish I would not have. He handed me this envelope and said, 'This is for you. Have a good day.' He then walked off. Here, look at what it is." Jenny handed Roy the stack of stapled papers along with the now empty envelope. Roy took them from her and began reading them.

The top of the front page had what looked like a court caption, though Roy had never studied one before. It said "IOWA DISTRICT COURT in and for LINN COUNTY." Below that were the names of the parties. The "Indianapolis Hawks National League Baseball Club" was listed as the plaintiff. Roy saw his name as the listed defendant. To the right in bold-faced text were the words "ORIGINAL NOTICE." Below that was a couple of paragraphs of text informing him that a lawsuit was now on file in the Iowa District Court and he needed to file an answer in the clerk of court's office in Cedar Rapids within twenty days.

Attached to that front page was a document that had the same caption but was titled "PETITION AT LAW." It did not seem long for a lawsuit, at least the way Roy thought of lawsuits. Roy read it.

~~~~~

Plaintiff Indianapolis Hawks National League Baseball Club (the "Team"), for its cause of action against Defendant Roy Adams (the "Player"), states:

1. The Team is a Delaware corporation with its principal place of business in Indianapolis, Indiana. It operates as a professional Major League Baseball team.

2. The Player is an individual with a principal residence in Cedar Rapids, Linn County, Iowa.

3. On November 2, 2012, the Team and the Player entered into a written contract whereby the Player agreed to play baseball for the Team and the Team agreed to pay the Player to do so, among other terms. The form of contract was a standard uniform player's contract as agreed to among Major League Baseball and the Major League Baseball Players' Association.

4. On Sunday, March 10, 2013, the Player was absent from team activities, including a spring training game and mandatory practice, without permission or proper excuse.

5. On Thursday, March 14, the Player informed the Team he would be absent again on Sunday, March 17, again without permission or proper excuse. The Player further informed the Team he would be absent from all team activities, including games, on all Sundays for the indefinite future.

6. The Player's refusal to play baseball on Sundays is a breach of his contract with the Team, is a breach of the covenant of good faith and fair dealing, and is an intentional interference with the Team's business relations.

7. The Player's breach has caused and will continue to cause damages to the Team through the date of the Player's normal career expectancy.

8. The Team's damages include, but are not limited to, reduced chance of postseason revenues, reduced gate re-

ceipts and concessions, and reduced merchandise sales. Additionally, the Team paid the Plaintiff a signing bonus, which the Player by reason of his breach of contract should be made to forfeit.

9. The Player's breach is a willful and wanton disregard for the rights of the Team, entitling the Team to punitive damages and its attorneys' fees.

10. The Team will suffer irreparable harm not fully compensable by an award of damages if the Player does not fulfill the obligations under his contract.

WHEREFORE, Plaintiff Indianapolis Hawks National League Baseball Club demands judgment against Defendant Roy Adams for its damages, now and into the future, together with punitive damages, plus interest as allowed by law, and the costs of this action, including reasonable attorneys' fees. Plaintiff further requests an injunction against Defendant requiring his specific performance of the contract, including his performance on Sundays.

Roy finished reading. It was simple enough. The team claimed he was in breach of his contract for refusing to play on Sundays and it wanted money from him. But how much? The lawsuit did not say. It seemed like it could be a lot when tickets, food, beverages, and jersey sales were factored in, given he was the team's best and—up until now—most popular player. He wondered whether the team could prove all the future damages. Baseball and business were so uncertain, and he could get injured. Roy supposed the team could hire some economist who would be able to factor all that in.

The team's demand that he pay it damages, though, did not immediately dominate his feelings. Instead, he felt anger boiling up inside him that the team had served the lawsuit papers on Jenny and not him. He had been at the ballpark all day. They knew where he was. Why come here and get her upset?

She had been looking down as he read the papers. When he finished she looked up at him. Her eyes were moist but momentarily had run out of tears.

"What does all this mean?" she asked.

"I do not really know," Roy replied truthfully enough.

"I thought you said everything would be okay?"

Had he said that? His memories blurred. If he had, he should not have. No one knows the future but God. If he had not, whatever he had said, Jenny had heard him say things would okay. Maybe they still would be. "I am not sure what will happen now," he said. "The team did not tell me it was going to do this. Whatever happens, God will work things out for good. We just need to trust Him."

Jenny was now staring away from Roy at nothing in particular. Roy was not sure Jenny heard him. She asked, "If the team wins this lawsuit and a jury makes you pay a bunch of money to the team, how will you pay it if the team will not let you play at least part-time?"

"I do not know. Maybe they will let me play part-time."

"Don't you think this lawsuit is their answer to that question?"

"Maybe."

"Malik's wife, Whitney, would hardly talk to me on the phone today. She wouldn't commit to getting together. Do you think she knew about this?"

"Maybe," Roy repeated.

He had no words that would comfort his wife. That realization depressed him infinitely more than the fissure that had opened with his team.

She stood and walked to a sliding glass door leading to a deck and looking out over the city. Roy set the papers down and walked over to her. Her arms were crossed. The tears were definitely gone. She was biting the inside of her lip.

Jenny did not turn to him, so Roy reached his arms around her and hugged her from behind. She remained tense. Both his words and his touch failed her.

He could have a game where he struck out four times and committed two errors and not feel as much of a failure as he did right now. Her coldness soon caused him to withdraw from her. She made no movement to beckon him back.

He went over to where he left the lawsuit papers and read them again. He realized reading those words again would not help anything. He went into the kitchen and opened the refrigerator door. He stood there staring in, not remembering why he had decided to open it in the first place. He closed the door.

The thought came to him that he needed a lawyer. But who? Roy did not know any lawyers, but he thought of someone to call. He looked at his watch. It was not too late in Iowa, not that the person he wanted to call would mind if it had been late.

Roy walked back into the living room. Jenny had moved from standing in front of the sliding glass door to a chair. He looked at Jenny. "I'm not sure what to do with this." He was not sure his wife was listening to him. "I suppose I should not be surprised. The surprising thing is that Earl or someone in the front office did not tell me it would be coming. Maybe Earl didn't know, though."

"He had to have known," Jenny replied.

She was listening.

"Yeah, you are probably right."

"What are you going to do?"

Roy looked away from Jenny and stared at nothing. After a pause, he said, "I think I should call Pastor."

"He is not going to know anything about what to do," Jenny protested.

"He will not know about the legal stuff, but I am sure he will have some good wisdom. He will help us move in the right direction."

"Okay." Jenny looked down, arose out of the chair, and walked to their bedroom.

Roy placed the call. His pastor picked up on the second ring.

18.

"This is Will Jacobson," Will said on picking up his ringing phone.

"Mr. Jacobson, this is Nate Sanders, the pastor of Pine Road Baptist Church."

"Yes, hi." Will became uncomfortable. It was against attorney ethics rules to talk to opposing parties represented by counsel. It took Will a moment to scramble around in his mind to confirm that Nate Sanders was unrepresented. Still, even with that confirmed, every time Will spoke with unrepresented parties he worried about being accused of taking advantage of them.

Sanders continued, "I am glad I caught you still in the office. I thought you attorneys went golfing on Friday afternoons. Here it is past five and you are still there."

"I think you are confusing us for bankers," Will responded light-heartedly.

"Eh? I don't know many of them either."

"Well, I suppose there are a few attorneys who find ways to make golf part of their practices. I have never seemed to manage to get to that point."

"I see. I'll try not to keep you long, and I know this may seem a little strange given your representation of the Association in its lawsuit against my church, but I have a legal issue I would like to discuss with you," the pastor continued.

Will stumbled over some words before saying something coherent. "I, uh, would actually have a conflict of interest in providing you any advice. If you need legal advice, I highly recommend you hire your own counsel, and that would have to be someone other than me or anyone in my firm."

"I'm sorry. I was too imprecise. The help is not for me. It is for one of the members of my church."

"Oh, okay. What is the nature of the issue?"

"Do you know Roy Adams?"

Will's mind raced. It seemed like a common enough name, but the only person his mind could settle on was the baseball player. "I certainly know the name because the baseball player by that name has been in the news lately. Other than him, I couldn't tell you."

"He's the one I mean."

"He is?"

"Yes, he's actually a member of my church, since October anyway."

"Wow. I figured he did not live in the area anymore."

"He still comes back when he is not playing baseball. Both he and his wife are from around here."

"Wow." Will realized he was repeating himself. "Well, whatever legal assistance he needs, I am sure our firm can provide it. With the number of lawyers we have here, we consider ourselves full service. There is not much we do not have experience with. Is he getting into some real estate in Iowa or wanting to have a will or trust prepared? Those are not my areas, but I will be able to refer him to one of our attorneys."

"Actually, I think what he needs is more in your area, but you can tell me if not. His baseball team has filed a lawsuit against him."

Will quickly recovered from his surprise and replied with a question. "Here in Iowa?"

"Yes. I haven't seen the papers, but he said in Linn County."

Will did not know what to say, so he repeated the pastor's statement as a question (something he found to be a useful device when he didn't know what else to say). "Really? Here in Linn County?"

"Yes. That's what he said."

"When?"

"Just a little bit ago."

"No, I'm sorry. I meant when was he served with the lawsuit?"

"Oh, uh, I believe they served his wife and he found out about it about an hour ago. He called me right away asking for advice."

The first thing Roy Adams did when served with a lawsuit by his team was call a pastor, Will silently thought with some wonder.

Sanders continued, "We talked for a bit, I prayed with him, and he asked me what I thought he should do. I told him to keep praying for wisdom, to keep doing what was right according to the Bible, and to hire a lawyer, which is kind of funny now that I think about it, since I did not have the church hire one. But we are sometimes willing to endure things we do not want others to go through."

"I understand. I recognize litigation can be life-interrupting and inconvenient. I do hope your time in being deposed in our office was not something too difficult to endure." Will said this sincerely. He quickly realized George Bannon would be upset if he knew what he had just said.

"No, it wasn't too bad. I mean, it wasn't something I enjoyed, but if that is where God wanted me to be, then so be it."

"You are the first I've had tell me that God wanted me to depose them."

"I did respect the way you conducted yourself during the deposition. You treated everyone kindly, not just George, but me, the court reporter, and your receptionist."

"I appreciate that."

"Anyway," the pastor continued, "Roy said he did not know any lawyers, would probably end up just searching the internet for one, and asked me if I knew any. I said his agent should know some lawyers who would be good for this, but he said he did not trust his agent to recommend a lawyer who would support him. I then said I knew you. He gave me permission to tell you about our conversation and ask if you could help. Thus this call."

"Thank you for recommending me," Will responded.

"Sure. As you said, sometimes God uses lawyers. Perhaps He will use you in this."

"Well, I don't actually know about that, but if I can help Mr. Adams I will try."

"Good. I will call Roy back and tell him to give you a call."

Will told the pastor he would be in the office another hour, but Roy could also call him on his cell phone. He gave the pastor his number and then said, "Wait. Can you give me a heads up on what his team is suing him for?"

"He has been skipping team activities on Sunday to attend church."

Again, Will found himself saying, "Wow," this time in a soft whisper.

The two ended the conversation and hung up.

Will was initially excited about representing someone famous. That gave way to anxiety. It was not easy to operate under the microscope of others. He had learned to be comfortable around his clients and colleagues, but he had never had to work with media and fan attention. That would certainly come by agreeing to represent one of baseball's biggest stars.

The other thing that bothered Will was what this lawsuit was about. He was certain he would feel more comfortable on the other side, if it was the team and not the church-going player that wanted to hire him. How would others view him if he represented someone who may be on a religious crusade? He knew there were lawyers—some not even religious—willing to defend those in need no matter what others thought of them. Will wasn't sure he was one of them. He had never been directly called on to be one.

Since he had not yet spoken to Roy Adams, there was still time to decide against representing him. It would be an easy though dishonest thing to tell Adams that it really was not his area of practice or he had too many other pending cases.

Certain things can bring an end to wavering and force a chosen path, for good or evil. This time, for Will, it was the ringing of the phone. The screen on his office phone told him the call was coming from Arizona.

"This is Will Jacobson."

A pause on the other end and then: "Uh, hi, uh Mr. Jacobson. My name is Roy Adams. I believe you just spoke to a Nate Sanders about my case. He thought you might be able to help me out."

"Yes. Is this the Roy Adams that plays for the Indianapolis Hawks?"

"Yes. At least I *was* playing for them. I am not exactly sure right now."

"Pastor Sanders gave me a little background, though I don't know much yet. Is it right that the Hawks have filed a lawsuit against you in Iowa, here in Linn County?"

"Yes."

Will extracted information on the named parties and the New York attorneys representing the team. He then asked, "When were you served?"

"Some guy served my wife outside our apartment building here a few hours ago. Is that allowable? Serving my wife?"

"Yes. Also, since you were just served, that means you have twenty days from today to file an answer to the petition. Without going into too much detail, can you tell me the team's complaint and what it is the team wants?"

"Last Sunday, I voluntarily missed team activities, including games and practices, in order to attend church. I told the team I would continue to miss Sundays for church. The team's petition accuses me of breaching my contract with them, breaching a covenant of good faith and fair dealing, and intentionally interfering with its business relations. I don't know what all that means. They say I have caused them damages and they want me to pay them, but they don't say how much. They also ask for an injunction to force me to stop going to church on Sunday when the team has games, which is every Sunday."

He signed a contract for a lot of money to play baseball, then he decides he doesn't want to play one day of the week, and so just stops playing that day? Yes, the team probably does believe he breached the contract. Will immediately saw this was going to be the most interesting case he had, but he did not see how it was a winnable one. He would rather be on the other side.

"Will you represent me?" Roy asked.

In the end, Will did not hesitate. Even if it was a loser of a case, Adams must have money to pay him and he seemed nice enough. He told Roy he was willing to represent him. He explained he first had to ensure his law firm did not have a conflict of interest, but he did not expect one. He was not aware of anyone in his firm representing the Indianapolis Hawks or someone adverse to Adams. He would know for sure by the morning.

He then felt the need to caution Roy about his own experience. "I handle civil litigation cases, including contract disputes like this, but I have never represented a professional athlete. I am sure there are lawyers who specialize in this sort of thing. Not necessarily the religious aspect, but in player contracts. I could ask around my firm to see if anyone knows someone like that. Or the people you know in the baseball world may be able to refer you to good lawyers with experience representing players in disputes with teams or leagues."

Will told himself he was not afraid of the case. No, he was simply doing the right thing by informing a potential client that there were other options besides him, others with more experience.

"I appreciate your honesty about that," Roy responded, "but I am not sure many of the people I know or many of the lawyers they would refer me to would have my best interest in mind."

Best interest? Will thought Roy was crazy, but as the client it was Roy's view of "best" that mattered. If Will was going to have Roy's best interest in mind, it would help if he understand Roy's mind. Right now he did not.

"Okay," Will merely replied.

"And," Roy continued, "if Pastor Sanders trusts you, I do, too."

"Alright, then, I will call you tomorrow. What is the best time to reach you? I won't be able to call right away in the morning, as I will need part of the day to allow time for others to respond to the conflict of interest check."

"Truthfully, I am not really sure right now. We have a game at one, which will be two your time. I don't know if the team will want me to play or allow me in the park or what."

"The team sued you, but didn't suspend you?" Will asked.

"If they suspended me, they haven't told me yet."

"Interesting. Okay. I advise you to not talk about the lawsuit or the issues in the lawsuit with anyone tomorrow. Even if you do not say anything wrong, sometimes words are turned around against you."

"I will keep that in mind."

"I will call you sometime tomorrow afternoon. If you can't pick up, I will leave a message."

"That sounds fine. You'll let me know what's next when you call?"

"Yes. Typically, I like to meet in person with a new client right away. It is the best way to communicate and get to know each other. I don't suppose there is a chance that you will be in Iowa soon, before the deadline to answer this petition?"

"No, not unless the team waives me or something, but I did think about this right before I dialed your number and I do agree it would be good for us to meet soon. I would like to fly you down here so we could do that."

"I am sure we could arrange that," Will said as he thought how in the world he was going to arrange that with the other work he had and the desire to spend time with his wife and kids during spring break, which had just started. "Before getting into that, though, it does bring up another issue I should've discussed before, and that is the cost of defending yourself in litigation."

"How much are you talking overall?"

"That part is hard, because there are so many variables outside of our control, the largest one being how hard the other side pushes, including how much discovery it requests of us. I think most attorneys you talk to would say the same thing. What I can tell you is you will be charged on an hourly basis, with monthly invoices, and my hourly rate is $250 per hour. To the extent legal assistants or other attorneys in the firm work on your file, their rates vary depending on experience, legal assistants being less than attorneys. That rate is probably less than half the rate the New York attorneys are charging your team. The only other things I can say are you should be prepared to spend in the low six figures and I will keep you informed of expected costs during each stage of the litigation. Frankly, the biggest cost is the trial and most cases never get there."

"Okay. I am not sure why I even asked. That won't be a problem. While I make just a little over the league minimum, that is still a lot, and more importantly I received a nice signing bonus out of college and have had some endorsements."

Those endorsements are going to dry up, Will thought to himself.

"Right," Will responded. "You never know with the stories we hear about athletes blowing their money."

"My parents taught me well. We are doing fine. Actually, I did not mean to just invite you. I do not want to take you away from your family, if you have any. Do you have any family?"

That was the first time a new client had asked him that during the initial conversation. "Yes, I have a wife and three children," Will answered.

"That's great! Please bring them as well. I will pay for their flights as well. There is a new hotel near my apartment. They have suites so your kids can be in a separate room. I know other players have put extended family members in there and they have enjoyed it."

"That is really nice of you. You really do not need to do all of that."

"I want to. I really would hate to take you away from your wife and kids. This is a way I can prevent that. Can they come? Or do they have school and work?"

"Actually, they just started spring break. The kids are off school this next week and my wife, Ashley, took the week off her part-time job."

"Oh, I guess I did not think about spring break. Did you all have a vacation planned already?"

Will grunted. "I'm not sure I can remember the last vacation I took. Ashley and the kids were just going to find some things to do around town. I was going to be around them when I could, but I had just planned on continuing to work."

"Well, if you do not mind working on my case, please come spend the week down here."

"That really sounds good. Let me talk with my wife. I will confirm our firm does not have a conflict of interest and call you back tomorrow afternoon."

~~~~~

Will arrived home after supper later that night. While the kids watched *The Tale of Desperaux* for what must have been the thirty-third time, he started to talk to his wife about his new client. "I had an interesting phone call today. Actually, two interesting phone calls."

Ashley did not look as she said, "Oh yeah?" With purpose, she was showing lack of interest in the husband who had shown so little attention to her.

Will continued, "First, the pastor of the church that is the opposing party of a lawsuit I filed on behalf of the Midwestern Baptist Association called. That's the same guy I deposed a few days ago."

"You deposed a pastor?" Ashley interrupted. She hadn't looked up yet.

"Yeah, why?"

"It just seems strange you would sue a pastor."

"No, I didn't sue a pastor. My client is a religious association and they sued a church. The pastor is just the representative of the church, not the actual defendant. It's a real estate dispute. He is a witness with information, so we had to depose him."

"You weren't mean to him, were you?"

"No, of course not. In fact, when he called me today he said he wanted to refer a client to me because he liked me so well."

Ashley looked up at Will. "So who did he refer to you?"

"Roy Adams."

"Who?"

"The baseball player. Remember? I was telling you about him the other night when the news was reporting he had skipped practice or a game on Sunday."

"Right. When you said you had to be working."

Will smiled. "Yeah. As I said then, I just needed a quick break. I am glad I was watching. I was able to know a little bit about what was going on. And he wants me to represent him."

"What for?"

"Are you asking why he wants my help or why he needs help?"

144 · Jason M. Steffens

Ashley giggled. "I'll say both."

Will smiled at extracting a smile from Ashley. He was certain her smile brought him more joy in life than anything. He marveled at why he spent so little time working on making her happy. This wasn't the first time he scolded himself for his short-sidedness, which caused him to see the immediate "problems" of his job and miss everything behind that job.

"Well, the 'why he wants *my* help' question has me stumped as well. As for why he needs a lawyer's help, I am sure it will be all over the media soon, but for now I can't say without breaking his confidence."

"Sometimes I wish your ethics rules didn't require you to keep everything so secret. I hardly know what you do." Ashley looked down again.

"I'm sorry, but I can tell you one thing."

"What's that?" Ashley asked, as it appeared to Will she was pretending to show lack of interest again.

"I will need to meet with Roy, he needs to stay in Arizona for spring training, and so he wants to bring us down there next week, for the whole week. The kids can come as well. There is a new hotel near his apartment building. I will have to do some work, but it will be a family vacation as well."

As he said this, Will hoped Ashley would latch onto the "vacation" part more than the "work" part, but he did have to temper her expectations somewhat, for he knew that—in addition to working with his new client—he would not be able to entirely abandon the other work he had planned to do over the coming week.

Will was both thankful and disheartened his wife was used to such tempered expectations. Disheartened, because he knew they came from his consistent failure to at least occasionally put aside everything else and just focus on her and their relationship. Thankful, because her reaction right now was excitement just over the word "vacation." She looked up and—in a voice that wondered whether it was really okay to display eagerness—asked, "Really?"

"Yes! He will pay for the whole trip. I just need to make sure our firm does not have a conflict of interest in representing him, but I do not think that will be a problem."

"Wow! When do we leave!?"

"Monday morning."

19.

Saturday morning

Nate and his wife and their four children ate breakfast to-gether and walked over to the church building. As his wife did some work in the church office and the kids ran around the small basement, Nate went to his office in the back of the building. He pulled out two small sheets of scrap paper on which he had written notes. He looked over them, made another note, and then prayed.

Shortly before ten o'clock, he stepped out of his office and went into the auditorium, hoping to see church mem-bers walking in. As usual, none came this morning.

It was a young church, Nate told himself. Or, at least, the congregation was now mostly made up of new mem-bers, some of them new converts. Many of the members here when he arrived had left. The change had been diffi-cult on them. Others had not yet developed the habit of coming on a Saturday morning or mid-week evening to knock on doors to share the Gospel and invite strangers to church.

Nate also considered that some of the members worked outside for their jobs. This March day was sunny and unseasonably warm in eastern Iowa. Their employers would have them working.

They would learn the importance of coming eventually.

Though no others came this morning, Nate's wife and their children did walk into the auditorium at ten. He was so thankful for them. He felt the enormous responsibility of leading them and insufficient in that task. "Lord, please help me," Nate silently prayed, trusting that He would.

After giving his family the challenge he had prepared, they split up in pairs. Nate took their youngest, his wife the next youngest, and the two oldest went together. They took their van to a neighborhood a few miles south of the church. It was one they had not knocked before. It sat in a triangle-shaped area between 1st Avenue and Williams Boulevard after Williams branched off of First Avenue. They were just south of an elementary school named after Grover Cleveland and housed in a now more than half-century old building still in productive use.

Nate and his youngest child knocked on doors along the north side of a street called Reynolds Avenue. They then crossed the street and walked back toward the area where they started. Near the end of the morning, they came to a house with a single-stall garage attached to an enclosed non-insulated side porch that was then attached to the house. The side porch had a door. There was also a front door to the house. Nate normally would have knocked on the main front door, but the vegetation growing around it showed its disuse. Nate knocked on the door to the porch. No one answered. Usually when no one answered he just left a tract in the door. It contained information about the church and the gospel message. Before doing that here, though, Nate saw through the door that there were two other doors inside. The one on the left led to the garage and the one on the right to the house. It was possible that whoever lived here did not hear the first knock given it had to travel through another door. Nate tried again, knocking harder. After a few moments, a young man slowly opened the inner door and walked to the outer door, cracking it open. "Yeah?" he asked as he looked at Nate and then down at the child with a skeptical face.

The prospect for a good conversation looked bleak, but Nate had learned to not trust first impressions.

"Hi. My name is Nate." He deliberately did not use his title. "I am from Pine Road Baptist Church. We are walking through your neighborhood this morning inviting people to church. I would like to invite you, especially if you do not already have a church home."

The young man appeared to wake up. He looked more intensely at Nate and said, "I know who you are."

"I am sorry," Nate replied. "You do look familiar, but I can't immediately recall where we have met before."

"We did not exactly meet, but I came to your church about a year ago."

Nate realized it was the guy who came to that first Sunday evening service, before the church even called him to be the pastor, when he was there canidating for the pastorship. "Of course," Nate said. "You are not wearing a ball cap now." The young man removed the rough look from his face and gave the hint of a smile. Nate continued, "That is why I did not immediately recognize you, but I certainly remember you. I have wished since that night we had learned your name and you would come back."

"Yeah, well, I meant to but things got busy, ya know?"

Busyness was merely an excuse. Nate had heard it many times before. We always make time for the things important to us. How we spend our time demonstrates our priorities. But Nate did not say that out loud.

"Was there anything about the service that caused you to not come back?"

"No. Just been busy."

Nate nodded.

So was this the court reporter's son? "Since I did not get your name when you visited us a year ago, could I get it now?"

"It's Donnie. My friends call me DJ."

"Last name Valenza?"

"Yeah, how did you know?"

"I know someone who is looking for you. Actually, two people."

"I am sure one of them is Jesus, but he did not tell you my last name."

Nate laughed. "That is right. I met your mother earlier this week. Through an unusual set of circumstances, I discussed the story of the visitor who came to our first Sunday evening service. She thought it might be you. Actually, I am not really sure how, but she seemed convinced it was you."

"Are you going to tell her where I am?"

"She asked me to, if I ever found you. It would be better if you did so. Is there some reason you have not? She misses you."

Many people open up to pastors, saying things they do not tell others. Hearing his mother missed him was the trigger for DJ. "I felt I let her down, my whole family, when baseball—the one thing I was good at, the thing that made people love me—was taken away from me because of an injury. I got bitter. I have spent the past three years of my life tryin' to make something of myself so my parents would have a son they could be proud of. I'm not sure I'll ever do that."

"Your mother's love for you has nothing to do with baseball."

"Maybe, but I'm not sure about my dad. Anyway, they were both depressed when they found out how severe the injury was. I think they thought I was going to make a lot of money and buy them things."

"I have only met your mother. As far as I can tell, if she was concerned about that once, her concern now is just you." DJ looked skeptical. Nate continued, "Look, this life is hard to live alone, but before you can live it victoriously, you must first know where you are going."

"I know what you want to know preacher. You asked the same thing at the end of that service. My mom took me to church every Sunday from the day I was born."

"You know it is not church membership that can overcome your sin and give you an eternal home with God."

"I know. It is nothin' but the blood of Jesus. When I was six-years-old, before bed one night, I told my mom I wanted to be saved from the penalty of my sin. Though I already knew them, she showed me again the Bible verses that talk about our sin and the penalty for that sin being death and hell, but how God loved us so much He sent his perfect son Jesus, who willingly died on the cross to pay that price for us, and then how He rose from the dead. Jesus saved me two thousand years ago. I called on the Lord and received that gift that night when I was six."

Nate had not run across people like DJ much. Though only God knew, DJ appeared to have made a sincere decision to trust Jesus for his salvation many years ago. Now, he appeared depressed, but DJ recognized that Jesus was looking for him and he had made one attempt to come to a service at a church that had not even invited him.

"Good," Nate replied. "There is nothing more important than that decision. But trusting Jesus as our Saviour gives us more than the promise of eternal life, though I do not mean to downplay that at all. It also allows us to have victory in this life. You feel the way you do because you are starving yourself."

"What're ya talkin' about? I eat."

"Physically." DJ looked at him with a modicum of understanding, but didn't say anything. He continued, "We need food on a regular basis for physical strength. We need other things for spiritual and emotional strength. If we neglect Bible reading, prayer, and church membership, we will be weak, even though we may be physically strong."

"I don't know. I know my Bible. I was in church a lot as a kid. I know all that stuff. I am doing fine now."

"You just told me you were *not* doing fine, that you felt like a failure. But even if you were fine, we will not have the right definition of fine without seeing things, and ourselves, as God sees them. And we will not see everything as God does without daily hearing from Him by reading his Word, daily talking to Him by praying, and regularly being around other believers, singing hymns, and hearing the preaching of God's Word."

The look of skepticism returned to DJ's face. There was nothing like trying to turn a person's life around to cause that person to put up all sorts of barriers, even if the path they were on was unpleasant.

"I will give it some thought. Maybe I will come visit your church again."

Figuratively, DJ had closed his door. Nate did not press him more. He was convinced DJ knew all this. It was a matter of acting on what he knew. But he did ask DJ about his mother again. DJ said he was not ready to contact her yet, he would give that some thought as well, but if Nate wanted to tell her where he was that was fine.

20.

Roy kept looking for someone from the team's front office, or one of the coaches, to come talk to him about the lawsuit or tell him that he was now suspended from the team. No one did.

He went through drills with the rest of the team. He then watched that afternoon's game, as he had a scheduled day off from playing.

His teammates reflexively avoided him for the most part, but it appeared none of them knew what was going on, except Malik.

After the game and after he had changed his clothes, Roy headed toward the door that led to the player's parking lot. Before he reached it, Roy saw his manager, Earl Vinson, approach him.

"See you tomorrow?" Vinson asked him, almost in a pleading manner. "I am going to give the Sunday fans a taste of what I think our regular season lineup will be, so all the starters will be in, and I may have to play you the whole game, as Bobby and Adrian are nursing some minor injuries." Bobby and Adrian were two of the reserve outfielders vying for roster spots.

Roy felt his heart pound. It was one thing to reiterate to the owner and front office staff his decision. It was another to tell Earl Vinson. Reinhold and the executives did not care about him except as a money and fame maker for them. Roy knew his manager cared about him. He also knew what he had to tell him would disappoint him, which made this so much harder. There was so much in Roy that wanted to please Earl.

"I will not be here, Earl," Roy responded. "For the same reason I gave last week for why I cannot be here on Sundays." His heart continued pounding as he waited for his manager to reply. Vinson's lips tightened.

"See you *tomorrow*," he said, this time as a forceful declaration rather than a plea. He then walked away. Roy stood there a moment watching him before exiting and heading home.

At home, Jenny did not greet him with a kiss, but she did have supper prepared. Roy tried to engage her in conversation. She was not talkative. After a few moments of silence, she looked up and said, "I saw Whitney today."

"You did? Where? I thought you were having difficulty setting a time to get together."

"We were at the game."

"You were?" Jenny had not mentioned she was going to the ballpark today.

"The players' wives had that memorabilia giveaway today to benefit the team charity."

"Oh, I forgot."

"She is really spiritual. I think we could become good friends and that I could learn a lot from her. She has been a Christian since she was a young girl. Her dad was a deacon in his church."

"That is wonderful!" Roy said sincerely. "Malik is a really good guy, too. Maybe we could do some double dates."

"That would be fun." Jenny momentarily perked up, but it passed. After a moment, she said, "She told me about Malik's idea."

"About the team chapel?"

"Yeah."

"What did you think about it?"

She hesitated. "Well, there are certainly good things and bad things about it."

"Yeah."

"But you told him 'no'?"

"I did."

"Do you think it is a bad idea?"

"I think they mean well, but it is not really church. And even if you could call it a church, it is not the church we should be in. Plus, it is important for us to be in church together. I want to lead my family in worshipping God. I cannot do that if I am not there, if I make baseball more important. It would send a mixed message to our kids when we have them."

"Okay. You are probably right."

"Don't you want to be seen in church with me?" Roy asked in a joking manner, hoping to lighten the mood.

Jenny did not catch that he was being facetious and answered seriously. "I do. It's just ..." She paused, appearing to search her mind for the words to convey her thoughts.

"It's just what?" Roy asked.

"It's just that I do not want to be the cause of taking you away, even for one day a week, of what you love doing."

"I love God and I love you."

"I know you do. I *do*. But you also love baseball. You always have, since you were a small boy."

"I do love baseball, but sometimes things change, priorities are rearranged."

"The team does not understand this. No one does. I just want you to know that if you want to play baseball, if you want to keep the team happy, I am fine with that. I can go to church on my own during the baseball season and then we can go together during the offseason."

"I love you so much. I know you would do that for me. But I do not want you to have to. I also do not want you to ever feel like you are keeping me from something. You are not. You make everything better, no matter what it is!"

She smiled. Then she smiled bigger and asked, "Like bacon?"

Roy laughed. She was reminding him of their first date. He took her to a 1950s-style diner. He ordered a bacon cheeseburger and fries. She ordered the same, but without the bacon, not because she did not like bacon—she later admitted—but because the baconless cheeseburger was thirty cents cheaper. She had grown up on a small farm. Her family was frugal. Roy had tried to get her to order the one with bacon, telling her bacon made everything better. They then had a long discussion where they tried to think of foods bacon did *not* make better. Roy had refused to move off his original position on any of them.

"Like bacon," he replied.

"I love you, too," she said back. "I just hope the team comes around to what you want to do."

21.

Roy sat with Jenny in church. He had taken a circuitous route there. After the conversations with the owner, the manager, and the reporter, he worried someone would follow him and his presence at the church instead of the ballpark would cause a circus atmosphere, but he did not see anyone.

In church, it seemed the congregation did more whispering about him and gave him more side glances than it had the past Sunday or Wednesday night. That may have just been his paranoia, though. It was hard to tell. Still, no one came up to him and asked for his autograph or, more awkwardly, asked him why he was not with the team. It was church as usual for them. There were a couple of other guests there that diverted the attention of many of them.

Roy had hoped he would receive something from the message that would confirm he was making the right choice. It was probably there, but he was not getting it. Instead of focusing on the preaching, his mind wandered. He allowed himself to think about what the team management would tell his teammates. How would they react? What about the press? When would they find out? How harshly would they react? Preston Edwards seemed to already know. Would he disclose what was going on? What was he waiting for? Beyond everyone's reaction, was his career now over because of this decision? Would the team even allow him in the ballpark tomorrow?

What Roy knew was lost in what he did not know. The uncertainty of the near future consumed him.

Roy glanced at Jenny now and then. She would glance back and give a small smile and then look back up at the pastor. She, too, seemed distracted.

They did not stay long after the service and drove straight home, mostly in silence. After they finished eating leftovers for lunch, Jenny glanced at the TV. "Should we turn the game on?" she asked.

The Hawks' spring training game that afternoon was about to start.

"I don't think we should," Roy answered, belying his curiosity.

"Will the announcers say anything?" Jenny wondered.

"They might not know. The only way they would is if someone from the front office or Earl told them. There are enough players still on the spring training roster that the dugout will be full and my absence will not be immediately obvious."

"After last Sunday, won't they be looking for you?"

"Maybe, though it is unlikely they would suspect that just because I was absent last Sunday that I would be absent this Sunday. They do not know the reason I was absent."

"Unless someone told them," Jenny observed.

"Yeah."

"So, don't turn it on?"

"Let's not. Whatever happens happens. Let's not let it distract us from enjoying this day." Roy left unsaid what was obvious—they were not going to enjoy this day.

They cleared the table and put the dishes in the dishwasher. Roy decided he would pass his afternoon before the evening church service reading. He went into a spare bedroom they had turned into an office. Reading would help him avoid media.

Fifteen minutes later, he heard the TV turn on in the living room. Jenny was flipping channels. She stopped at the game.

Roy could hear the announcers, but could not make out what they were saying. He refrained from going into the living room. After a few minutes, he picked up his book again. He did his best to focus on it. It was a crime thriller, which helped. If the announcers said anything important about him, Jenny would come tell him.

Jenny kept the game on all afternoon. She never came and got him.

~~~~~

To help Roy—or any client—Will needed to know what precedent existed concerning the issues in his case. How judges ruled in the past often foretold and sometimes dictated how they would rule in the present. Even beyond decisions by the courts, it was helpful to know how similar instances had played out.

There had been athletic stars of long ago who refused to participate on Sundays, among them Olympic sprinter Eric Liddell (one of the subjects of the 1981 film *Chariots of Fire*) and women's tennis player Dorothy Round, but that was in a day in which events on Sunday were much less common.

In most major cities, Sunday baseball games had not been legalized until the early twentieth century. Philadelphia was a holdout despite legislative attempts and court battles to overturn Sunday blue laws, but by 1933 it, too, had legalized Sunday baseball. By the 1950s, many teams held doubleheaders on Sundays to maximize attendance.

Roy was not just joining the losing side of a societal debate over Sunday sporting events. He was joining the side that had already lost, with most people alive not knowing there had once been a battle.

There had been others. In 2009, London's *Daily Telegraph* reported that Scottish rugby star Euan Murray would miss a match against France that fell on a Sunday as a result of his Christian faith. He had played a Sunday match the previous year, but his faith had since deepened. Neither he nor the team would comment on his contractual situation. The same thing happened in 2011, according to the *Sydney Morning Herald*, when Murray missed a Sunday Rugby World Cup match against Argentina. Murray was quoted as once saying: "It's basically all or nothing, following Jesus. I don't believe in pick 'n' mix Christianity. I believe the Bible is the word of God, so who am I to ignore something from it?" He also reportedly said, "I want to live my life believing and doing the things He wants and the sabbath day is a full day. It's not a case of a couple of hours in church then playing rugby or going down to the pub, it's the full day."

The team knew Murray's position about Sunday play and went on without him. The precedential value seemed minimal. If Roy's case went to trial or arbitration, Will did not see a United States judge, arbitrator, or jury paying much attention to someone playing a sport with little following here and that only played Sunday matches irregularly.

There were some examples outside Christianity, including among Jewish and Mormon athletes. The closest parallel to Roy was Sandy Koufax, the great Jewish Dodgers lefthander. He did not pitch on the Jewish holidays Rosh

Hashanah and the first day of Passover. In 1965, Game One of the World Series fell on Yom Kippur and Koufax refused to pitch. He was still able to pitch Games Two, Five, and Seven, throwing shutouts in the latter two with the arthritic pain that would lead to his retirement after the next season. However, Koufax's refusal to pitch for religious reasons was limited to major holidays. He regularly pitched on the Jewish Sabbath throughout his career. The biggest difference was that Roy was not a pitcher. He was an everyday player.

Thirty-one years earlier, another Jewish star, Detroit Tigers first baseman Hank Greenberg, anguished over but ultimately decided to play in a key pennant race game against the New York Yankees on Rosh Hashanah. Greenberg later sat out multiple Yom Kippurs. Dodgers outfielder Shawn Green later followed the example of Greenberg and Koufax in sitting out Yom Kippur.

The Mormons had an entire institution—Brigham Young University—that did not participate in athletic events on Sundays. That created some scheduling issues when, for instance, the BYU men's basketball team made the NCAA Tournament, which held games on Sundays, but college games were spaced apart enough that those issues were capable of being worked out without forcing the forfeiture of games. Some smaller Christian colleges followed the same practice with less fanfare outside of the money and popularity involved in Division I college athletics.

In 2006, the *Los Angeles Times* reported that a Utah Little League baseball team mostly comprised of Mormons forfeited rather than play a Sunday game during a Little League World Series qualifying tournament. According to the report, some of the parents were more upset than the kids about the forfeiture.

Even though BYU does not play on Sundays, there have
been many BYU alumni that became professional athletes
who played on Sundays. One who did not was an offensive
lineman by the name of Eli Herring. Herring had told National Football League teams not to draft him because he
would not play on Sundays. Nevertheless, the Oakland
Raiders took him in the sixth round of the 1995 draft, hoping to entice him with money. He turned the Raiders down
and became a teacher. Professional football was different
than baseball in that almost every game was played on a
Sunday. There was no option to play sometimes. It was either play on Sunday or almost never play.

There were lots of examples of Christians with strong
professions of faith who said they felt God wanted them to
remain in their sport as a witness.

While all of these situations had similarities to Roy's,
none of them involved a professional athlete in the midst of
his career suddenly refusing to play on a certain day each
week for religious reasons. And none of them involved a
team suing its player in an attempt to force him to play. Unlike Scotland's accommodation of Euan Murray, the Indianapolis Hawks appeared to have no intention of accommo-
dating its player.

Will reached the conclusion that there was no precedent
for Roy Adams.

~~~~~

On the way to the Sunday evening church service, Roy confirmed with Jenny that the announcers did not say anything
about him. He had preferred to not know anything until
Monday. The knowledge that Jenny had watched the game
destroyed his resolve to keep his mind away from the field

and on church. As he expected, her not coming to get him meant they had ignored him. The television company employed the announcers, but only with the team's permission. It was possible they knew and kept silent at the team's request. It was also possible they still did not know.

Roy and Jenny sat through the evening service much as they had the morning service, distracted by thoughts of what their world would be like the following day. Roy realized he was putting Jenny through a lot of anxiety. He hated that.

When they arrived back to their apartment that night, Jenny turned on her cell phone. They had both kept those off all day. Jenny mentioned there were several voicemails on her phone. Before she could check them, it rang. Roy could tell Jenny did not recognize the number, but she answered anyway. "Hello?" he heard her say. Then: "Uh, just a minute."

She covered the phone and said, "It's Bill Armstrong. He says it is important. Do you want to talk to him?"

Bill Armstrong was Roy's agent. He was a decent guy who did his job well, but *no* Roy did not want to talk to him. Roy took the phone anyway.

"Hi Bill."

"Roy, I am glad I got ahold of you. I have been trying to reach you since early this afternoon."

"I had my phone off."

"Okay, well, you need to know the team is going to suspend you."

"How do you know?"

"Kevin Absher called and gave me a heads up. It will happen tomorrow sometime." Absher was one of the team's assistant general managers.

"Suspend as it did last Monday?" That had only been for a day. If it was the same suspension this time, it would mean there was still a possibility the team was open to coming to an understanding about him having Sundays off.

"No," the agent answered. "I don't know the details. Either they were still working it out or Absher knew but did not tell me. Whatever the case, they wanted me to know so I could try to talk sense into you. Of course, it would help if I knew what was going on. Why haven't you showed up the past two Sundays?"

Roy had not told him. He told him now. The agent was initially dumbstruck. Then he unleashed every persuasive argument he could think of to get Roy to stop this. Having faced down his owner, his manager, and his best friend on the team, the agent had no chance of convincing him, but Roy had to spend the next twenty minutes beating back his agent's pleas. Finally Armstrong gave up and Roy was able to give Jenny her phone back.

Jenny had heard Roy's side of the conversation, which was enough, so there was no need for Roy to explain to her what the agent had called about. They ignored their phones for the rest of the night, which was not a restful one.

In his tossing and turning, Roy made one decision. It was time for this story to be out in the open, if for nothing else than to remove some of the uncertainties.

22.

The Hawks had not informed the security guard of Roy's pending suspension. He allowed Roy in the players' parking lot at the stadium.

Roy had awoken early that morning, well before Jenny. It was not hard to wake so early after not sleeping well.

Before leaving his apartment for the team's spring training facility, he sent text messages to Preston Edwards and the team's beat reporters. There were three sportswriters in town covering the Hawks full-time. One worked for the *Indianapolis Star*, one for MLB.com, and one for an upstart sports blogging network. In the text, Roy merely told them his plan to hold a press conference that morning before the team's activities got underway. He felt Edwards would come if he was available. The Hawks' beat reporters would grumble about having to get to the park earlier than normal, but they would definitely come.

Roy had written a short statement he would read to them before taking their questions. They would have lots of questions. He did not want to be one of those who read a statement on something important and then ignored the questions that provided the real answers.

166 · Jason M. Steffens

Roy walked into the facility. He did not see any other players or coaches there yet. It was still early. A few of them may have been in the locker room receiving treatments from trainers. Instead of going there, Roy headed straight for the small press conference room. The three beat reporters were present, as was an uninvited Associated Press reporter who had seen the *Star* reporter in the continental breakfast area of the hotel in which they were both staying. Roy did not know him well, but that was fine.

Preston Edwards was not there. Something must have kept him from coming.

One of the reporters grumbled about there being no coffee ready in the room. Usually the team set out beverages for press conferences. It seemed to be less a real complaint than an attempt to reduce the tension in the room. They all knew this was unusual. "Sorry," Roy replied. "This was not planned, at least until I decided to do it late last night. As you may have guessed, the team does not know I am doing this."

"What's up, Roy?" one of them asked. "Are you going to tell us why you were missing last Sunday?"

"And why you were not around yesterday?" another asked.

So at least one of them had noticed his absence yesterday, Roy thought. He had not bothered to check the media members' web sites this morning to see if any of them had reported that fact.

"I have a statement I prepared I would like to read first," Roy said, "and then I will answer your questions."

Roy went behind the desk set up for interviewees. The reporters took their seats and prepared to record the press conference. Roy looked down at what he had written on the paper and read it aloud:

"The baseball season is around two hundred games when you count spring training and the playoffs. The regular season is six months long. Spring training and the playoffs add another month each on the front end and back end of the regular season. During that time, there are almost no days off. The days we do have off are in the middle of the week, never on the weekend, and half of them are in cities outside our hometown.

"I do not say this to complain. I am not complaining. Though physically difficult and requiring intense mental focus, it is not grueling work compared to most jobs in the world. It is, after all, a game. It is fun. And we at the major league level are paid lots of money to play it.

"I say this because I can no longer give baseball a couple of the things it currently demands: primacy and time.

"This past offseason, while back in Iowa, I met a man who showed me from the Bible my eternal condition, how I fell short of God's standards, and how I could not earn my own way to heaven. I put my faith in Jesus and his payment for my sin. Since that day, I have tried to live more and more for God, so I please Him and bear good fruit.

"I have a long way to go. One thing has become obvious: I cannot be the man God wants me to be if I let things get in the way of serving Him.

"Church attendance is an essential aspect of being a Christian. It is where we worship Him collectively, hear preaching from His word, serve Him, and receive encouragement and edification from other believers. If I forsake church attendance, I will have told myself, the world, and God the lie that God is less important than my own priorities.

"As a result, before last Sunday, I informed the team I would be absent on Sunday in order to attend church. I attended the morning and evening services of a Baptist church here in Phoenix. That is the reason the team suspended me for one day last week, on Monday. During the week, we attempted to work out our differences. I was again absent yesterday in order to attend church, which the team knew beforehand.

"We have been unable to come to an understanding that reconciles the team's desire to have me seven days a week and my desire to set aside one day a week for church attendance. I have been informed the team will announce an indefinite suspension of me today. Additionally, though for some reason it has not publicized this, it filed a lawsuit against me back in Iowa asking for an unspecified amount of money from me.

"I want to continue playing baseball, and to do so for the Hawks. I am willing to take less money. I just want the ability to do what many Christians do, which is attend church at least one day of the week."

Roy finished. His voice had started off shaky due to his nervousness, and then had steadied, but now his heart pounded harder. He had never before been so open about his still relatively new faith. He did not expect this crowd to be sympathetic, but as he looked up he hoped they would at least understand him and treat him fairly. If they did, there was a chance, however small, the public would see his side and then pressure the team to accommodate his request.

The questions came fast. Initially they were basic. *What church? What man in Iowa? What teammates and coaches know about this? What do they think?*

Roy's answers were as short as honesty allowed. For some of the questions he did not have answers, such as how long his suspension would be or if the team would ever allow him to play every day but Sunday. He was asked about the lawsuit. No, he did not know for how much the team was suing him, but the team was trying to force him to play on Sundays. Yes, he had a lawyer—Will Jacobson of Cedar Rapids—and yes he intended to defend himself if the team pursued the court case.

The questions then became more accusatory. *Are you saying it is wrong to play sports on Sundays? Can't you just go to church or have a Bible study during off-days?*

One reporter asked, "Are you saying other players have less faith than you because they choose to play on Sunday?"

Roy thought, *How do I state what I believe to be best without necessarily implying other choices are wrong, or at least less right? Maybe I can't.*

"I am not judging the faith of anyone else," Roy answered. "I have just determined that attending church services on the day my church has scheduled them is important to my faith."

The same reporter then asked, "Are you trying to be Chuck from *Amazing Grace and Chuck?*"

"I am not sure what you mean," Roy responded.

Another reporter smirked as a third looked at the questioner with puzzlement and asked, "Yeah, what are you talking about?"

The reporter said, "You know, the 80s movie? In it, this star little league baseball player named Chuck quits baseball as a protest against the existence of nuclear weapons. He will not play again until the world disarms itself of them. A pro basketball player played by NBA star Alex English joins his protest, and then other athletes start quitting other sports. They all moved into a barn outside the boy's hometown."

"Did the protest work?" one of them asked. In this informal press conference, the reporters were now asking themselves questions.

"Well, if you want me to spoil the ending," the movie buff reporter responded, "not exactly. Someone killed the Alex English character, the president met with Chuck and kindly explained to him what a dumb protest it was, and Chuck went back to playing baseball with nuclear weapons still in existence."

"So Roy," one of them asked, "are you trying to be the leader of a big protest against Sunday sports?"

Before Roy could respond, the Indianapolis Hawks' Vice President for Public Relations, Sally Folding, opened the door. Roy looked in her direction. Her gaze was directed toward the reporters. "This press conference is over," she announced. "I need you all to leave." The reporters sat there for a moment like they were going to object. She continued her stare. They started to collect their things.

Roy asked her, "How did you even know this was going on, Sally?"

She turned to Roy, appearing to use all her effort to intensify the harshness of her stare. "One of these guys is reporting this on Twitter. Everyone now knows this is going on."

The reporters from the traditional media outlets looked at the one from the upstart blogging network. They realized he had not asked any questions. He had been busy posting portions of the interview of the press conference on the Internet and thus had the story out before they did. They scrambled faster and started out the room. As they did so, one of them thought to ask Ms. Folding, "Does the team have a comment on this story?"

"The team will issue a statement soon," she answered. "If it decides to hold a press conference following that statement, you will be notified."

The reporters left. Sally Folding looked at Roy and said, "Go see Earl." She then walked out of the room. As the person who was often the face of the team and who helped the players with public relations, Sally usually had an endless supply of smiles. Roy had never seen her so angry.

He left the room and walked through the locker room. Thankfully, it was still early enough that most of the players had not yet arrived. Roy knocked on his manager's office door. "Come in," he heard from the other side.

Roy opened the door and walked in. He saw Earl Vinson standing by the side of his desk. His arms were crossed. His arms were always crossed when he had something serious to say. He had not yet changed into his baseball uniform. "Sally told me you wanted to see me," Roy said.

"You are no longer welcome here," Earl said without turning to face Roy. "Get what personal effects you want out of your locker and go home. This suspension is without pay, of course, and indefinite."

Roy did not know what to say back. He stood there for a second, but his manager never turned to look at him.

Roy left. He walked back through the locker room in a daze, forgetting even to stop at his locker. Everything was happening so fast. Roy had figured if things fell apart they would do so abruptly, but that expectation did not lessen the shock.

He reached the players' parking lot and saw Malik getting out of his car. Malik saw Roy. He looked like he would have rather avoided him. Roy would have preferred that as well, but their paths had to cross as Malik headed toward the facility and Roy walked to his own car.

"The report is already on sports radio," Malik said as they stopped when they reached each other. "Are you suspended?"

"Yeah," Roy answered.

"How long?"

"Indefinitely."

Malik paused and then said, "It did not have to be this way."

Malik's declaration awoke Roy out of a stupor of self-pity. Malik was not on his side. "I had to make the right decision. The consequences are not up to me."

"There are going to be a lot of opinions about that."

"That's fine."

"You can still end this and get things back in order."

"No, I cannot."

"Alright. I gotta go take care of my family. You take care of yours. Maybe I'll see you around."

Without further word, Malik continued toward the door of the facility.

23.

Will arrived at the Phoenix airport with Ashley and their three children. He instinctively checked his phone as the plane parked. There were lots of emails. He ignored them for now because he saw two text messages had come in back-to-back from Roy. The first message said simply, "Let me know when you arrive. Please come straight to my place with your family. Situation changed this morning." The subsequent message provided his address.

Will wondered what was going on. He sent a text message in reply, saying they had just landed and he would get there as soon as possible.

It took them close to an hour to disembark, pick up their luggage, and take the kids to the restroom. Will then found them a cab and directed the driver to Roy's apartment building. Another half-hour later they arrived.

Roy authorized their entrance with the security personnel. Will was uneasy about bringing his whole family up to his new client's home. "Why don't you and the kids hang out down here in the lobby while I go up and see what is happening?" he said to Ashley. "Maybe he will have a suggestion about where you all can go while I try to do whatever I can this morning. My guess is we cannot check into the hotel for a few more hours."

"Okay," she replied. "But try to figure it out quickly. The kids are going to be hungry for lunch soon. If they do not get it, they will either start fighting with each other or eating the lobby furniture."

"Got it. I'll be right back. I promise."

Will took the elevator up to Roy's floor. His client greeted him as soon as the elevator door opened. "I am so glad you are here," Roy said to him. "It's nice to finally meet you."

They shook hands. "You too," Will replied.

Roy brought him into his apartment. Inside, a young woman rose from where she had been sitting. "This is my wife, Jenny."

"Hi, thank you for coming," she said with a smile.

"Yes, glad to do so."

"Where is your family?" she asked.

"I left them down in the lobby for now."

"Oh, we can't have that," she replied cheerfully. "I will go keep them company while you two talk. I really hope you can help us." With that, she left, which saved Will from having to explain to her that sometimes lawyers cannot help, except to the extent that explaining choices among multiple bad options is "help."

"So what's going on?" Will asked as Roy shut the door behind Jenny.

"I am not sure this was the best thing, but last night I decided to get everything out in the open. I held a press conference this morning."

Nothing in that explanation comforted Will. Rarely did good come out of clients taking action in the middle of disputes without first consulting a lawyer. On the other hand, nothing about this case was usual and Will was uncertain he could help Roy anyway.

Roy explained what happened at the press conference, including the team's premature ending of it, and his subsequent meeting with his manager.

"Has there been any reaction so far?" Will asked, though he knew there had to have been.

"Yes. A lot."

"Have you paid attention to it?"

"It's all Jenny and I have done."

"Has it been bad?" Again, Will thought he knew what the answer would be.

"Yes." Roy walked over to his couch, picked up his TV remote, and brought up a recorded clip. "This has been typical, though Preston Edwards is more articulate than most." Roy hit play and for the next five minutes they watched the baseball reporter interact with a couple of anchors about the story. Edwards first confirmed what the team's beat reporters were saying—the team was suspending Roy indefinitely. Edwards added that the team had tried to work with Roy but that team sources said he had been uncooperative. The team was now working with the commissioner's office on its options.

After the facts, Edwards offered his opinion. It was devoid of compassion for Roy's position, seeped in sympathy for the team's. "From my vantage point," he said at one point, "the Hawks' front office and its manager Earl Vinson have been exceptionally gracious to Adams, offering him chances beyond what a player, even of Adams' talent, would warrant. Adams has been given good advice, but he has rejected it. From somewhere, he is getting bad counsel about what it means to be a Christian and a baseball player in today's age." One of the anchors wondered whether this was all the doing of Adams' wife. Edwards replied that he did not have information on that, but that possibility remained open.

Roy stopped the clip. His phone beeped. He picked it up and looked at a text message. "Jenny says she is taking your family out for lunch. There's a quick order Mexican place down the road."

Will looked at his phone, which had been on silent. Ashley had texted him as well and said the same thing. That would be good, as it would keep the kids from grumbling.

Will then listened to Roy explain that the team had been updating Edwards on the situation, but had reigned in his reports somehow until now. Edwards had requested an exclusive interview with Roy if Roy decided to discuss the situation publicly. Roy had invited him to the press conference this morning but he had not come.

"That commentary from Edwards was actually kind compared to what others have said," Roy continued. "Some of the sports talk radio people are saying this is the result of me not being able to handle the pressure of the expectations this season. A few are quite seriously wondering whether I have a mental illness."

"It is interesting that Edwards did not mention the lawsuit. You had talked about that in your press conference, right?"

"The rush of emotions is starting to cloud my memory, but I am sure I did."

Not having a further response to how this impacted Roy's legal situation, for Will had no experience on something this high profile, he asked how Jenny was taking this.

"It's hard on her," Roy answered. "Earlier, she saw that bit about maybe this being her doing. Other members of the media have tried to bring her into it as well. Each time she hears her name, she withdraws into herself a bit. I wish I could protect her."

"When she greeted me, she seemed to be taking it well," Will offered.

"She's tough," Roy said and then paused. "She's really great." Will nodded.

"She is also hoping you will be able to fix all this," Roy continued with a bit of a grin. "The hope this can all be worked out is keeping her going."

"Yeah, uh, well ..." Will searched for a response.

"Don't worry," Roy saved him. "I am not expecting miracles from you. I am prepared for you to say there is nothing you can really do. Perhaps the situation does not need fixed."

Will was struck by Roy's attitude. He had realistic expectations *and* was content.

"That is a good attitude," Will responded.

"But I am still interested in what you can tell me about the lawsuit."

Will told Roy about the other athletes who had refused to play on certain days for religious reasons and also how none of their situations were quite like Roy's.

"So, you think the team's lawsuit has merit?" Roy asked. "Jenny is worried the team is going to take all our possessions, plus everything we would ever earn in the future."

"But you are not worried?"

"I would be lying if I said I was not a little worried."

"You are in a tough position legally speaking, but that does not mean the lawsuit necessarily has merit. Litigation is so unpredictable. A lot of it is about managing risk. I wish I could be more sure. I will tell you what I think, though. I think there is a reason the team sued you but did not publicize the lawsuit. Your contract has a specific procedure for the resolution of disputes between you and the team. The remedies in the contract appear to be exclusive."

"What does that mean?"

"It means if the team has a dispute with you, it needs to follow those procedures and not choose its own, such as filing a lawsuit against you in Iowa."

"The team has smart people on these legal issues. They have to know that. So why would they file the lawsuit?"

"I wonder if it was a scare tactic," Will offered.

"To get me to back down ..."

"It is possible."

"That would explain why they served it on Jenny rather than me. They wanted her to know about it."

"Yes, that would fit," Will replied. "The team may have sought to use her anxiety over the suit to put more pressure on you."

Will could tell Roy was trying to refrain from showing too much anger.

"Can we get a judge to dismiss the lawsuit then?" Roy asked.

"Perhaps. Again, I cannot guarantee anything. It is possible an Iowa judge who has never seen a Major League Baseball player's contract before will interpret the contract differently. Either way, it will take time." Will went on to explain the commissioner had certain powers that, if exercised, could cause the Iowa District Court to allow the lawsuit to continue, at least for the time being.

"The owner of the Hawks and the commissioner are reportedly good friends," Roy said.

"That could complicate matters," Will responded. "That said, the more likely scenario is that the team now realizes its strategy of scaring you and your wife by a lawsuit has failed. It may just drop the lawsuit and focus on the grievance procedures under the contract."

"If the team wins under those, what will happen?"

"The consequences could be similar: Loss of pay, return of signing bonus, et cetera. Forcing you to pay damages for things like lost ticket sales seems to me a lot less likely. On the other hand, the team may be able to keep you suspended without pay for the rest of your career, preventing you from signing with anyone else."

"It's doubtful any team would want a six-day-a-week player."

"That is probably true."

"So what are the chances we can convince the judge or arbitrator or whoever decides this that the team should allow me to play on every day but Sunday, with reduced pay."

Will detested this part of conversations with clients with bad cases. He was asking such clients to pay him lots of money only to reach an unpleasant end. There was value in honest advice, but clients often had a hard time seeing it.

Will looked at Roy and said with as much compassion as he could convey, "Under your contract, there is almost no chance."

"Almost!" Roy exclaimed with a smile. "That is better than zero chance. I thought you were going to say there was zero chance."

Will had not meant to create false hope. He wished he had said zero chance. But that would not have been truthful. As he had told Roy, litigation was unpredictable. Like life.

"One thing that will help me as your attorney is to know what you want out of all this. I cannot promise we will achieve them, but your goals will help determine our strategy. So what do you want the end result to be?"

Roy thought about it. It was the question he never had the chance to answer at the press conference. There were some obvious things—people acknowledging God, his wife happy, the team letting him go to church, and a good end to the lawsuit. But there was something more. The reporter who had asked whether he thought he was Chuck from *Amazing Grace and Chuck* had really been on to it. Roy did not know the movie, but the reporter's description seemed to fit, though Roy's motivations were different. This was not about a political point or national security. It was so much bigger. It affected everything.

Roy offered his answer, what he really wanted: "A return to the time when Sunday was set apart for church and family."

Will was confused. "What does that look like? A mandatory day of rest, with no work or play?"

"No," Roy immediately answered. "Church and family time often involves both work and play. I am not asking for a return of the Sabbath. I want the first day of the week, not the last. I want people to have the liberty to be in church and with their families on Sunday. I want those in professional sports and other industries who have taken Sundays from us to voluntarily cede it back, to lead in recognizing that money and entertainment is less important than our relationship with God."

Will nodded and considered what he had heard. "You want all of baseball—and football, and whatever else—to stop playing on Sundays, so that the players are free and the fans are not distracted by it?"

"Yes."

"You know that will never happen," Will protested in an attempt to get his client to reduce his unachievable goal. "I mean, think about football. The National Football League would go out of business. And golf. All the PGA tournaments end with a round on Sunday."

"They could change their businesses," Roy countered.

"That will never happen," Will repeated.

"None of us knows what will happen other than what the Bible tells us will happen. It is up to us to do our part, giving our best, for God and not for ourselves. And, even if it does not happen, it will have been worth trying."

Will had no response.

24.

It took Jenny, Ashley, and the kids a couple of hours to get back from lunch. During that time, Roy's agent called. "The team has formally suspended you, without pay," he told Roy. He made sure to emphasize "without pay." It impacted the agent's commission.

"Okay," Roy said. "Is there anything you can do to help me?"

"Yes," the agent replied. "I can give you this advice—Prove those who are calling you mentally ill wrong by telling the team you are sorry, this will never happen again, and you will dedicate yourself to bringing a World Series title to Indianapolis."

"Thanks," Roy replied with sarcasm. "You are a lot of help."

"I *am* helping you, Roy." Roy sensed the bitterness in his voice. They hung up.

Roy turned the TV volume back up. The anchor announced that the Hawks had just issued a statement. He read it: "The Indianapolis Hawks today suspended without pay center fielder Roy Adams for his refusal to play baseball and participate in team activities, as required in his and every other Major League Baseball player's contract. We attempted to work with Roy to satisfy his concerns, including offering him special accommodations. He refused those efforts. The entire Indianapolis Hawks organization remains concerned for Roy's well being. We remain ready to assist him in whatever way possible to get him the help he needs. In the meantime, our team must continue preparing for the season. We are prepared to play it without Roy."

Roy turned down the volume. "Wow," he whispered.

"What accommodations are they talking about?" Will asked.

"I don't know, unless it is Malik's suggestion of having a team chapel service."

"That did not interest you?"

Roy stared at Will. "Team chapel is not church." Will nodded his understanding. Roy was not certain he really understood, but he appreciated his lawyer's willingness to try. He also wondered how many times people could call him crazy before he started to believe that he was.

"Any suggestions?" he asked Will.

"We should find out what the players' union thinks. Who is the union representative on your team?"

The representative was one of the veteran relief pitchers. Roy could not remember if he was scheduled to pitch in today's game. Even if he was not, he was probably in the dugout or doing some running and so Roy would not be able to immediately reach him. Roy sent him a text message to call him when he could. He also tracked down the phone number of a union employee involved in player-team disputes. He called her, but the employee did not answer. Roy left her a message.

Soon after, Jenny and Ashley returned with the kids.

Will suggested there was nothing else to do until they heard back from the union on how it would help. Roy thanked him for coming and then drove them to the hotel a few blocks away.

~~~~~

Will watched his kids run in the room and jump on the bed. They were, to say the least, excited to be here. He smiled at their joy. He saw Ashley smiling, too.

"How was your time with Jenny?" he asked her.

"Jenny is great!" she replied. "She is so nice, down to earth, and easy to talk with. I think we could be great friends if we had the chance. She probably already has a lot of close friends, though."

"What did you two talk about?"

"A little about Iowa. She grew up in Jones County. Until she was about in high school, she thought Cedar Rapids was a *really* big city."

"That's funny."

"We also talked about kids. She wants them, though it sounded like she wanted to wait a bit, spending more time enjoying being married without them. Our kids were a little bouncy at the restaurant. I hope they did not scare her off."

"Did you discuss the case at all?"

"A little. It seemed like she wanted to avoid that topic. I think it worries her. I hope you are able to help them."

"That is not going to be easy."

Will saw Ashley look at him sympathetically. She hardly understood what he did as an attorney, and he knew it was hard on her when his thoughts continually drifted to his job, but she so often seemed more concerned about the stresses he faced than her own. He felt undeserved of her patience.

Allie, their oldest, bounced off one of the beds in the three-room suite and came up to them. "So what are we going to do?" she asked. "Are you going to have to work the whole time we are here Dad?"

"Not the whole time," Will answered and then thought he better add a qualification. "I hope."

"How much will you have to work?" she asked.

"There is something I need to do that will take up a good part of tomorrow. And then I also need to be on-call for the client, Roy Adams, who brought us here. I will probably have to meet with him a few more times. We are waiting to hear back from someone."

"So what should we do first?" she asked enthusiastically.

"Let's check out the visitors' guide the hotel has. Maybe there is something close by we can do until supper."

~~~~~

Roy returned to his apartment. "Is he going to be able to help?" Jenny asked him.

"Depends on what you mean by help. He thinks the lawsuit is improper, but can't guarantee anything about it." He also explained to her the lawyer's comments about the team having other procedures that could keep him out of baseball and unpaid, and how they were waiting to hear back from the players' union.

"So for now we just wait?"

"Yeah."

"That is hard."

"I know." A thought came that would have been foreign to him a year ago. "We could spend some time praying."

Jenny did not respond immediately. Finally, she said, "Yeah, okay."

Praying together was not something they had done much since becoming Christians last fall. Since then, Roy had learned enough from Pastor Nate Sanders to know that the Bible was the way God communicated to them and prayer was the way they communicated to God. Still, it did not come natural to him, especially when he prayed with someone else. Nevertheless, he knew he needed to make it a more consistent part of his life.

Roy kneeled down in front of their couch. Jenny joined him. Roy prayed first, holding Jenny's hand. He thanked God for his salvation, asked Him for wisdom, and asked Him for peace no matter what happened. He stumbled through a few other requests. After a few minutes, he concluded, "In Jesus' name, Amen."

Roy continued to hold Jenny's hand. She did not speak. "Is there anything you want to add to the prayer?" he asked her.

She opened her eyes. "No, not right now."

"Okay," Roy replied.

They got up. Jenny shuffled off without a further word. Roy watched her open the door to the outside deck. As she stepped outside, she left the door open, closing just the screen. He saw her sit in a chair. Then he heard what sounded like yelling, but from some distance away. Jenny got up and walked inside. "I think I will lie down in our bed for a bit." She headed to their bedroom. Roy walked to the screen door and peeked outside. There were several people gathered on the sidewalk on the opposite side of the street below. They were looking up toward Roy's apartment. It took Roy a moment to realize they were yelling at him. Somehow they had found out Roy lived in this building and they had come to heckle him.

He closed the screen door so they could not see him again, but he stood there listening for a minute. They swore at him, mocking his faith, mental health, and baseball ability. These same people had probably cheered for him a couple of days ago. Now they would actually spend time standing outside his home yelling at him because he would not play a game. He felt both anger and pity toward them. He was tempted to walk down and argue with them, but realized that would not result in anything good. Roy closed the door, blocking out the remaining taunts.

He picked up his phone. There were more missed calls and text messages than he wanted to wade through. Lots of reporters had been trying to contact him for comment.

He pulled up the news. Within the last hour, the commissioner's office had issued a statement. The commissioner was continuing to investigate the situation, but based on preliminary information it supported the Hawks' decision to suspend Roy without pay. That was not surprising. The commissioner, after all, was an employee of the owners. Plus, there was the issue of Reinhold and the commissioner being friends.

What was more troubling was that, according to the statement, the commissioner was also considering actions he could take against Roy for Roy's harm to the game of baseball. The commissioner viewed Roy's conduct as undermining the financial integrity of the game and as a direct attack on baseball's long-standing tradition of upstanding, family-friendly entertainment available on all days of the week during summer months. The commissioner would reserve full judgment, though, until after receiving all the facts.

He realized he should go through his text messages and missed calls to see if anyone from the union had tried to reach him. It took him twenty minutes, slowed down by additional messages that came in, before he determined the union had not responded.

John Reinhold and the commissioner were buddies, but it was open knowledge the president of the Players' Association and the commissioner were on unfriendly terms. They rarely agreed. They often found ways to annoy each other. The lack of friendliness between two seemed likely to help Roy now. He was thankful for that, but he also felt guilty for being thankful two men despised each other.

25.

There had been no call from the union. It would never come. Disruptive events can make enemies into friends.

Roy had the TV on mute, but saw the banner at the bottom of the screen. It read, "PLAYERS' UNION HEAD SPEAKS ABOUT ADAMS."

Roy turned the volume up. The screen split between the anchor and the president of the players' union.

"Does this mean the union will not be supporting one of its players?" Roy heard the anchor ask.

The union president responded, "Like the commissioner, we are still gathering all the facts, and will reserve full judgment until that is done. However, Mr. Adams cannot consider himself one of our players if he chooses to intentionally violate his contract with his team."

"Do you believe Adams intentionally violated his contract?"

"Based on Adams' own statements this morning, that appears to be the case."

"So, just to be clear on this, if everything is as it appears to be, the union will not be supporting Adams in any grievance or arbitration process?"

"That is correct. We intend to convey to Mr. Adams that we are here to assist him get back on the field in a full-time capacity. However, if he chooses to continue to violate his obligations to his team, he is on his own. We support the game of baseball and we support players, not deserters. Mr. Adams' apparent actions are a betrayal to all other players, and to the game itself."

"What is the union doing to reach out to Adams?"

"What I have said so far is really all I am prepared to comment on right now. I will just reiterate that the Players' Association is committed to building up the game of baseball. It does that by being advocates for players. If Mr. Adams wants to be a baseball player again, we will work with him."

The anchor thanked the union president for his time and ended the interview. He then brought in Preston Edwards via satellite link to comment on the union's position. Edwards explained that the union could not support Adams if it wanted to support all other players. If it were to request Adams be allowed to play less for lesser pay, it would open itself up to having to advocate for all sorts of special requests, which could only cause fan antagonism toward the players, as well as less money for them.

Roy turned the TV off. He was alone. *No, that was not true.* There were a lot of people who would support him: His wife, his pastor, and his church, among them. And there would be fans who would understand his motivations. It was just that many who had supported him in the past, people he had developed close relationships with, were now abandoning him. He did feel bad for involving the lawyer, who would now be known as the lawyer for the most unpopular baseball player in the world.

Roy walked back to the bedroom to tell Jenny the news about the union. She walked out of the room and met him in the hall. Her cell phone was in her hand. Before he could say anything, she said, "My dad is on the phone. He wants to know if he can talk to you."

Roy gave her a quizzical look, but not wanting to keep his father-in-law waiting he immediately took the phone. "Hello sir," he said.

The man on the other end said, "Roy, I gotta say I wish you would have told me about your plans. I could have helped you through them."

"Yes sir. Things have happened fast."

"That's what I mean. You have let things get out of hand. It is time to slow things down."

"How so?" Roy asked.

"I am concerned you have not thought through the consequences of your actions." Roy was starting to realize that was the sort of thing people said when they did not agree with him. His father-in-law continued, "I am even more concerned about my daughter. You are putting her through stress she does not deserve, that she did not sign up for when she married you. And if you continue down this road, how do you plan to provide for her? You think you are going to be ostracized from just baseball? You are setting you and Jenny up to be ostracized from all sorts of business and people."

Roy was shaking. He mustered all the calmness he could and replied, "I am certain I am making the right decision. You know I love Jenny, sir. I will always provide for her. I know God will provide for us."

"Roy, listen to me!" Jenny's father's voice continued to get more forceful and loud. "Stop this *now!*"

His shaking would not stop. Roy was sure it showed in his voice when he calmly replied, "No sir. I cannot."

Roy heard the phone on the other end disconnect. He pulled Jenny's phone away from his ear and looked at it, confirming his father-in-law had hung up on him. Roy had never had an open disagreement with him.

Roy looked at Jenny. She was crying. "You gave me your phone so your father could scold me," he said to her in a voice louder than he had used with her father.

"I didn't know what he was going to say!" she pleaded.

"You may not have known exactly what he was going to say, but you knew he was just going to criticize me!" Roy yelled back.

Jenny cried harder and ran away from him, into their bedroom. She slammed the door shut.

A lot of people said the first couple of years of marriage were the hardest. Roy had no idea what they were talking about. He and Jenny had almost no problems, were happy, agreed on just about everything, and hardly ever fought. He could not remember the last time he raised his voice to her. He was ashamed he had just done so. At the same time, he allowed his anger over the call from her father to prevent him from asking for her forgiveness. He told himself she was probably not in the mood to receive it anyway.

Roy took out his own phone and hit the number he had recently added to his favorites.

~~~~~

Will watched his wife take a stroke with her putter as he said into his cell phone, "Yeah, sure, we will make it. Are you sure you want us to bring our kids? ... Yeah, I am sure they would love to play some new video games. ... Okay, we will see you around five."

Will disconnected the call and put his phone back in his pocket. His wife's golf ball had entered a miniature castle and she had hopped around to the other side to see which of three holes it would exit. On the hole ahead, Will's three kids were breaking all the rules, such as they were, of miniature golf. They laughed at the obstacles, but used their putters as hockey sticks, guiding the ball into and away from the obstacles, depending on what struck their fancy. Will loved listening to them laugh at themselves making up their own fun together.

Ashley watched her ball come out of one of the castle gates and asked, "So your new client needs to see you right away?"

"Soon," Will answered. "He invited us all to come to his place for supper, though. It won't be fancy. He is ordering something in."

"He remembers we have three kids, right? Are you sure it would not be better if I took them and found something else to do?"

"Roy said 'no,' that everyone should come. He has a game room. Ping pong table, air hockey, foosball, video games, even a couple of old arcade games. The kids can take their food in there and eat and play while we sit at the adult table."

Ashley smiled. "I like this client. I have never been involved in your work before."

"Yes, this is definitely different. And I like having you around when I work."

"Maybe after I finish beating you in this round of miniature golf, I'll take you down in foosball."

"We'll see about that," Will said as he took a stroke with his putter and watched his ball go inside the mouth of a fake hippopotamus and spit back out at him.

~~~~~

Roy and Jenny had not made up as they sat with Will and Ashley eating pizza. Jenny had not come out of their bedroom until their guests arrived, at which point she put on a happy face. Roy knew she was not happy. Her self-exclusion meant Roy had been responsible for supper. Not knowing what kind of pizza his lawyer and his family liked, he ordered enough kinds no one could be disappointed, which meant there was enough to feed all of them for about a week.

As they ate, Roy explained the statement from the commissioner's office and the interview with the president of the Players' Association. Just before Will and Ashley and the kids arrived, Roy had also received a text message from the Hawks' representative to the union. The relief pitcher said he was not in a position to help Roy.

As a result of the call from her father and the subsequent verbal fight, Jenny had not yet heard any of this. She sat silent. Roy sensed she wanted to say something as he explained these developments, but that she did not want to give away to their guests that she was not on speaking terms with her husband. In fact, it appeared she was not on speaking terms with the world, for she had hardly said anything to Will and Ashley or their kids since they arrived. Roy wondered if they noticed. They had to, given how cheerful Jenny had been to Ashley and the kids earlier.

"So it appears we are not going to get outside help," Roy concluded. "I was wondering what your thoughts might be on what can be done from here," he asked his lawyer. "If anything," he added, not wanting to place undue expectations on what Will could offer.

"To be honest, it is disappointing your union is apparently taking the owners' side in this already. This would have been better with its help. I could look into whether your rights as a union member could force its assistance."

"It's okay really. I do not want the help of people who do not want to help."

Will nodded and Roy continued, "I do not want you to take this the wrong way, but that goes for you as well. This has to be more than what you thought coming in. If representing me no longer interests you, I will not be hurt if you tell me that."

"The thought never crossed my mind," Will responded immediately. Roy was relieved and hoped Will had meant it. He seemed to.

"Thanks," Roy said.

The lawyer continued, "I do not know how this will all end. We will dispute the lawsuit as we discussed before. We may or may not get it dismissed. If it is not dismissed, we will proceed to defend against it. We can also initiate procedures under baseball's grievance process to try to get the suspension overturned and your pay reinstated, at least partially. As I said before, I think the team has a good legal position, so unless it softens up for other reasons, our chance of success is low. You should be prepared for all of this to take a long time. And we might want to hire a public relations firm. Fan support might be our only hope."

Roy thought about what Will said. Everyone was picking at their pizza, but not eating it. The only sounds came from the other side of the apartment where the kids were running around the game room. He remembered the hecklers that had stood on the street below his apartment that afternoon. There will not be enough fans to support me, he thought. They like Sunday baseball. They have shown that for a hundred years. He could fight this, fight for their support, but how long would that take?

"I can't have this go on a long time," Roy finally said out loud. He looked at Jenny, who was looking down at her plate. "We can't."

"I understand," Will said. "Litigation is hard and life interrupting." Roy could tell Will was looking for the right words to express sympathy.

"It is not just the litigation," Roy said. "If it was just that, I might be willing to go through it. But this will play out in the public. ... There has to be some way to end this quickly."

At this, Jenny looked up and spoke. "There is only one way and that is for you to play." Jenny looked back down at her plate. Roy could not tell if playing was what she really wanted him to do.

After a moment, Will said, "There is another way." They all turned their eyes on him.

"What is it?" Roy asked.

"Retire."

"Retire?" Roy asked.

"He means quit baseball," Jenny answered.

"I know what he means. I just ... I don't know. It seems so final and drastic. How would it work?"

"You provide written notification to the team of your intention to retire," Will answered. "The team then has to place you on the Voluntary Retired List. It ends your contract, meaning you no longer have to meet the team's expectations and it no longer has to pay you. The team gets to use your roster spot on someone else. You are prevented from playing baseball for anyone else, at least in the United States, without applying for reinstatement. In essence, you announce your career as a professional baseball player is over. There won't be a grievance process and the team will have nothing left to fight over in the lawsuit, if it ever meant to do anything other than scare you with it."

As he listened to Will, Roy began to imagine his life without playing baseball. He did not need baseball, he told himself. It struck him as absurd that he had spent so much of his life thinking he would be incomplete without baseball. Will was right. He had been trying to hang on to baseball on his own terms. There was no way the other people associated with the game would allow him to do that. He had no right to expect they would. Yes, he could leave the game. Isn't that what he had been doing anyway?

Jenny's voice broke Roy's thoughts. "You are considering it, aren't you? You are considering quitting. I cannot believe you would just walk away from what you have always wanted and worked for."

Roy did not reply. He watched her get up from her chair and walk the short distance to the kitchen, which was separated from where they were eating by an open window, so he could still see her when he shifted in his chair. She got out a pitcher of water from the refrigerator, pulled a glass down from the cupboard, and filled it, even though she had a beverage at the dinner table.

Roy turned back around. That was the influence of her father, he thought. His words—whatever he had said before she handed Roy her phone with him on the line—were still fresh in her mind. Her feelings would pass. She would see there was so much more to their marriage than baseball. She had loved him before she had even known much about the game. As his guests took small bites of their food, Roy returned his thoughts to retirement. He did not know what he would do if he did not play baseball. Few players did. But he knew lots of people did lots of different things. It could not be that playing a game was his only option. It could not be that he was defined by the game. God would provide for them and they would be happy because they loved God and loved each other.

Jenny remained in the kitchen. Ashley got up and joined her in there.

"You really think retiring would end all the legal stuff?" Roy asked Will.

"I do," Will answered. "Actually, it probably will not be long before it ends all the media stuff as well. Fans and media are fickle. As long as you are a suspended player who may return, you will remain on their minds. If you retire and disappear from the game, they will soon start talking about something else. There is always something else to talk about."

"And all I have to do is give the team written notification I am retiring?"

"Yes."

Roy then heard Jenny raise her voice in the kitchen. It was directed toward Ashley and it was harsh. "You don't know anything about me and you are telling me what I should do? You try having your own husband turn every-thing you know and expect upside down!"

Ashley responded in a lower voice, "You were so kind earlier. Selfishness is less becoming on you."

Jenny turned out of the kitchen and again shut herself in the bedroom.

Roy and Will stood. Ashley walked back toward them. Roy had never seen someone criticize his wife. It hurt him. "Please," he said to Ashley, "what you saw out of her earlier today was real. This is hard for her, as it would be for anyone."

"I am sorry," Ashley said. "I was trying to help. I should not have said anything."

"We should go," Will said.

Ashley nodded. "I'll get the kids." She left them to go end the kids' fun in the game room.

"You have a lot to think about," Will said to Roy.

"I am not sure I do," Roy replied.

Will tightened his lips and nodded in understanding.

Roy felt bad for how awkward things now were between them all. He had to defend his wife, though. Will's wife really should have just left her alone.

Will's three kids came groaning down the hall, though they quieted as they reached Roy. Ashley followed behind them.

"Call me if you need anything else," Will said to Roy as they headed out the door.

"I will."

"And let me know once you have made a decision."

"I will."

26.

Will got his family to their rental car. They had nibbled, but had not really eaten. The kids had been too busy exploring the game room and he and Ashley had been too busy talking with Roy and Jenny. As the kids acted wound up in the back seat and he and Ashley sat silent in the front, he drove them to a restaurant with a bakery. He ordered dessert for them all and put his kids in a separate booth.

"So, what did you say to her?" Will asked Ashley out of earshot of their kids. As he spoke, he could not prevent a grin coming from his face. He had never seen his wife say something to cause someone else to storm off. Away from the scene, the awkwardness had turned to comedy in his mind, despite the apparent damage to his relationship with his client. Ashley's ears turned red when she got excited. One was still pink. They both started to redden again.

"First, I just asked her if she was okay."

"Was she?"

"No! But she said she was."

"But what did you say to her to cause her to get so upset?"

"She shouldn't have gotten so upset."

"Undoubtedly."

"I mean it!"

"I actually cannot imagine you saying anything to cause someone to get so upset."

"Don't be sarcastic."

Will gave a mock look of hurt, then laughed. His wife was so worked up she had lost all ability to read him. "I meant that," he said. "Seriously."

"Okay, well, she should not have gotten so upset. There must be something else going on or something wrong with her."

"But what did you say?"

Ashley blushed. Her cheeks were red now. "I suggested to her that her husband needed her support. I said even if he decides to quit baseball in order to be a squirrel trainer, her life would end up happiest supporting him."

"You did not!"

"I did! I was trying to be helpful, to say something profound with a little humor."

"She obviously didn't think it was funny."

"Or profound."

"What made you say that?" Will asked her.

"She needed it, though something is preventing her from seeing it. If she does not support Roy now, he will either stop trying to do what is best for them or he will keep trying and they will live in continual conflict. Either way, he will resent her and she will be bitter toward him."

"Where did you learn that?"

"My mom."

Will smiled at his wife. "What?" she asked.

"So if I decided to quit my law practice, sell our house, and move us to wherever it is people learn how to train squirrels from master squirrel trainers, would you follow and support me?"

Ashley laughed. "It sounds like a fabulous life! When do we go?" And she laughed some more.

Will stared at her in amazement. "You really would, wouldn't you?"

She stopped laughing and simply smiled at him. "I would," she said.

He knew she was telling the truth. It puzzled him how he had ended up with a wife who loved him so much. He felt so unworthy of her devotion.

He loved her, but how did he show her that love? He bought her things—clothes and shoes when she wanted them, something for the house, gadgets, dinners where she did not have cook; on this night, a milkshake. But Will knew those were not the things she really wanted. It was not things that made her feel loved. She wanted his attention, the one thing he was truly terrible at giving.

Will sat across from his wife with a desire to tell her he was sorry and that he would be a better husband. He *was* sorry, but he was not sure he would ever be a better husband, the husband she really deserved, so he kept silent, lest he promise something he failed to deliver. She was happy in this moment, anyway, Will told himself, as they spent a long time eating their desserts and talking.

~~~~~

Roy knocked on the bedroom door. It had been two hours since the Jacobsons left and Jenny still had not come out. There was a bathroom connected to the room, so there was no need for her to leave.

"What?" came the reply on the other side. She said it in a tone that indicated she still wanted Roy to leave her alone, but he had to talk to her.

"Can I come in?"

"It's your room, too," she answered.

Roy opened the door. Jenny was walking back to the closet. On the bed was a small bag. Jenny had started to put clothes in it. He ignored the bag for the moment. "There are a couple of things I need to tell you."

"What are they?" she asked without looking at him.

"First, I am sorry."

She looked at him. "For what?" she demanded to know.

"For yelling at you. I should not have accused you of turning your father on me and I should not have raised my voice at you. That was wrong of me. I am sorry."

"Oh. That's fine. It was just part of the craziness of the day." Her tone said something different than her words.

"It's *not* fine," Roy said back. "I should not have done that. I hope you will forgive me for it."

"I forgive you," she replied. "What is the other thing?"

"I emailed the front office staff, Earl, and my agent. Just now. I told them I was retiring. I have retired from professional baseball."

She nodded and then moved to continue packing. "That is what this was always heading to. We should have recognized that earlier. We should not have gotten our hopes up that the team would ever allow you to be part-time. It is probably for the best."

"It is for the best," Roy tried to say convincingly. Then he asked, "What are you doing?"

"I am flying back to Iowa early tomorrow morning."

"Why?"

"I will get out of your way. You can finish up what you need to with the lawyer and with the team and getting us out of this lease and selling the stuff in here. Everything. I will just be out of the way. Plus, I need to think about some things. I will stay with my parents."

"What do you mean you need to think about some things? And you would not be in the way. I would rather have you here. I need you here. Please don't leave because I got upset at you. I really am sorry about that."

"I know you are," Jenny replied, now with some sympathy. "It's not that."

"What is it then?" Roy asked.

"It is everything. Our lives. What each of us is going to do now."

"We can figure that out together."

Jenny shook her head. "You need to figure things out. It is better if you do that without me. Dad said I could come live with him and Mom for awhile. I could work for him in the farming operation. He needs help with the planting and the bookkeeping."

Roy realized Jenny's dad was offering her a way out of a life with Roy, now that Roy had chosen a life outside of baseball. It was not the baseball her dad loved. It was the knowledge his girl was married to someone kind, respectable, rich, famous, and universally loved. *Kind* was proving to be the least important of those characteristics, or at least insufficient without some of the others. Roy was certain Jenny's dad knew what he was doing in offering this to her. Did Jenny see her dad's plan?

"How long?" he asked her.

"I don't know," she answered.

"I will be back in Cedar Rapids soon," he said.

"Okay."

Roy walked out of the bedroom. He had nowhere to go. He could drive around, but getting out of his vehicle would risk someone recognizing him and he did not know the reaction he would receive. He turned the lights off and laid down on his couch. He left the TV on mostly for the glare. He pulled out his cell phone and sent a text message to Will—"It's done. I am retired from baseball. Let me know once you find out what the team will do with the lawsuit." He then turned off the phone and spent most of the rest of the night staring at the ceiling. He did not know what time he finally fell asleep, but when he awoke early in the morning, Jenny had already slipped out on her way to the airport.

27.

Will drove north toward North Phoenix Baptist College. He pulled out his cell phone and called Roy. Roy answered and Will said, "I wanted to let you know I got your text last night. I certainly understand your decision."

"Thanks," Roy responded.

"I think the team will drop its lawsuit. I will try to reach its lawyers to see what the team intends to do. I will let you know as soon as I know anything about that."

Again Roy thanked Will.

"What do you plan to do today?" Will asked.

"Jenny left to go back to Iowa this morning," he said.

"I see. Do you intend to go back to Iowa soon?"

"I am driving to the airport right now," Roy answered. "There is nothing for me here. I will stay there until I get a flight back to Iowa."

Will started to say "good luck," but caught himself. Did someone as dedicated to his faith as Roy believe in "luck"? So he said "Godspeed" instead. *Was that the right thing to say?* It came out awkwardly, at least in Will's mind.

Roy again said, "Thanks," but distantly.

Will wanted to tell him he thought he was making the right decision for himself and he admired him and his convictions. It was true. Will felt he believed certain things as much as Roy, though he had never acted on them like Roy had. But his client was distracted right now and Will was not confident Roy would think much of compliments from him. So Will ended the conversation with, "Okay, I will be in touch. You can always contact me with questions."

After disconnecting the call, Will made himself focus his attention on what he had set out to do today. He had managed to have breakfast with his family this morning, which was rare. The hotel they were at opened its restaurant for breakfast and served meals to order. His kids were so surprised at having their dad eat breakfast with them, and even seeming him in no particular hurry, they sat quiet for some time. Eventually Allie, the oldest, started talking. The younger two soon followed, so that for the final forty-five minutes of their meal together there was hardly a moment when at least two of them were not trying to talk to him at once. It occurred to Will he may have learned more about his children at breakfast that morning than he had learned in the past year.

That is a problem, he thought. *I need to fix it. But how?*

He would not fix it today, for after breakfast he convinced his family to spend time at a mall so he could come up to this college. He wanted to see what it could tell him about the lawsuit in which his client was trying to kick a church and its pastor out of the property they used, property in which the church had always been.

As a result of reading through its website, Will knew a number of things about the college before he arrived that morning. The college had opened just fifteen years ago. Pastor Nate Sanders had been part of its second class. It had grown some. To meet that growth, it was starting to build a new academic hall and add onto a residential hall. There were no large endowments or benefactors, so the project was moving along slowly. The campus otherwise consisted of a small set of connected buildings that had once housed an alternative school for troubled students. The public school system that had run the school closed it five years before the sale to the new Bible college. The school's closing had followed a drug ring scandal involving both teachers and students. The scandal negatively stigmatized the school. Given that enrollment had been declining to that point anyway, it was an easy decision for the district to simply close the school. It did so without a plan or buyer for the buildings. The new college came along and proposed to rent the deteriorating and unfashionable buildings for the cost of their maintenance. In counter, the school district said the newly incorporated college could become the owner of the campus for the nominal price of one dollar. The college's founders saw a miracle in receiving property no one wanted.

Will figured his first and perhaps only stop would be the college library. He hoped the library would have historical information about the college and its students, as short as that history was. He thought going through those reference materials would be the least intrusive means of finding more out about Nate Sanders and George Bannon.

Will pulled off the highway, turned east, and quickly saw a small sign pointing the way to the college. At the entrance to the drive leading to the campus were two poles with flags at the top, one a United States flag. The other one Will did not recognize, though it appeared to have some Christian symbols. Perhaps it was the banner of the college.

The driveway leading to the buildings was about five hundred feet long. Will looked for a sign saying which building was the library, but he did not see one. At what looked to be the main academic building was a sign that said simply, "Main Hall." He would ask someone in there.

After parking in the nearby lot, he walked across the drive and up ten steps that led to the double doors of the Main Hall. Inside there was, appropriately enough, a main hall with closed rooms on each side until an exit on the other end.

It was a dimly lit and uninviting hall. The designers designed this for function and not aesthetics, Will thought, though we often miss the beauty in function.

The first door on the left had a sign above it that said "ADMISSIONS." The sign above the first door on the right said "GENERAL OFFICE." Will chose the general office.

As he turned to his right and put his hand on the doorknob, Will realized he might need a story if asked why he wanted the location of the school's library. Before arriving, he assumed he could just walk into the library, which would be its own building. That he had not found a building marked "Library" started him wondering whether the school restricted library access to students and staff.

Will's imagination failed him. He found himself unable to quickly concoct a false but plausible story for his snooping, and then realized he was ridiculous for trying. Why would he lie, especially on something so minor, and inside of a Bible college no less? What was wrong with the real story? The worst that could happen is the college would refuse his request. What was so bad about that?

Will opened the door and walked in. Inside the room, there was a long counter. Behind that was a desk, behind

210 · Jason M. Steffens

which sat a woman, about 50-years-old, with long, graying, brown hair. She looked up and smiled at Will. She got up from her desk and came up to the counter. "How can I help you?" she asked pleasantly.

"I came to do a little research," Will replied. He would reveal more if she asked him. "I was hoping you could tell me where your library is. I did not see it when I drove in."

"That is because there is not much to see, at least not yet. Come on, I will show you where it is." She started to step around from the counter.

"That is okay. If you just tell me which building it is, I am sure I can find it without taking you away from your job."

"My job is to help the people that come in here. Plus, our library is not a building." She continued around the counter and started out the door before Will could reply further. "Don't worry. It won't take me long to show you."

She exited the door. Will followed her out. She turned to her right, walked twenty-five feet, and stopped at the very next door. Above it was a sign reading "LIBRARY".

The woman opened the door and announced in a loud voice, "Charles! You have a patron."

Will walked in behind her and saw a desk to the right with an empty chair behind it. To the left were four rows of free-standing bookshelves eight feet high and about thirty feet in length. There were also shelves attached to each of the walls of the room. From behind the second free-standing shelf from the entrance, the man who must have been Charles appeared. Charles looked to be about eighty. He was tall and had thin-white hair. "Welcome!" he said. He also made no attempt to quiet his voice. Voice control was not a feature of this library, Will thought.

The woman, whose name remained unknown to Will, looked at him again and said, "The president of the college loves libraries, so he put the college's library next to his office." Will surmised that the president's office must have been in an adjoining room of the General Office, the place they had just come from. "Charles here is our head librarian. He can help you find what you need."

"Head librarian, yes," the man said. "Also, the only librarian. Someday maybe they'll even pay me."

"You know your problem there, Charles. You love what you do so much that if it came down to it I think you might pay the college to keep doing this job. You don't have any negotiating power."

Charles smiled as if the woman had just proclaimed an open secret. Having accomplished her task, she walked back out the door.

"So, what can I help you find?" Charles asked Will.

"I am doing some research on the history of the college."

"That should be easy enough. It's not a long history. How far back do you want to go?"

"The beginning."

"All the way back there, eh?" Charles asked in a good-natured, sarcastic manner. "Follow me."

As Will followed Charles behind the last shelf, he decided to continue in conversation. "So how long have you been head librarian?"

"Since the college was opened."

"Has the library always been in this room? I expected it to have its own building."

"Yes, always in here. The college does continue to grow, though, and we hope to at least have a bigger room, with more books, someday soon. It is not cheap building a good library. But it is better to have this than no library at all. The next trick is to increase the number of students who check out and read the books."

"I figured that would be more common at a Baptist college."

"Why is that?"

"I don't know. Less television or something, I guess."

"There actually is *no* television in the dorms, but our students really are not all that different from students on any other campus when it comes to reading. They think reading textbooks takes care of their self-assigned quota, that they do not need to read other types of books. They don't see that the amount of time they have for reading will never be greater than it is while they are in college, at least until their own kids are out of the home and they reach retirement age. Their lack of reading good books shows in their writing."

Will liked Charles. He was clearly still sharp. Loving books and writing, requiring the exercise of his mind, had to have something to do with that.

"I know what you mean. Most lawyers can't write very well either."

Charles had reached the end of the bookshelf. He pointed to a row of books. "Each year, the college's media students produce a yearbook and the administrative staff produces an annual report. Here is that collection. That is about all there is to the written history of the college. Maybe someday I will write one."

Will thanked him. Without anything further to say, Charles nodded and sauntered back toward what he had been doing before Will arrived.

Will took the first annual report. It had been completed after the end of the first school year. It was thin. There was a description of how the college came into existence, some limited financial information, and a page listing the staff and mostly adjunct faculty, followed by a few pages of biographical information about them. The president of the college was Dan James. He had brought his family here to help start the college after having been a Vice President of a larger Baptist college in North Carolina.

The first class had thirty-five students. The report did not say much about them. Will picked up the first yearbook. He quickly found George Bannon's photo. Bannon had been elected student body president.

Will grabbed the second yearbook. The second incoming class had just thirty students. The college did not exactly experience immediate growth. Will found Nate Sanders' picture. He had entered a year after Bannon. With just fifty-nine total students (apparently six from the first class did not come back for a second year), they must have had classes together, but there was nothing in the first two yearbooks that provided any clues to their interactions.

A glance at the third yearbook showed that Bannon was still student body president, but nothing else was significant.

By the fourth yearbook, the college's growth had begun. The incoming class was up to one hundred students. The incomers—if they were allowed to vote—must have been as impressed with Bannon as everyone else had been. Four-time student body president had to have been a rare achievement in the history of American higher education. This yearbook had two full pages dedicated to Bannon and his tenure. He had done quite a bit to help the college grow through various recruitment initiatives designed and implemented by him. He also finished as valedictorian of his class and was voted "most likely to succeed in the ministry."

He was unequivocally the college's star. It was a little hard to believe looking at him now, but he was even the college's best basketball player, though the team had little success.

Following the two pages of dedication to Bannon, there was a black-and-white photograph of him and a young woman, their faces filling most of the page. The look on Bannon's face was one of forced sophistication. The woman's face bore a cheerful, affecting smile. Beneath the photograph was a caption that read: "Senior George Bannon and Sophomore Tara James led a team of students on a short-term missions trip to Caborca, Mexico." James was the last name of the president. Perhaps she was his daughter or niece.

The yearbooks were getting thicker. Everyone seemingly received at least a couple of mentions. But again there was nothing about Nate Sanders, now a junior, other than his profile photo. It was as if he did not do anything but register for the classes and show up for picture day. That was hard to believe. Will looked back at the masthead. It listed just one editor: George Bannon.

Will was about to reach for the fifth yearbook when he heard a voice that caused his heart to jump. "What kind of case are you working on anyway?"

Will turned his head and saw Charles coming down the row. His voice had boomed in the small library, which was apparently still unoccupied except for the two of them.

Will did not immediately know what to say. What came out was that paragon of intelligent questioning he so often heard out of his children. "Huh?"

"You said you were a lawyer," Charles explained, "and had research to do. I figured you were working on a case. Can't imagine there would be too much of an exciting case involving this college, but I guess you never can tell."

Will silently scolded himself for having mentioned anything about being a lawyer, but Charles might have some more information. He measured his replied. "I cannot talk about it too much for confidentiality reasons, but yes I am doing some research for a case. It doesn't have to do with the college, except a couple of the people involved once attended here. They are not the parties, but they are witnesses."

"Oh, what are their names?"

Will hesitated, but came back to the attitude he had just before entering the general office. The librarian might be able to help. Truth and openness was best. "George Bannon and Nate Sanders," he answered. "Do you remember them?"

Charles smiled. "They are battling it out again, eh?"

Again? What did he mean by that?

"Well, as I said, they are not the parties, but they might as well be, and they are definitely not on the same side." Will reasoned he was not revealing anything Charles could not find out from public records. "Have they disputed with each other before?"

Charles ignored Will's question. "Where did you say you were from?"

"I actually had not said where I was from, but I am from Cedar Rapids, Iowa."

"You came all the way here to do research in our library for this case?"

"No. I never would have come if I had not been in the area for an entirely different case. But what was it you said about them battling again?"

Charles appeared to ignore the question again. He merely responded with a "humph" and then stood there staring at the books with his arms crossed. After a moment, he said, "Well, we better go see Mr. James. He's the one you want to see."

216 · Jason M. Steffens

"What?" Will asked as he saw Charles turn his back to him and start to walk away.

"Dan," Charles said with his back to Will, still walking away. "The president. You want to know about George and Nate. Dan can tell you about 'em."

28.

Will had no cordial choice other than to follow the librarian. They exited the room and turned down the hall back
toward the general office. On entering, Charles looked at
the woman behind the desk. Before she could get up he
asked in stride, "Dan in?"

"Yes," she responded. "His door is open." Charles continued through the short swinging door separating the areas
in front of and behind the counter, barely holding it open
long enough for Will to pass through as well. For an eighty-
year-old, Charles moved fast.

The door to what was apparently the president's office
was open, but Charles stopped before entering and tapped
on the door.

"Dan, do you –"

"Hi Charles! Come on in!" the man behind the desk said
before Charles could even complete his question. Will
watched Charles almost trot in. He followed behind more
slowly.

"I have a man here who needs some information and I
thought you would be the best source for him."

"Sure, please, have a seat," the president said kindly, as if
he did not have anything else to do. As Will took one of the

two guest chairs and Charles took the other, Will observed that the walls to his left and behind the president's desk contained bookshelves to the ceiling. The wall to Will's right was almost entirely a glass window. The shades were open and it looked out into a courtyard.

Charles had not shut the door behind them. There would not be any secrets from the secretary Will had met when he first arrived, if she chose to listen.

No one spoke. Will realized they were done with their introductions. Charles the librarian and Dan James the president were simply waiting for him to speak. To them, it appeared to Will, everyone was already friends. He wondered if his story would end that friendship as quickly as it had apparently started. He also realized that by bringing him in here, Charles had both prevented him from snooping anonymously and informed the president of his visit.

The truth, Will said to himself. Besides, these men probably could tell if he was making something up.

"My name is Will Jacobson," he opened. "I am an attorney from Cedar Rapids, Iowa. I was in Phoenix on other business, but I have a case involving a couple of witnesses, both of whom attended this college. Frankly, my suspicion is there is some history between them affecting their motivations in the lawsuit. So I came to your library this morning to see if I could find out anything about their history together. Charles here was kind enough to show me the section of the library containing the yearbooks and annual reports. He then said perhaps you would be the best person to speak to and he brought me in here. I hope I am not interrupting you or inconveniencing you in any way."

The president grinned at Charles and then said to Will, "No, no inconvenience at all. We enjoy having visitors here.

Who are the two people you are researching?" Will told him.

Dan James nodded his head. His grin was gone, but it did not appear to Will that he was surprised. Instead, it appeared he knew something and was now measuring how much to reveal. "Were you able to find out what you needed from the yearbooks and annual reports?" he asked.

"Not exactly. I looked through the first four before Charles was kind enough to bring me to see you. I mostly learned George Bannon was a star student, leader, and good athlete. I did not learn much about Nate Sanders."

The president paused. He looked contemplative. He then asked, "Did you see the photo?"

Will had seen the photo of Bannon and the woman—Tara—who had the last name as the president. Was that the photo to which he was now referring? It had to be. Will described the photo to the college president and asked him, "Is that what you mean?"

Dan James nodded and said, "Yes."

Charles spoke up. "It is not Dan's favorite photograph in the world."

The college president chuckled. "Yes," he said. "In moments of weakness, I have thought about ripping it out and burning it. But then I would have to track down each copy around the world—some of that year's students are now missionaries—and burn those as well. And that might look a little silly. I actually approve every page of the yearbook each year. But that year I was on a trip visiting churches with our singing tour group. The yearbook was finalized in my absence. I had one of our faculty take my place in looking it over. That was the last time."

"Is Tara James related to you?"

"She is my daughter."

Will still was not sure how this all related to the lawsuit and the apparent animosity between Nate Sanders and George Bannon, or rather more accurately the animosity Bannon had toward Sanders. Then James said, "Let's call her. She will be able to clear this lawsuit up for you."

"Call her?" *Had he heard him right?*

"Yeah, that okay?" James responded without looking up from his laptop, which he was now opening.

Will mustered out an affirmative. Before he thought to ask how Tara James could help, the college president had opened a video chat app and started calling her. A woman answered and said, "Hi Dad!"

"Hi Tara," Dan James replied. "I need your help with something. I have your grandpa in here as well, along with a guest he was showing around the library."

A connection—Charles was Tara's grandfather. Since Dan had called the librarian "Charles" rather than "dad," Charles must be James's wife's dad. If they were all not such nice people, Will would have thought they were devising some trick on him.

The president got up from his chair and came around to the other side of his desk where Will and Charles were sitting, swiveling the laptop so it faced them. Will could now see the woman on the other end of the video call. It was definitely the woman from the photograph in the yearbook, now about a decade older. In the background were four kids eating breakfast at the kitchen table.

"Tara, this is Will Jacobson, the lawyer from Cedar Rapids working on the church case."

"Hi Mr. Jacobson," she said. "Nice to meet you."

"Yes," Will replied. "Hi. Nice to meet you as well." He

was missing something, like he had been daydreaming during an introduction that would have explained the relationships among all these people.

"You are the lawyer representing the Association," she said matter-of-factly.

"Yes," he answered. Will looked at the president. "You know about the lawsuit," he said as a half-question, half-declaration.

Dan James nodded. He looked back at the screen. "Is Nate at home?" he asked his daughter.

He had to be asking about Nate Sanders. Will got it now: Tara was the pastor's wife, which meant Dan James was his father-in-law.

Tara answered, "No, he is at the church."

"That is probably for the best," James responded. "Mr. Jacobson here thought there might be something underlying the Association's lawsuit against your church. He came here to look through the library. Your grandfather noticed and brought him in here."

"Hi Grandpa," Tara said. "Way to keep your eyes on the lawyer."

"He saw the picture," Dan James continued toward his daughter.

"What picture?" she asked.

"You know—*the picture*," her father replied.

"Oh," she said. "You mean the missions trip picture of me and George in the yearbook? I had forgotten about that."

"It is hard for your father to let that one go," Charles said in a partially scolding tone. The son-in-law sighed and offered a half-grin in admission of his weakness.

"I think we should tell him what is going on," James said. "It might help him find a peaceful resolution to this lawsuit."

"Are you sure we should do this without Nate?" Tara asked. "I could have one of the kids run next door to get him."

"You can tell him about this conversation later," her father responded. "This won't take long and you know he has always thought more highly of George than necessary."

"George does have good qualities," she said sincerely, but without any hint of affection.

Will sat there feeling like these people were having a conversation as if he were not present.

"Yes, he does," James admitted with resignation in his voice. "Anyway, the worst that could happen is Mr. Jacobson here continues to believe, if he ever did, that George is motivated by principle, and the lawsuit continues as it always has to whatever will come. But I think he wants to see the right thing happen or he would not be here."

At this point, Will felt like he had to say something, to interrupt what had been an intra-family conversation. "Look, it appears you already know this, but I want to make sure we are all working off the same page. I am an attorney and I represent the Midwestern Baptist Association in a lawsuit against the church pastored by a person to whom you all are apparently related by marriage. There is no court reporter here, but by speaking with me so freely it is possible you could say something I could use against the church in the lawsuit. Also, feel free to call me Will."

"Yeah, we know. Nate said you had good character, though. And we know you are helping Roy. Thank you for that. You can use this information as you see fit, but you should know it."

Tara's face showed she was following her father's lead. She sighed and then began, "I entered college two years behind George, one behind Nate, so when George was a senior and Nate a junior, I was a sophomore. It was not a big college at the time. We all had some activities together and, of course, chapel every day.

"Anyway, George started to show some interest in me. I had never had a boyfriend or anything close to one. George was smart, ambitious, very nice looking, and well respected by everyone in the college. It was very flattering to me. He started eating lunch and dinner at the table I ate at, with other people of course. Everything at the college was always very open and group oriented in order to inhibit inappropriate relationships. Then there was that missions trip, the one where that photograph you saw was taken. There were college staff chaperones and other students on that trip, but George spent a lot of time talking with me. Alone, though in the sight of others. At the end of that trip, before we returned to the college, we sat down together on a stone bench and George told me he was going to ask my father for permission to begin courting me –"

"Which he was really already doing," interrupted her father.

"Yes, well, that is true," Tara agreed.

For the third time in a week, Will felt he was witnessing people from an alternate universe. A pastor willing to risk his church's property and his own home, a baseball player giving up millions of dollars so he can go to church, and now talk of college students that like each other but do not go out alone.

"Wait," Will interjected. "Where I come from, many people still ask a father for permission to *marry* his daughter, but I really am not familiar with the concept of asking permission to engage in courting. I am also not even sure I know the meaning of courting."

Charles sprung forward in his seat as if a bee was about to sting him from behind. "Dating is like someone opening a box of chocolates and taking a bite out of each one before reaching the last one." The elderly man sat back as if he had just completely solved Will's ignorance, along with a few world problems. It was a treatise by one sentence analogy. Or maybe the bee just went away. The thing was, Will sensed that Charles's analogy *had* fully solved Will's puzzlement, but at the moment he was in some way prevented from recognizing how.

To avoid making it obvious that he remained without understanding, Will kept silent, but Tara must have recognized the confusion on his face. She said, "Most people start dating in high school. They give their hearts away to someone during that time, but they do not marry that someone. They then date other people in college and perhaps well into their twenties, giving away their heart multiple times, so by the time they walk down the aisle they only have part of them left to give."

"Half the piece of chocolate," said Charles.

"The other person may not hold that against them," Tara continued, "and the marriage may thrive, but it is not the best way. Dad taught me from the time I was a little girl that I should keep my heart pure. I could do that by devoting myself to God first and to my dad second, so when the time came for him to give me away to my husband on my wedding day, he would be giving away my heart. My devotion would be transferred from my dad to my husband, with God always first. The wedding ceremony handoff is a beautiful picture, especially when the bride has not allowed her heart to be stolen by those who do not deserve it and will not keep it. Courting, then, is where a man spends time with a woman and her family in order to show himself worthy of her love and devotion. Where dating offers no promise of marriage, courting is for the specific purpose of marriage. Now, much of what some people call courting is really just dating, but my dad would have none of that. I am so thankful for that, as is my husband."

"I think I understand," Will said. "At least as well I can without seeing what it looks like in real life. So did George follow through with his statement that he was going to ask your dad's permission to begin courting you?"

"Yes."

"What was the answer?" Will looked back and forth between Tara and her father, not knowing where to direct the question or who would answer. It was the father who responded first. "I told him I would pray about it and get back to him. I also needed to speak with others. He understood."

"Who did you speak with?"

"Me, for one," Charles answered. "I gave him my advice. I may look like I have lots of wisdom, but I said the wrong thing then. God gave daughters a dad for a reason."

"What did you say?"

"I told Dan that of course he should say 'yes' to George. George was the best student at the college and the best we ever had. Still is. In many ways he helped build it. I thought he was the best. Dan, though, likes to ask my opinion and then do something else. I am glad he did not listen to me in that instance."

"I usually do listen to him," Dan said to Will.

Will began to wonder whether Tara had any say in the matter. As politely as he could, he asked "Was Tara one of the people you had to speak with?"

"Of course she was," her father quickly answered. "She was the most important person. None of what I thought would have mattered a bit if Tara had a mind to reject it. Whether she ultimately married one or the other or neither of them was always up to her."

"What did she think?" Will asked Dan and then thought maybe he should ask Tara directly, and so did.

They all sat there in silence. Will realized that whatever that conversation had been, they were not going to disclose it to him. He decided to move on to avoid further awkwardness. "I suppose it doesn't matter now. Can you tell me what happened next? I am still not sure how all this relates to the lawsuit."

Dan spoke. "What happened next was that some other guy came into my office the next day and asked me the very same thing: permission to court Tara."

"Nate Sanders," Will offered.

Dan nodded. Tara smiled. Charles shook his head.

Dan continued, "It was the most awkward conversation I ever had. Maybe the shortest, too. His request came out of the woodwork and he was not the best conversationalist at the time. Nate had been on campus almost three years, but I hardly knew who he was. About the only thing I knew was he was shorter, paler, and less athletic than George. He also could not talk or write as well. He was quiet. We often miss the character of the quiet ones."

"Or mistake greatness for loudness," Charles piped in.

"Yes, true," Dan agreed.

"Hey," Tara protested, "you are all talking as if Nate looked like an ogre in college. He was very handsome and he, of course, still is."

"You know," Dan said, "many people would hear her and say 'love is blind.' Actually, infatuation is blind. True love opens our eyes. It helps us see things more clearly, as they really are."

Will had been around Bannon working on this case and had deposed Nate the prior week. The physical descriptions these people were giving of them in college appeared to have been reversed ten years later. Outwardly, Nate had taken care of his body. George had let his slide. George was certainly still taller, but that was about it. Nate looked like an older version of what he had been in college, more mature looking. Looking at George now, it was hard to believe he had been the college's athletic star.

"Anyway," Dan continued, "I did what I did with George. I told Nate I would get back to him after I had prayed about it and spoken with some people."

"And spied on them," Tara said.

"Yes, well, there was some of that, too, though spying is not quite the word I would use. I followed them around the next week and observed them in public. What they were like alone, in private, only they and God knew. Even in public, though, it was not exactly possible to observe them closely for a full week all by myself, so I enlisted the help of a few others."

"You did?" Tara asked. "I did not know that. Who did you have help you?"

"You never knew?" her father asked. "I guess I always assumed you did. Your mother helped. I also had a couple of staff members help. And, of course, your grandfather."

"Even after observing them closely," Charles said, "I still told Dan he should give permission to George, but you might say the strength of my conviction had weakened. Dan was, of course, right to ignore my opinion."

"I did not ignore it. I definitely considered Charles's advice. But at the end of the week I knew Nate was the right man for my girl and that George was not. I was a little worried when I told Tara, as I knew that she had gotten to know George well, thanks to George's efforts before he even came to see me. It did not appear to me she had interacted with Nate very much."

"I cannot really explain it," Tara added, "but I knew Dad was right. Certainly, my initial reaction was disappointment. All I knew was that George had come to him for permission and my father was considering it. When he told me his decision, that was the first time that I knew Nate had asked as well."

29.

He got the girl.

That was why George Bannon had the Midwestern Baptist Association sue Nate Sanders and the Pine Road Baptist Church. At least that was the way Dan James and Charles the librarian saw it. They were probably right.

Will was now driving south back toward Phoenix. Dan James and Tara Sanders, with Charles interjecting periodically, had finished telling him how Nate's humility, genuineness, and strong desire to serve God—no matter where that might lead and even if it meant no notoriety for himself—had won them over. It had actually taken him a week after James gave him permission to court Tara to work up the courage to approach her and have something beyond a "good afternoon, sure is nice weather today" conversation.

George initially appeared to accept the decision, especially after he was able to confirm Tara's agreement with it out of earshot of anyone else. It was not long, though, before George started displaying subtle forms of jealousy, undermining Nate, but never in so overt a way he could be accused of it. Putting that photograph in the yearbook of him and Tara had seemed to them to be another in a series of pokes. They were not certain if George actually thought

Nate and Tara's courtship would end in failure and a determination that George was the better man all along.

Nate never really recognized what the rest of them thought George was doing. Though he was never close with him, Nate had continued to view George as a friend with many qualities worth admiring.

Notwithstanding Dan's intense dislike of that yearbook photograph, the three of them spoke of George less out of bitterness than pity.

When they had given Will all the information they thought he needed, Will thanked them for being so forthright with him. They ended the video chat with Tara and Will left the campus. He now had to decide what to do with the information they had given him. He always thought the Association had a legitimate case or he would not have filed it. It was possible Dan's intuition about Bannon's motives was wrong. Still, Will had never really understood the point of the lawsuit. Religious institutions that mostly saw things the same way fighting over land, which was really just a fight over money? Was there not a better use of everyone's time and resources? On the other hand, Will thought, much of his work came down to that: the shifting of money, justified or not.

The two organizations clearly needed to go their separate ways, but did that have to involve a lawsuit? There had to be a peaceful resolution that recognized the Association's original purchasing of the land and building of the original structure, and the church's decades-long maintenance of and adding on to that structure. Was Bannon's envy of Nate preventing that? Motivations are complicated, and sometimes the actors themselves do not fully understand why they are acting the way they are. It was not as if Will could ask Bannon about this.

Before reaching the city limits, Nate pulled off the highway into a gas station to fill his car. It was now early afternoon. As he stood by his car while its tank filled with fuel, Will looked up into the sky. There was not a cloud in sight and the sky appeared blue and limitless. It was eighty degrees and there was no humidity. This would not be a bad place to live, Will considered, but then he remembered August in Phoenix would be a little less pleasant. He had grown up and learned to love the change of seasons and incredible growth of everything green in Iowa. *We only covet something else when we turn our eye away from the goodness before us*, Will said to himself. That was probably something one of his Sunday School teachers had taught him when he was a child.

After the car was done fueling, the receipt printer at the pump jammed. Will walked inside the convenience store to ask the clerk for one. There was a person ahead of him in line. The clerk was male and looked about thirty. He was tanned and had blond hair hanging a little long, if not quite to his shoulders. He looked unimpressive, having gone nowhere in life and going nowhere. The customer ahead of Will paid for his items. Will stepped to the counter. "I need a receipt for pump 2. It would not print."

"No problem brother," the clerk said. He began punching buttons on a machine to get it to print a receipt. "Sorry about that."

"That's okay," Will replied.

"What a gorgeous day today, eh? You here to watch spring training?"

Will wondered how the clerk knew he was not from the area. Perhaps he had seen the rental car company's logo on the car outside. "No, that would be nice, but I am here on business."

"Oh man. Well, while you are here, if you don't go to the baseball games and have some free time away from your business, there are some good bike trails and paths. When this shift is done, my wife and our girl—she's seven—are going to ride part of the Grand Canal trail. It's a great day for it."

"Thanks. I will keep that in mind."

"Here is your receipt. Sorry about that again. I will get out there and check on that machine, so hopefully it will not happen the next time you are here. Have a great day."

"Thanks," Will said as he turned and exited the store. He walked to his car in a bit of a daze. He opened the door and sat in the driver's seat. His quickness to assess the clerk, to decide who he was before he knew him, resulting in a false assessment, depressed him. For all Will knew, the clerk was the owner of the store. Or perhaps he was just here doing this job for a month to help out a friend or family member during the busy spring training season. Maybe this really was what he did for a living.

The point was that Will certainly did not know, yet he had defined the clerk by his job. Even the phrase that had just gone through Will's mind—*what he "did for a living"*—was wrong. The clerk had acted with purpose in doing his job well, but the job was not him. He was serving others and he did it with joy. There were probably a thousand other jobs he could've done to earn money and he would've done those with joy. But he was also a husband and father. The clerk fulfilled those roles with joy and purpose as well, probably much better than he did. Will could not remember the last time he planned an activity that he, his wife, and his children could do together.

Will started the car and pulled it away from the gas pump, parking it along the edge of the store's parking lot.

He got out of the car again and pulled out his phone. He found the number he was looking for and hit "call." The receptionist connected him to Spencer Frieden, George Bannon's boss.

"Mr. Frieden, this is Will Jacobson, the attorney representing the Association regarding the dispute with Pine Road Baptist Church. We spoke once about that dispute when your Association first retained my firm. I have been dealing with George Bannon since then."

"Yes, Will, what can I do for you?"

"I have some new information that may impact resolution of the dispute. I would like to discuss it with you. Is there a time you have available?"

"I would make time for you now if I could, but I am sorry I really cannot. In-person meetings are better anyway. It just so happens I will be in Cedar Rapids tomorrow for a meeting of eastern Iowa Association churches. I could make some time to meet with you before or after that meeting."

Will explained he was in Phoenix. Then he realized there was nothing more keeping him here. He would try to get back on a flight that night. They set a meeting time and place and agreed that if Will was not able to get back to Cedar Rapids tonight or early in the morning that Will would call back and they would set up a new date.

After they hung up, Will found a flight back that would arrive in Cedar Rapids that night. He then reached Ashley on her cell phone. She and the kids were finishing a late lunch following an indoor amusement park excursion. The disappointment of having to return so soon was evident in her voice, but she did not complain, especially after Will explained the benefactor of their trip no longer had the income that would justify paying for someone else's vacation.

The clerk inside the convenience store was smiling at his customers, looking forward to a bike ride this afternoon with his family. Will was telling his wife to hurry and pack up their stuff so they could cut short their vacation and fly back to Iowa. *So he could work.* Will would buy them all a piece of pie in the airport restaurant. For that brief moment, he would look the part of an involved dad. Will had been wrong about the clerk. Anyone looking at him in the airport with his family would be wrong about him. When it came down to it all, he was his job and not much else.

30.

The last minute, one-way, first-class plane ticket—the only one available—had cost Roy a lot, especially for a person now unemployed and whose income prospects had gone from seemingly unlimited to seemingly nothing, but it had gotten him to Iowa, where he needed to be. He turned onto Interstate 380 heading north. Within minutes he reached the Highway 30 interchange. Taking it east would have taken him toward Jenny, but he continued north into Cedar Rapids.

He passed through the downtown area and took the 42nd St. exit. He reached Kennedy High School, turned right onto Wenig Road, and drove north until it ended at Pine Road, just south of Highway 100. He pulled into the parking lot of the Pine Road Baptist Church. There were several cars in the lot and people walking outside of the small church building. Roy knew they were here to go out and knock on doors to share the Gospel and invite people to church, just as Pastor Sanders had knocked on his door on a Tuesday night last fall.

He parked his rented car and stepped out. There were some new people he did not recognize. They did not immediately recognize him, either. A few others noticed him and said "hi." Roy asked them if Pastor Sanders was there. Just then, Roy saw him walk out of the church doors with his wife Tara.

"Hi Pastor," he said.

~~~~~

Nate looked up and saw Roy Adams. He smiled at Roy and shook his hand. "What are you doing here?" Nate asked.

"I just got into town. I was hoping I would catch you. Looks like you have a good group going out tonight."

"Yeah, we sure do, but what are you doing here?" Nate asked again.

"Do you have some time?" Roy asked him.

There was someone Nate wanted to visit tonight, but he could see Roy needed to talk. He had not spoken to him since before the media reports of the past two days.

"I am going to try to see someone who visited our church some time ago and has not been back. Why don't you come along and be my partner?"

"Sure," Roy responded.

"I will go knock on doors with one of the ladies," Tara said to Nate.

"Thank you," Nate replied and gave her a kiss on the cheek.

Nate led Roy to his car. As they left the parking lot, he said, "The news today said you retired. I suppose there was nothing left for you in Arizona."

Nate listened as Roy talked about the events of the past couple of days. He was glad to hear Roy was so complimentary of Will Jacobson. He was sad as Roy told him of Jenny's decision to come back to Iowa alone. By the time Roy finished talking, they had arrived where Nate was taking them, which gave Nate a little more time to determine how to best counsel Roy.

There was a car parked in the driveway, so they parked the car on the street. They got out of Nate's car and began walking up Donnie Valenza's driveway. Before they got up to the door, Nate saw the young man he came to visit walk outside. "Hi Donnie," Nate said to him.

The young man looked up and saw Nate with recognition. "Hi Pastor," he replied.

"Are you headed somewhere?" Nate asked.

"Yeah, I have to go in for work. I have a few minutes, though. What's up?" Nate then saw Donnie do a double take at Roy. "Wow, man, you look a *lot* like Roy Adams."

"Donnie," Nate said, "let me introduce you to Roy Adams."

"For real?"

"No joke." Nate laughed. When he had invited Roy to come with him, he had forgotten it was possible Donnie would recognize Roy. The two of them shook hands and said it was nice to meet the other.

"You really have a lot of guts," Donnie said to Roy.

"Thanks," Roy replied. "I appreciate that."

"We will not keep you if you have to work," Nate said. "But I came by to invite you again to church. We have a midweek service tomorrow night starting at seven. Do you have to work tomorrow night?"

"No. Maybe I will stop by."

"I talked to your mom again today," Nate continued. "I had talked to her on Saturday as well. She said today that she tried to visit you here, but no one was home when she came."

"Yeah, I got the note she left in my door."

"Her church does not have a midweek service. She said she would come to our church tomorrow night."

"I see. You are trying to reunite us at the church house."

"Church is a good place for reconciliation," Nate offered.

Nate watched Donnie think for a minute. Then Roy, who had been silent, said, "You should come."

Donnie looked at Roy, but remained silent a moment more. Then he nodded and said, "Okay, I will try to come."

They said goodbye and got in their respective cars. As they drove away, Roy said to Nate, "I hope that was okay to speak up. It seemed like he needed to hear it from someone other than the pastor."

"It was perfect," Nate replied. Nate thought about it some more and then said, "You know, you might be able to be a lot of help to him."

"You think so?"

"He apparently used to be a really good baseball player. He had to give it up because of an injury. He is still bitter over it. You gave up baseball voluntarily. Perhaps you could help him see there is more to life than baseball. It may be that he agreed to come because you encouraged him. He has wanted the thing you gave up. If you were willing to let it go, perhaps he will."

Roy was silent. Nate could not see his passenger's reaction as he drove. He thought about the anxiety that had been in Roy's voice as he talked before they had arrived at Donnie's house. "Are you regretting your decision yet?" he asked.

Roy gave an awkward chuckle. "Yet?"

"If it has not happened yet, there is a good chance your mind will be attacked about your decision."

"I think the attack has already come," Roy replied.

Nate desperately wanted to help Roy. Nothing in Bible college had taught him to deal with famous baseball players who decided to quit baseball and whose wife may be on the verge of leaving him because of it. *No, that's not true*, Nate thought. Bible college had given him the most intensive Bible training he had ever received, *and the Bible applies to everything*.

He said, "I read this once: 'Our greatest fear as individuals and as a church should not be of failure but of succeeding at things in life that don't really matter.'* The Bible says our love should abound in knowledge and judgment, so we will approve things that are excellent.† Choose the things that matter to God. See things as He sees them. Whatever results, that is the best way."

Roy was silent for a moment and then responded, "I believe that. As clear as I saw that yesterday when I made the decision to retire from baseball, I still see that. There is nothing special about a game compared to things that matter for eternity, and if baseball was going to hinder my service with God, I had to leave it. It is just that —"

Roy paused. "What is it?" Nate asked.

"What if the only way to save my marriage is to go back to playing baseball on Sundays?"

Jenny had come to church with Roy from last fall until the time Roy went down to Arizona to prepare for spring training. They had always seemed so close and devoted to one another. Nate had seen a lot of wives openly critical of their husbands, often poorly disguised behind humor, but he could not recall Jenny ever doing that. On the other

---

* Quoted in Francis Chan's *Crazy Love* and attributed to Tim Kizziar.

† Philippians 1:9-10

hand, Nate admitted to himself, he did not really know her. Sometimes it takes a dramatic change in circumstances to reveal true beliefs and character.

"Do you think it has reached that point?" he asked Roy.

"It is just that she seemed so cold in her decision," Roy responded. He paused. "Yes, I think it is at that point. I really cannot believe that, but it is true. Outwardly she was fine until there was no hope left that the team would allow me to have Sundays. I thought retiring would relieve the pressure on her. It did, but it was as if my status as a baseball player had become the connection between us. When that was gone, so was her affection."

Nate knew it was best not to pretend things were okay when they were not. "You can only control your own decisions," he responded. "It is possible that no matter what you do, the relationship will not be what it once was."

They had arrived back at the church. Nate parked his car and they got out.

"Well, that's hardly reassuring," Roy said with some light-heartedness. "Aren't you supposed to offer words of encouragement?"

"Yes, if it's the truth."

"What about all things working together for good, as it says in the book of Romans?"

"That's true, if the conditions of the verse are met, but we must realize two things our short-sightedness causes. First, we often do not recognize what is good. Second, the verse does not tell us when the good will come. Remember, 'by faith the walls of Jericho fell down,' and also 'through faith' 'others had trial of cruel mockings and scourgings, ... bonds and imprisonment.' Worldly victory is clearly not the product of faith in every instance. In fact, the product of faith may be worldly defeat. But if you want to please God, you must have faith, and he will reward your faithfulness.‡

~~~~~

Roy knew his pastor was correct. After all, there had been Christians throughout history who had suffered real persecution. Their end had not been good from a worldly perspective. But they had not denied their faith. That was certainly good properly understood. Just because all things work together for good did not mean all things that happened to a person were good.

The look on his face must have expressed doubt, though, for Pastor Sanders worked to find another way to talk through this after they arrived back at the church. "I read a story recently," he said. "Let me get it." As Pastor Sanders looked for the story on his phone, he continued, "I saved it because I thought it would make a nice illustration in a sermon. Perhaps I will still use it, but perhaps it was just meant for you. It was from this guy who was an official in the State Department when Reagan was president."

A pause.

"Here it is," Pastor Sanders continued. "Yes, his name is Elliott Abrams. In 1984, he was Assistant Secretary of State for Latin America. He wrote that 'in 1984 there were many signs that the Soviet Union was planning to introduce advanced combat jets into Nicaragua.' Then look at these two paragraphs."

Nate handed Roy his smartphone and Roy read about Abrams' recollection of a National Security Council meeting:

---

‡ Hebrews 11:6, 30, 36

I recall an NSC meeting around that time where this subject was discussed, and there was a unanimous view that we would not permit Russia to put advanced combat jets into Nicaragua and change the power balance that had existed in the region since the Cuban missile crisis. Everyone agreed. I was then assistant secretary of state for Latin America and remember reading formally to my Soviet counterpart in 1985 or 1986, from written talking points, that we would not tolerate Cuban combat troops, or Soviet combat jets, being sent into Nicaragua.

But what preceded such talking points was the NSC meeting. There, after everyone said yes, let's deliver that message, James Baker spoke up. As I recall it, Baker said something like this: Look, we are not agreeing here on sending a message. We are agreeing now that if they act, we will act. We're not going to come back here in a month or three months or six months and say, now what do we do? If you are agreeing on taking this line and sending this message to the Soviets, you are agreeing now, today, that if they put those jets in, we will take them out. That's what we are agreeing. Today."§

Roy finished reading and gave Pastor Sanders his phone back. "Forget about the rightness or wrongness of the military decision," he said to Roy. "Think about the point James Baker was making. What is your message?"

---

§ Elliott Abrams, "Of Presidents and Bluffing," weeklystandard.com, May 5, 2013.

Roy thought for a moment and then replied, "That I will yield my life to God."

"That is a good message."

Roy smiled. "I got that from you."

"I am glad to know that someone listens to me!"

"I did listen to you."

"More importantly, you listened to God. I never told you to quit baseball. On your own, you came to realize that baseball hindered your service to God. At some point before then, you had not just decided to send the message that you would yield your life to God, you had decided to, in fact, yield your life to God."

"No matter the consequences."

"Right. The consequences are not up to you. What is up to you is to decide whether to do the things that please God, to show Him your gratitude for saving your soul."

"So don't back down, even if my marriage fails."

"Lots of people have lost family because that family separated from them after they fully committed their lives to God. It may be the hardest decision of priorities that Christians face. That, or money, though I don't sense that money is the draw for you." The pastor paused. "Here is the other thing: None of us knows the future. You do not know your marriage will end. It is possible that going back to baseball would not save your marriage. It is also possible the only thing that will save your marriage is not going back to baseball. Be the husband God called you to be, that He asks you in His word to be. Your wife needs that more than she needs you to be a baseball player, even if she does not see that right now."

Roy thanked his pastor. He knew what he had to do.

He would not let Jenny walk away so easily.

31.

Will found the Pine Road Baptist Church and pulled into the parking lot. He saw Pastor Nate Sanders walking over to the church building from what Will assumed to be the parsonage. Will walked up to him and greeted him. The pastor immediately told him of the kind words Roy Adams had spoken about the legal work Will had done for him.

"That is nice of him," Will replied. "I was not quite sure how he felt after the way things ended somewhat abruptly." Will decided not to get into the conversation between his wife and Roy's wife.

"It is quite a transition for him," Nate said.

"Yes, it sure is. Thank you again for referring him to me. I actually did not come to talk about that case, though. I came because of the Association's lawsuit."

"Have you come to tell me it has gone away?" Nate asked facetiously.

"Actually," Will answered, "perhaps in a way. The ball is at least now in your court."

"What do you mean? Has George softened?"

"Well, he will. Sometimes circumstances, or knowledge getting out in the open, has a way of softening people."

"That is certainly true," the pastor agreed.

"I just had coffee with Spencer Frieden, George Bannon's boss."

"I have never met him."

"I think you would like him. He's a nice fellow. Anyway, he does not want this dispute to go on. He would like some recognition of the Association's efforts, financial and otherwise, in starting this church, but he is also willing to recognize this church is its own body, has contributed to the property, and is headed in a different direction. In exchange for a $100,000 purchase price and an agreement to continue operating as a church, even if independent from the Association, the Association will deed the property, including the parsonage, to the church and drop the lawsuit."

Will saw the pastor processing the offer in his mind. He did not know the pastor well enough to guess his reaction with confidence, but the offer was a great one for the church. Not only would it remove the cloud of the possibility of losing everything, but with the parsonage the property was worth five to seven times that price. Will saw the realization of what the Association was offering appear on the pastor's face. A smile grew. "The church will have to vote on it and we will have to get financing," he said, "but I will recommend it, and it will pass. No strings attached?"

"None. The property will be yours and everyone walks away and goes about their church business."

"What did George say about this?" Pastor Sanders asked.

"I haven't told him," Will answered.

"He's not going to be happy.

"We do not always get what we want. George will have to get over it, though he probably won't ever hire me again."

"This is really incredible. I knew God would provide for us as a church, but it is always amazing watching Him do so. You had something to do with this, didn't you? How did you convince the Association to settle? George seemed so intent on kicking us out. Did this have anything to do with your conversation with Tara's father?"

"I cannot really disclose that," Will answered with a smile.

"I don't know how to thank you."

"I don't usually get thanked by the opposing party," Will replied, still smiling. "But maybe you can help me with something."

"Name it."

"I am curious—How did you get one of the best baseball players in the world to give up a game in which he was almost certain to earn hundreds of millions of dollars?"

"I didn't."

"Then what made him do it?"

Roy had tried to explain it to Will, but Will did not completely understand.

"Nothing and no one made him do it," the pastor answered. "He chose to give up baseball because there were other things more important to him."

"But what is really wrong with baseball?" Will said, almost in argument. "He could have done a lot of good remaining in the game."

"Yes, and there is nothing wrong with baseball, unless baseball replaces God and the things God cares about." Will displayed his confusion by the look on his face. "If Roy had stayed in the game, at least as the game exists in the form it does today, it would have consumed him and defined him."

That made sense to Will as he thought about his own life. But there was something Roy had that Will did not. Maybe what he lacked had more to do with motivation than understanding. As Will thought about the pastor's words and Roy life's compared to his own, Nate asked him, "Do you go to church anywhere, Will?"

Will explained his church background. He was too ashamed to admit he rarely attended anymore. "Why? Should I become Baptist?" Will asked half-jokingly. He did not really know what a Baptist believed or how it was different from the religion which he had always known.

"We would certainly welcome you to visit our church, but I am not concerned about that yet."

"What is your concern?"

"I am concerned that you are standing too close to things you think you know, or perhaps just the one thing you think you know," the pastor answered. "All you see are the things immediately in front of you."

"I am still not following you," Will said.

"I think you know what I mean."

The two stood there in silence. Will wondered whether he should press the pastor's meaning. Maybe he did know. What were the things to which he was standing too close? Or the one thing? His job? Before he figured out a way to continue the pastor's thought, Nate turned to him and said, "Come over here." Nate walked from the middle of the parking lot to a spot two feet away from the side of the church building. Will followed him. Nate faced the building and said, "What do you see?"

"Some bricks."

"Right. Now, walk back with me to the middle of the parking lot and look in the same direction." They did so.

"I can now see the full building." Was that all this was? Seeing the tree, but missing the forest? If so, what was the tree and what was the forest?

"Most people put themselves in Roy's shoes and only see the fame and money. Roy sees Jesus and is learning to see things as Jesus sees them."

Will stood there silently, not knowing how to respond.

The pastor's next question seemed an abrupt change of topics, though Will knew later it was not. "Do you know what will happen to you when you die?" Nate asked.

Will admitted to the pastor he did not know.

"Last fall, Roy did what you need to do now."

"Do I have to quit my job to go to heaven?"

"Roy did not quit baseball last fall, and quitting baseball had nothing to do with the cleansing of his sin. Roy quit baseball because he refused to make his life about baseball. He loved God more, and so wanted to do what God preferred. And he loved God because God first loved him. No, what Roy did last fall was realize he had no hope without Jesus."

"Why am I without hope?"

The pastor continued, "God once prepared a place called Tophet to hold the Assyrian army because it had attacked God's chosen city.** Every single one of us is in rebellion against God's standards and are bound for our Tophet. Alone, we are without hope."

Will had been in Sunday School enough to understand Nate's reference. "You mean we are bound for hell?"

"Eternally," Pastor Sanders continued, "the Bible calls it the lake of fire. There are also present consequences of our sin, including lack of peace and joy. Most people admit they

---

** Isaiah 30:33

have done some things wrong in life, that they have transgressed God's standard of holiness. Surely you have seen it in your own children, where they have fallen short of the standards you have set for them."

"Yes," said Will.

"The harder thing for people to accept is that there is a punishment for that transgression."

Will searched his brain for any other Bible he knew. "But God is love. Doesn't love forgive?"

"Yes! But on His terms, not yours. God chose a path to redeem man out of his rebellion. That path was through His perfect Son and the sacrifice he offered on the cross. Jesus suffered, bled, and died for you, to pay the price for your sin. That payment is a gift you may accept or reject, but know that choosing some other way is a rejection of that gift, leaving you to pay that price yourself. Will, I urge you now to repent. Turn away from your sin and everything you have trusted to gain favor with God other than Jesus, and receive him now as your Saviour. It is only then you will realize why Roy has done what he has done. More importantly, it is only then you will be reconciled with God."

Will felt paralyzed. He knew this is what his life had been missing, but he also sensed that what the pastor was saying would change him forever. That scared him. Will tried to tell himself there was no one else watching; he could do what the pastor had said. After a moment's silence, Pastor Sanders spoke again, "Remember, this is not about you doing something to earn your salvation. Jesus has done it for you. It is a gift. Receive it now."

What did he have to lose? Will thought. *Maybe a lot, but nothing compared to what he would gain.* "I will," Will finally said.

"Seal your decision by calling on God in prayer now."

"I will." The pastor kneeled to the ground and Will followed his lead. The pastor prayed for him and then Will prayed awkwardly but sincerely, receiving the gift of eternal life only Jesus provides.

32.

Roy had driven east from Cedar Rapids through the small towns that dot Highway 30—Mechanicsville, Stanwood, and finally Clarence—before turning off onto a county road headed north. Partway to another small town called Oxford Junction he had pulled into the short gravel driveway in which he now stood.

Jenny's father's farmhouse was modest but well cared for. It anchored 160 acres of farmland, on which her father planted and harvested corn, mostly on his own. Jenny was an only child. Her mother had died of cancer when Jenny was fourteen. Her father—his name, like the owner of the Indianapolis Hawks, was John—had done well to both keep the farm running and prevent Jenny from living rebellious teenaged years. If it had been up to him, Roy was sure, Jenny never would have left the farm, but when she fell in love at age seventeen with a high school baseball player from Cedar Rapids, John had embraced Roy.

It was John who now saw Roy first. He had been coming from a barn toward the house. "Hi Roy," he said without pleasantness. Whatever love John once had for Roy was absent.

"Sir," Roy said in acknowledgement. "Is Jenny here?"

John ignored his question. "You change your mind about baseball yet?" he asked.

"No sir."

John looked away. "She's upstairs in her room."

"Thank you."

Roy started toward the door, but then he saw out of the corner of his eye Jenny's father turn back toward him and say, "You know what happens if there is a divorce, right?"

The question pained Roy more than if John had struck him physically. He recovered and said, "I do not plan on there being a divorce. It will not come from me."

"It does not matter who it comes from," Jenny's father continued. "If you continue this there *will* be a divorce. And if there is a divorce, she will have the right to ask for a portion of your future earnings as alimony. The amount will be based on your *potential* earnings."

Roy grasped what his father-in-law was saying. Jenny could ask the judge to make Roy pay her half of what he would have earned had he continued playing baseball. *Was it true? Had John learned this from a lawyer?* Roy had no idea, but he was not going to argue with him.

"Is it okay if I go up and see her now?" Roy asked him. John waived his hand to indicate his permission and walked away.

Roy went inside and walked up the wooden stairs. They creaked with each step. He reached the top, strode to Jenny's door, and knocked. "Come in," came her voice from the other side. Roy opened the door. Jenny was sitting at her small desk, the same one her father had built for her when she was a girl. It sat against a wall in front of a window. There was a short lamp on it, along with several closed books, including a tall Bible, held up by bookends.

Jenny turned to look at Roy. "Hi Roy. What are you doing here?" Roy could tell she was surprised to see him, or at least surprised to see him so soon after she had come back to Iowa. She had been resting at her desk with her head down on her folded arms. Roy could see the imprint of the pattern of her long-sleeved shirt on her forehead. She looked sleepy and unkempt and beautiful.

"I was just in the neighborhood." It was something Roy used to say to her after they first met. She had come with friends to the Linn County Fair. Roy's friends and her friends ran into each other. They went on some rides together and exchanged phone numbers. After that, Roy would find an excuse to drive into southern Jones County and surprise her by stopping by her farm. "I was just in the neighborhood," he would say.

Roy walked over and sat down at the edge of a rocking chair close to Jenny's desk chair.

"I did not expect you to come back to Iowa so soon," she said.

"This is where *you* are, and so this is where I am."

She gave a small smile and looked outside.

Roy continued, "Let's go home to Cedar Rapids."

"Right now?" she asked.

"Yes, right now."

"I can't."

"Why not?"

"I just can't. Not right now."

"We are still married."

"I know." She looked like she was going to say something else, but nothing came out. She closed her lips and continued looking out the window.

"We still love each other," Roy pleaded. "God is still good. Everything will be fine."

"Everything won't be fine. It's not fine. Everything has changed, Roy."

"Lots has changed, but not everything."

"You are not the same," she said, "and neither am I."

"That is true," he admitted. She was right, but what had changed about him had caused him to love her more.

"I never loved you because of baseball," she said. "I hardly knew anything about baseball when I met you."

She was protesting against an accusation he had not made or thought. "I know," he said.

"But you are not who you were then. Maybe we got married too young."

Roy saw her searching for explanations for why she did not want to be married to him anymore. They did not make sense to him, but he did not want to argue with her. He had not come to argue. He had come to take her home.

She went on. "I cannot take the way people look at me. People used to want to be around us. Now they don't want anything to do with us. They see us as believing we are too good for them. We are losing our friends."

"We will have new friends. We will have friends at church. We will have each other. We will have God."

"It's just not the same."

"I don't want it to be the same. I want it to be better."

"Everything I saw for us is gone."

"It is okay. There will be new things."

"You should go, Roy." For the second time since he had arrived, words crushed him. He had not anticipated being so powerless. He thought he should be able to convince her, but nothing he said was working.

She loved him. She had to. Why was she withdrawing from him? Roy continued to sit at the edge of the rocking chair, silent, looking down, frantically trying to figure out the thing to say to change her mind. Nothing came. Silent moments passed.

"Roy, you should go," she repeated. He had nothing left, nothing he could say to convince her.

But there was one more thing he needed her to know. He looked up at her. "I will go. Can I say one more thing before I do?"

Jenny looked at him as if she was going to protest, but then she sighed and said, "What?"

Roy had never felt so defeated. He gathered all of his remaining emotional strength and said, softly, "I will wait for you."

Jenny shook her head. "I will not make you wait long. This is the way it is. I am not going to change my mind. We just got married too young and now everything has changed."

It was Roy's turn to shake his head. "There was no qualification to what I said. I did not mean I will wait for you to make some final decision. I think you have already made that."

Jenny looked at him quizzically. Roy continued, "I want you to know I will wait for you. I am your husband and will always be willing to serve as your husband, even if you never again choose to be my wife. Nothing will change that. Not sickness. Not disability. Not even if you divorce me. It is the vow I took on our wedding day. I will keep it. If you find yourself ninety-five-years-old, and whatever new husband you have found has left you or died, I will welcome you back without a word and care for you as your husband. I will love you, even if you never love me again. That is what I mean by 'I will wait for you.'"

Roy stood and walked out of the room, leaving the door open behind him.

Outside, he looked for and found Jenny's father in the barn. "John!" Roy said to announce his presence to his father-in-law. The man turned and looked at Roy. "If she divorces me, other than some money to give to the church and to buy some food, she can have every dime I earn for the rest of my life. No dispute in any divorce proceeding will stand in the way of her knowing I love her and I will take her back."

Roy turned, got in his car, and drove back to Cedar Rapids.

33.

Will stood and looked at Pastor Nate Sanders. "This is going to change everything, isn't it?" he asked.

Nate smiled and said, "Yes. And that is a good thing."

Will started to wish he would have lived his life differently. For so long, he had deceived himself into believing he fully provided for his family by meeting their material needs. Mostly he had just met his own pride. He needed to be so much more. Standing in the parking lot of the Pine Road Baptist Church, he knew God forgave him. Yet, he regretted so much. Most people who say they live without regret are not telling the truth or have amnesia.

Will mentioned his feelings to the pastor.

"Cheer up, my friend," Nate replied. "Whatever has come before, it does not mean our choices today cannot be the right ones. By Jesus all things consist. That includes you. God has begun a good work in you and He will perform it until He calls you home or Jesus returns. Let him have control of your life from this day forward."

"That simple, huh?"

"Simple, yes. Easy, no. But easier if you are in the right places around the right people."

"Where do I start?" Will asked.

"A good place to start is by staying for church tonight. It starts in a half-hour. Can you stay?"

Will looked at his watch. Ashley and his kids were having dinner at her parents' house tonight and were not expecting him. He also needed time to figure out how to explain all this to Ashley. Will said he would stay.

A car then pulled into the parking lot. "Do members always arrive this early?" Will asked Nate.

"No," Nate answered. A young man got out of the car. "He came," the pastor whispered.

"Who?" Will asked.

"His name is Donnie Valenza."

"Did you say Donnie Valenza?"

"Yes. Why?"

Before Will could answer, the young man walked up to them. The pastor greeted him, said his mother had not arrived yet but he hoped she would be here, and then introduced him to Will.

"Is there any chance you are the Donnie Valenza that used to work for Johnson Engineers?" Will asked him.

"Yes," the young man answered. "Why? What is it that you do for a living?"

Will had always answered that question the way he was expected, the way he knew how. "I am an attorney." As the words came out of his mouth this time, he knew he needed a new answer. There was so much more to living than his job.

Donnie just stared at Will, so Will filled him in on his representation of Johnson Engineers and the lawsuit against it. Donnie had not been aware that someone was injured at the site. The company had fired him before the injury.

Will continued, "I knew about your involvement on the project because the other day I came across an email you wrote. All you wrote was that 'the lane to the hoop is open.'"

At this, Donnie finally spoke. "Yeah, that's a phrase I used growin' up. Some of the guys at the company picked it up as well. It means there is a problem that has not been fixed. Someone has to stop the ball, if you know what I mean."

A basketball analogy that seemed apt to his own life up to that point, Will thought.

"What was the problem that had not been fixed?" Will asked.

"The design team had not designed a guard along the edge of the roof near the air handling unit. I am not sure if the design code required it, but it seemed like the right thing to do given where we placed the unit. Designing it had been discussed, but when I saw the final plans it was not there, so I sent that email."

Donnie proceeded to ensure Will that the design team would have known what he meant by the statement in his email. Will would need to have a conversation with Johnson Engineers President Bill Smith tomorrow. It would not be a pleasant one. Smith had either lied to him about Donnie's email or did not know the truth.

For that matter, George Bannon would probably call tomorrow, making two unpleasant conversations to which Will had to look forward.

Hopefully the conversation he would soon need to have with Ashley—about the decision he had made tonight and the change in direction their lives needed to take—would go much better. He silently prayed she would understand.

At that moment, another car pulled into the lot. They all watched it. Nate was the first to recognize who it was. "She's not with him," he said sadly.

Roy stepped out alone. He walked over to them. Suddenly a smile came to his face. "Donnie!" he said. "You came! I am so glad you are here."

Donnie, who had moments before taken on the look of someone who realized he was going to have be a witness in a lawsuit, smiled at Roy's enthusiasm. As Will watched the interaction between the two, he was amazed that someone going through the difficulty of having his marriage fall apart could still possess such joy.

Roy then turned to Will. "And what are you doing here?" he asked with excitement. "Are you going to join us for church?"

Will smiled and responded, "I am."

"That is great! I can't tell you how happy that makes me, and just when I needed it."

Will looked at Nate. "Did you know this was going to happen?"

"What?" the pastor asked.

"When you referred Roy to me, did you know all this was going to happen? Us standing here?"

"I had no idea, but God did."

Will turned to Roy. "Thank you, Roy. I am here because of you."

"Yeah," Donnie agreed. "I suppose I am, too."

Roy shook his head, astounded, and let out a small grin. "Now we need to work on getting our families here," he said, and the four of them walked inside the church building.

Epilogue

About one year later

"I cannot believe you turned me into a divorce lawyer," Will said to Roy as they got into the elevator.

Roy smiled for the first time that day. "Thank you for doing this," he replied. "You know you are the only lawyer I could trust with this. Plus, no other lawyer would allow me to do what we are going to do."

Will grinned and nodded. He had never handled a marriage dissolution case before, but Roy was now a great friend, so when Jenny filed her petition requesting a divorce six months ago and Roy asked for his help, Will agreed. He conducted a crash self-education on Iowa divorce law and asked some of his former law partners about strategies for reaching the best settlement in such cases. As Roy had done before, though, he made all normal legal strategies worthless. His goal was not compatible with them.

The elevator doors opened. The two stepped into the reception area of a Cedar Rapids law firm located in what is known as the APAC Building in downtown Cedar Rapids. Will explained to the receptionist who they were and why they were there. She stared at Roy for a moment before asking them to take a seat.

Soon a secretary entered and ushered them into a small conference room. She left them after making sure they had the beverages they wanted. Roy asked, "Will we meet with her and her lawyer in the same room?"

"I don't think so," Will answered. "The mediator will likely keep us separated."

A man walked in. He nodded at Will and introduced himself to Roy. "Hi Roy," he said. "My name is David Thorn. I will be serving as the mediator for this mediation session today."

"Good to meet you, Mr. Thorn," Roy responded. Thorn explained that the procedures in the county in which the divorce petition was pending required the parties to attempt a mediation prior to a trial. Though the mediator could not force a settlement, the hope was that the couple could agree on how to divide up their assets. That way they would avoid a contentious trial, during which unpleasant things would be brought up and both sides would likely walk away despising each other more than they already did. Thankfully there were no children and so no custody and visitation issues to work out. Those issues made reaching a divorce settlement a lot harder. Property and alimony issues were easier, as long as everyone was reasonable. As the mediator, Thorn would go back and forth between them today to try to get them to reach an agreement. He would work for as long as it took.

Of course he will work for as long as it takes today, Will thought. *He is charging by the hour at a high rate, just as I used to do.*

"Before we really get under way," Thorn continued in Roy's direction, "I would like to ask you about one thing. What is your main goal for this mediation? What would you like to see at the end of the day that would allow you to walk out of here satisfied?"

Will knew what the mediator was asking. He would ask
Jenny the same question. If he could get Roy and Jenny
what they each wanted the most in the divorce settlement,
everyone involved would be happier with him, happier to
pay his bill, and more likely to recommend his mediation
services to other divorcing friends and clients. Unfortunately for the mediator, Will knew Roy's answer was something the mediator could not deliver.

Roy looked at Thorn and said without quiver or stutter,
"The *only* thing I want is my wife back."

Thorn was experienced. It could not have been the first
time he had been involved in a divorce mediation in which
one of the parties did not want the divorce. But if he had
heard people answer his "goals" question like Roy just had,
he had not yet developed a natural reaction to it. He sighed
in a way that told Will he was disappointed with the answer.
He probably thought Roy's answer meant he was going to
be as difficult as possible so as to prolong the divorce pro-
ceedings as long as possible. Thorn awkwardly acknowledged Roy's answer without validating its legitimacy. He
then excused himself to go speak with Jenny and her lawyer.

Will and Roy were only alone for a few minutes when
the mediator returned, leaning just his head and torso inside
the room. His feet remained planted on the outside. "Will,
could I speak with you?" he asked. Will picked up a manila
envelope he had with him, got up, and followed Thorn out
into the adjoining hallway, shutting the door behind him.
Jenny's lawyer was standing there. His name was Rocky
Samson, as if his parents had thought a name could make
him become a physically imposing man. "Rock," as he was
called by those who knew him, ended up looking like the
opposite of Sylvester Stallone's Rocky and the Old Testa-

ment's Samson. His most defining characteristic was enough oil in his black, slicked back hair to match the cost of his suit. How Jenny came to hire him as her lawyer was a mystery to Will, though Rock tended to find himself in the middle of cases involving even the hint of celebrity.

Thorn began. "Will, I wanted us lawyers to meet so we can figure out where this is headed. Let me just give you my initial impression. It appears you have a client control problem."

"I do not have any intention of controlling him," Will responded. "He has enough self-control for all of us."

Now it was Rock's turn. "Will," he said, "I know you are new to divorce cases, but your client is aware he cannot stop the divorce, right? We have no-fault divorce in all fifty states. If Jenny wants a divorce—and she does—a divorce is what she is going to get, no matter how loudly Roy protests."

"Roy knows," Will replied.

"Then what does he hope to gain by making this difficult?" Rock asked.

"You two have formed your impressions of Roy too quickly. He does not see things like most divorce clients. It is true he does not want the divorce, but he has no intention of making this difficult. In fact, I have in this folder a copy of a settlement agreement I drafted that Roy has signed. It gives Jenny all of the assets the two have: the house here in Cedar Rapids, the car, and their remaining cash, except for enough to allow Roy to make a security and first month's deposit on a one-bedroom apartment and buy some Ramen noodles for a couple of weeks. If Jenny wants alimony, there are blanks for her to fill in the amount and for how long it will continue, subject to the standard stipulation that it ends if she remarries. Roy's signature is good no matter the amount she fills in, though you should know his ability to pay very much is limited."

"That is because he quit baseball," Rock protested. "If he goes back to baseball, she should be entitled to a portion of his salary. In fact, he should go back to baseball in order to pay her an appropriate amount."

"Are you taking orders from Jenny's father?" Will asked.

"No!" Rock answered. "I don't take orders from a person who is not my client!"

He was protesting that accusation too loudly, Will thought.

"I don't think that is really coming from Jenny," Will said, "but no matter. As I said, she can fill in what she likes and Roy will sign it. This agreement gives her everything she could ever want in this divorce, materially speaking."

The mediator, apparently feeling like he needed to show how important he was to this process, piped in. "What's the catch, Will?"

"No catch. However, Roy would like to see Jenny. She has ... uh ... not been returning his letters or calls."

"So in order for Roy to agree to this, Jenny has to meet with him?" Thorn asked, more as a summation than an actual question. Before Will could respond, the mediator looked at Jenny's attorney and said, "Seems like a pretty good deal, Rock. Jenny should really consider it." Thorn finished his interjection with a look on his face like he had just shared a profound conclusion. *He was really earning his hourly rate today*.

"I'll present this to Jenny," Rock said, "but I am not sure she will agree with that condition." Now Rock was trying to justify *his* rate, Will thought. Of course he would present the agreement to her, and he would probably try to give her the impression it was all due to his incredible negotiating skill.

"It's not a condition," Will said.

"What's not a condition?" Rock asked.

"Roy has already signed this," Will answered. "Jenny does not have to see him in order for him to agree to this settlement. She gets everything and whatever alimony she wants. If she really wants this divorce, there is nothing more she could request in the settlement, and she does not have to do or say anything for it. Here you go." Will handed the folder containing the agreement to Rock. He took it hesitantly, like he expected it to be snatched back and he did not want to look like a fool for thinking it was real. Will released his hand off the folder and continued, "Roy is simply asking to meet with her. Will you please ask her if she will?"

Will did not have any leverage with which to negotiate. Roy had not given him any and that was the way Roy wanted it. Will had never before negotiated on behalf of a client not just *willing* to give the other side everything, but *wanting* to give the other side everything. It was bizarre, but it was also fun and came with a sense of freedom. There is a lot of freedom in not being tied to material possessions.

"Yeah, uh, I'll ask her," Rock responded. "But if there is a meeting between the two of them, I am sitting in on it."

"No you are not," Will said back. "The meeting can be out in the open. It's a nice day outside. They can talk along the sidewalk below. But if Jenny agrees to meet, she is agreeing to meet with Roy without us getting in the way."

Rock harrumphed his way back toward to the conference room where Jenny was waiting.

~~~~~

Roy's wait for Will to return, and then his wait for Jenny's decision, had seemed longer than it was. She had agreed to the meeting. He now sat on a bench outside. He saw her walk out of the office building with her lawyer. The lawyer said something to her, she nodded, turned, and started walking toward Roy. The lawyer headed off in the direction of where his car was likely parked.

Roy stood. When Jenny got to him, he could not help a smile. "Hi," he said.

"I got your letters," she replied. "I know you have called. I meant to write back or call you. It's just with this proceeding ... I just ..." Her voice trailed off. Roy saw she did not know what to say.

"It is really good to see you," Roy said. "Thank you for coming out here."

"Sure." There was silence before Jenny asked, "How have you been?"

How should he answer that question? he wondered. He had been good and terrible. God had met all his needs. He had been able to find work, he and Donnie had done some coaching together, and he had been able to spend a lot of time doing things for Pine Road Baptist Church. He felt unworthy of all the good in his life. He had no right to complain. But he missed his wife. Her abandonment still hurt. Her absence meant that part of him was missing. Unsure if he could express his feelings without causing her to become guarded, "I am fine" was all that came out of his mouth.

She nodded and looked away. *Was she wondering what the point of this conversation was?* Roy asked himself. He was not sure he knew himself.

"How about you?" he asked her. "How have you been?"

"Okay." She paused. "No, not really okay."

Then she sat on the bench. He had not expected that.

So he sat as well. They were on separate ends of the bench. There was enough room for two people to sit between them, but no passerby with any perception would have dared.

They each stared out in front of themselves. Jenny looked down and asked, "Have you been seeing anyone?"

The question startled Roy. He looked at her to see if her expression conveyed whether she hoped he had, but she continued looking forward and he could not tell what was behind the question. "No," he answered. "And I won't." He did not ask her the return question. If she had dated anyone, he did not want to know.

"Preston Edwards called me a couple of months ago about a one-hour special he is producing. 'Roy Adams, One Year Later,' he calls it. His network offered me some money if I would participate. I shouldn't have, but I agreed. I gave them a couple of interviews on camera, walked them around my dad's farm, showed them where in Cedar Rapids we used to hang out before we were married, that kind of stuff. They asked a lot about what caused you to change your mind about baseball and they asked a lot about the church. After awhile, by the way they talked to me and the questions they asked, I got the impression they had their minds made up, that they are going to paint you as strange, maybe a little crazy, and claim your life is now a wreck. They wanted me to confirm all that. I didn't. I really didn't. But I am afraid when the show comes out you will think badly of me. I am sorry. I shouldn't have talked to them."

"It's okay," Roy said. Edwards had not called him, so this was a surprise, but Roy did not know how to respond.

"Please believe me that I did not mean to be involved in anything that would harm you," she said.

"I believe you."

They were silent again. Then Roy asked, "Do you think I am crazy?"

Jenny smiled for the first time. "Yes, but not because of the baseball and church thing."

"Are you going to church anywhere?"

She shook her head.

After a pause, Roy asked her, "So why do you think I am crazy?"

She turned to look at him now. "Why won't you just forget about me and go find a new wife?" she responded with her own question. "What if I never come back to you? You can't just live your life waiting for me!"

"Yes, I can live my life waiting for you."

"Who I am is not what you expected! You could find someone better!" A couple of faces across the street turned their way.

"That's not how it works," Roy responded.

"I just abandoned you when you needed me most," she said softer.

Did she really see she had done that? Or was she just using that argument to push him away? Roy no longer trusted his ability to read her.

"Jenny, I cannot give you the life you came to expect. But in the important ways it will be a better life."

"We are going through a divorce, Roy. What are we going to do? Get married again? That would look a little silly, don't you think?"

"I think you know I don't care if something looks silly to others."

"I know."

"But," Roy continued, "we do not have to get married again. The divorce is not final yet. You could still withdraw your petition for a divorce."

"We hardly know each other anymore," she said.

She might be right, Roy considered. But he was willing to learn about her again, if only she would be willing to learn about him again.

She paused in silence, her face staring down into her lap.

Roy then asked the question to which he had wanted an answer since she walked outside. "Did you sign the settlement?"

Her eyes briefly looked up at him and then glanced back down. She didn't answer right away. *She has not signed it*, Roy thought.

"I told my lawyer to look it over more, make sure everything looked right, and I would get back to him," she said.

"You saw it, right? There is nothing really to look over."

She grinned. "Yeah," she replied. "That is what my lawyer said, too."

Roy nodded. "Well, I suppose it is a good idea to have him look it over. We wouldn't want Rocky to run out of work and not be able to buy his hair grease."

Roy saw her giggle and then suppress more laughter.

"You meant what you said back on my dad's farm, didn't you?" she asked.

"Yes. And that won't change."

She stood and said, "I should be going."

Roy stood as well. "Okay," he responded, "as long as you don't offer me your hand to shake."

She giggled again. She nodded, kept her grin, and then pivoted on her right heel.

Roy watched her walk away for a moment and then sat back down on the bench. He pulled out his phone and sent a text message that simply said "ready".

A minute later, Will pulled up in his car, rolled down the window, and said, "You are going to have to take a seat in the back. Look who I picked up wandering around Green Square Park."

Roy saw Nate in the front passenger seat and smiled. He opened the rear door and got in the car. "What are doing here, Pastor?" Roy asked.

"Tara dropped me off earlier so I could pray while you were having your mediation. Will found me while he was driving around waiting for you to get done with your meeting with Jenny."

"I should have known," Roy said.

"So?" Nate asked, turning around to look at him. Roy saw Will look back at him in the rearview mirror as well.

Roy smiled. "There is hope," he said.

Will and Nate smiled back. Nate nodded and said, "Yes, there is always hope."

P.S.

About the Author

Jason M. Steffens grew up in eastern Iowa. He graduated from the University of Iowa College of Law. For nine years he practiced in the civil litigation division of one of Iowa's largest law firms, becoming a partner at age 31. At age 35, he withdrew as a partner and ended his law practice so he could become reacquainted with his wife and children. They live in Cedar Rapids, Iowa. Jason is a member of Twin Pines Baptist Church. *Never on Sundays* is his debut novel.

Follow Jason on Twitter: @j_steff

Follow Jason on Goodreads at goodreads.com/steffens

Find out more about Jason by visiting about.me/steffens

Like *Never on Sundays* at facebook.com/ NeverOnSundaysNovel

How This Book Came to Exist

That I came to be a lawyer felt like a slow-motion accident. That I came to write a novel was hasty and purposeful.

The fall semester of my senior year at Wartburg College, I served as a student teacher at a nearby high school and discovered I did not want to be a high school teacher. That was a problem in that I was going to graduate with a double major in history and education. If I was not going to use the education part, what was I going to do with the history part?

I had a minor in religion as well, but it was not as if I could make a career out of that, especially since I had become a Baptist while attending the Lutheran college.

With one semester remaining to figure it out, I learned law schools accept students with all sorts of undergraduate backgrounds. (I had a law school classmate tell me he majored in theater in undergrad. He seemed more prepared for legal work than me.) My then-fiancé (now wife) was going to be attending graduate school for physical therapy, so I signed up for and took the Law School Admissions Test (LSAT) and applied to the three schools to which she was applying. Two of the three offered me full-ride merit scholarships based on that LSAT score. In retrospect, I am not sure why I did not just play golf for the four years I was in undergrad and then show up for the LSAT.

We ended up at the University of Iowa. I spent three years there doing the things law students do: reading some of the reading assignments, "outlining," cramming for the finals, clerking for a law firm during summers, writing and editing for a law journal, and buying into the false notion my life in law school was busier than what real life would be. (There are these things called "work" and "children" that throw all prior notions of "busyness" out the window. Thankfully, the latter of those, at least, is a fount of joy.)

I initially thought working in a law firm was a nice thing to do during summer break, but was not something I would do as a career. I am not sure when that thought changed. It was probably when I was offered a good amount of money to do work I found myself capable of doing. Also, it was nice not having to search around anymore for a career.

So for the next nine years—five as an associate, four as a partner—I was a civil litigation "trial attorney." That meant I spent a lot of time organizing and reviewing paper and electronic records, writing briefs and letters in which I accused the opposing side of not understanding the law or the facts, and living in Microsoft Outlook. I spent only a little time actually in a courtroom (nine trials in nine years, in addition to smaller, more regular motion hearings; most clients for whom I worked were risk adverse, preferring settlements to the uncertainties of trial).

There is good, worthwhile work done in law firms by good people. Many of those people are able to balance work and family and other interests. I was unable to do that. I spent my days in the office wondering how I got there and wishing for a client who actually wanted to hire and pay a lawyer and then do what that lawyer suggested. I spent my evenings and weekends working, or—if not working—thinking about working. My wife and kids talked to me; I barely listened and rarely talked back. They found things to do without me. I did the things Christians are supposed to do: I attended each church service, did volunteer work in the church, and invited friends and strangers to the services. But it was unusual for me to do those things while fully focused on them. Most of the time I thought about work. No matter how much I got done, my to-do list only got longer and it consumed my thoughts. Things got worse as I acquired more responsibility, as I worked on bigger cases.

I was so absorbed with who I was and what I had to do as a lawyer that I lacked the ability to think about what other possibilities existed. I knew I had to extract myself to even begin to think about what else there was. More importantly, I knew if I did not extract myself, I would never be the husband and father God called me to be.

I was thirty-four-years-old. It was late summer. I wrote a one paragraph notice of withdrawal as a partner in my firm. It sat on my computer for a couple of months.

There was no one triggering event. But I did feel it was change course then or remain what I was for the rest of my life.

So, one weekday morning in mid-November 2012, I printed off that notice of withdrawal and signed it. With my door closed, I then walked around my office for an hour before finally mustering the will to find a member of our firm's board of directors and hand him the notice.

It took me until mid-February to complete or transition my pending cases. It was a slow process. One day, there was just nothing left. I stopped coming in to the office. I stopped thinking of myself as a lawyer.

I had wanted to write a novel since I was in college, maybe high school. I had a problem: I did not write well enough to put down some of the stories that were in my head. Part of the reason for that was I only read good literature when made to by teachers. That meant I did not read good literature enough. Reading good literature is essential to writing well.

A number of things helped me become a better writer. I started reading the Bible more consistently. I watched less television. And I wrote a lot, in law school and then as a lawyer.

So when I "retired" from the practice of law, I decided to write a novel.

I discovered I like the life of a novelist. It was not easy crafting the story, but it wasn't stressful. I wrote at home a couple of hours a day, sometimes more and sometimes less, depending on what else was going on. I had meals with my wife and kids. I talked to them during those meals. I played with my kids at night. I listened to my wife without thinking about work. I mowed my lawn regularly. I paid attention during the sermons at church and was able to perform a lot of tasks to help our church buy a much larger facility. I am still not the husband and dad I should be, but things are better. I have not once regretted my decision to withdraw from the practice of law.

The novel is, of course, about a lawyer, as well as a baseball player and a pastor: the thing I became, the thing I wanted to be as a kid, and the thing I admire the most. As the lawyer, you will see a lot of me in "Will." But there is also a lot of me in "Roy" and "Nate." Those characters tell the story of how our jobs and our associations can come to define us and about how there is both hope and division in choosing the best path God has for us.

Like any writer, I hope people read this novel and like it. Also, I hope people buy it. Yes—people buying it would be nice. But whatever happens, I know two things. One, I have created something. Two, I am not just a lawyer.

Jason's Favorite Novels

(in alphabetical order)

Always in His Keeping by Unknown

The Count of Monte Cristo by Alexandre Dumas

Ishmael (and its sequel *Self Raised*) by E.D.E.N Southworth

A Tale of Two Cities by Charles Dickens

True to the Last by Evelyn Everett-Green